A Contrived World

JUNG YOUNG MOON

A
CONTRIVED
WORLD
A NOVEL

TRANSLATED BY MAH EUNJI AND JEFFREY KARVONEN

DALKEY ARCHIVE PRESS

Originally published in Korean as *Eotteon jagwiui segye* by Moonji Publishing Co., Ltd., in 2011.

© 2011 by Jung Young Moon
Translation copyright © 2016 by Mah Eunji and Jeffrey Karvonen

LIBRARY OF CONGRESS CATALOGING-IN-PUBLICATION DATA
Names: Jung Young Moon, 1965- author. | Eunji, Mah, translator.
  | Karvonen, Jeffrey translator.
Title: A contrived world / by Jung Young moon ; translated by Mah Eunji and Jeffrey Karvonen.
Other titles: Eotteon jagwiui segye. English
Description: First edition. | Victoria, TX : Dalkey Archive Press, 2016.
Identifiers: LCCN 2015040708 | ISBN 9781564789556 (pbk. : acid-free paper)
Classification: LCC PL992.2.Y625 E6813 2016 | DDC 895.73/5--dc23
LC record available at http://lccn.loc.gov/2015040708

Partially funded by the Illinois Arts Council, a state agency, and published under the support of Literature Translation Institute of Korea (LTI Korea).

www.dalkeyarchive.com
Victoria, TX / McLean, IL / London / Dublin

Dalkey Archive Press publications are, in part, made possible through the support of the University of Houston-Victoria and its programs in creative writing, publishing, and translation.

CONTENTS

A Contrived World

1. The Time I Spent Drinking Tequila and Shooting at Cacti

IT WAS NOT MY FIRST TIME in San Francisco. I had stayed there briefly on my trip to the United States five summers earlier. On that trip, I was traveling with a woman I had dated for some time a while back and her boyfriend. A short but well-built Mexican-American, he mostly played driver to my ex-girlfriend while living off her, though I suspected his true function was in the bedroom. Although I consciously tried to be critical of the man who was living off my ex-girlfriend, he had a certain charm, and we became friends. He readily took a liking to me and insisted on calling me "brother," the way black men often call one another, even though I told him not to. In the end, I let him, and I called him brother, too. When I later switched to calling him "sister," he called me sister in return, and so we became sisters, but we didn't act like sisters.

The first time we met, I noticed the tattoo on his arm—a bird being engulfed in flames. It was an ordinary bird, specifically what kind even its wearer didn't know. It was small and colorful, more like a fairy pitta than a phoenix. I thought the bird looked singed. It seemed to be roasting ever so slowly, imperceptibly. Looking at that bird, I imagined that rather than soaring up from his arm like a phoenix, it would one day become a charred mass. This man, with a tattoo of a small, smoldering bird, had a somewhat comical demeanor. He acted and walked sort of like a gangster, a "gangsta" to be exact. He wore sagging, wide-legged pants, exposing a little bit, sometimes too much, of his underwear. Watching the way he walked, I thought that

3

it was only because he was not a real gangsta that he could act and walk sort of like a gangsta. He wouldn't act like a gangsta if he actually were one. It would be ludicrous for someone to try to act like himself. By that logic, a real gangsta wouldn't act like himself, though he might impersonate another gangsta only to make other gangstas laugh.

He had the quintessential face for a part in a dull western movie in which many people are shot to death, particularly a Mexican man who meets the death that serves the least purpose but fits into the plot so naturally that he is not given a chance to feel victimized. I'm bending the truth, actually. His mixed ancestry had given him rather attractive facial features. And those rather attractive features made for a remarkably attractive face. As soon as I saw him, I thought that I wasn't a match for him, although this was a viewpoint that I shared with no one. My feeling this way could have caused the kind of awkward wariness or nervous tension that can arise between a woman's past lover and her current lover, but disappointingly there was none, and this wasn't only because of his attractive face.

Years earlier, my ex-girlfriend had become fed up with Korea and left the country, saying that she could no longer live among Koreans. I'd felt as though it was somehow my fault. Upon departing, she'd made me promise that I'd leave Korea later and come to her. By visiting her, I had half kept my promise, or so I thought. While we were still seeing each other, she said one night that she'd decided to go to the United States. Her words had sounded to me like she wanted to go out alone, at night, for a walk from which she wasn't sure whether she'd return. One week later, she did go on a long walk and never returned. She'd started a business in the United States and was rather success-ful. Making life-changing decisions effortlessly, or so it seemed from the outside, was one of her finest qualities. That aspect of her character hadn't changed much, and perhaps that was the reason for her success.

I couldn't tell exactly what her business was. She told me only that she was importing goods from Mexico. Most of her busi-ness involved the telephone, and sometimes she'd take her calls in the bathroom. Her operation seemed shady, but that was only because everyone who's successful in the work they do, everyone who works, everything people do for work, and everything in the world is shady in my eyes. To me, even a fisherman catching fish, a salesperson selling shoes, a teacher teaching students, an author writing, a singer singing about joy and sorrow, a bird singing, and a chipmunk collecting acorns seem shady, as do the acorns collected by chipmunks, the songs sung by singers and birds, the texts written by authors, the students taught by teachers, the shoes sold by salespeople, and the fish caught by fishermen.

If I set my mind to it, they can seem as shady as I want them to be. But then I can just as easily set my mind to seeing them as legitimate. Looking at it that way, her shady business didn't seem all that shady. Still, remembering that she had been my girlfriend, I tried to believe that she was involved in some great shady business. She was just as kind as she had been when we were together. She ran a business, but she didn't act like an entrepreneur. She didn't take her work seriously, which was probably why she never explained exactly what she was doing. Ironically, this made me trust her more. I don't really trust people who take their business seriously, or those who believe that life is a serious business.

After a few days at her house in Los Angeles, the three of us traveled to her vacation home, which was somewhere southeast of the city, quite some distance away. It was the kind of place one could find on a map but whose location one couldn't possibly guess without looking at a map. We drove for a long time through a bleak landscape that barely changed, and so the place where we ended up seemed as though it existed only on a map.

The place was in the middle of a vast wilderness. The daytime sun was as intense as in the desert, and we frequently spotted scorpions. Upon arrival, we were greeted by a scorpion in the empty house, and our chasing it out created a small ruckus. The scorpion was not big, and it was kind of cute. In the heat of the day, scorpions tried their best to come into the shady comfort of the house. They especially like to roost in the dark, cozy interior of a shoe, so we had to shake our shoes out before putting them on. I could guess why my ex-girlfriend had gotten a vacation home in a place that got as hot as the desert during the day: she wanted the langour of that hot climate, to naturally feel like everything was a bother, to be lazy and do nothing, but to do whatever it took to chase out scorpions that came into the house.

The air conditioner was emitting lukewarm air and it was too hot in the house, but none of us liked air-conditioning enough to do anything about it. We stayed half naked most of the time, both inside and outside of the house. The houses in the surrounding area were far apart from one another. What few trees there were were clustered around the houses, which made the houses look like oases in the desert. From the nearest house, which was quite far away, I often heard a dog. Sometimes it barked like a dog, and other times it howled like a wolf. I thought that when the dog howled like a wolf, it was reminding itself of its wolfish ancestry, and that when it barked like a dog, it was trying not to forget its dogness by differentiating itself from wolves.

Once, in a park in Los Angeles, I saw dogs that normally barked like dogs but would start howling like wolves, completely changing their voices and registers, whenever they heard an ambulance siren. One dog would start, and the rest would follow. Even the pug among the larger dogs joined in, but the pug couldn't quite howl like a real wolf. It would instead make a strange wolf-like noise. The pug was wearing an Elizabethan collar, the so-called "cone of shame." I couldn't tell whether it was recovering from an injury or being punished by its master, as in a cartoon. American ambulance sirens are particularly loud and sharp, to the point that they hurt my ears. It made me want to howl like a wolf, and I wondered if the dogs howled for this reason. I was curious to know what, other than a siren, makes a dog howl like a wolf, what returns a dog to its wolfish state, however temporarily. The sound of the dog howling near my ex-girlfriend's vacation home did not provide me with any clue whatsoever.

My ex-girlfriend talked about a pug she had once raised, how it was as stupid as it was unsightly, how it snored loudly, and how she had to be careful not to get sprayed when it sneezed. She said that it was so lazy that she'd always find it sprawled out in the most unrefined positions, and that she accidentally stepped on the dog on numerous occasions. He had lived a long life, repeatedly evading death by crushing. At different times in her life, she had raised various breeds of dogs. The other pugs she had kept were no better. She said that although it would be unfair to generalize about all pugs, it was difficult for her to imagine a stately pug.

Our Mexican friend wasn't a nudist, but he'd occasionally walk around as though he were. One morning, I woke up and looked out the window to find him, the boyfriend of my once long-term girlfriend, shoveling naked in front of the house, with his very black erect penis in plain view. I thought, *What a very large black penis!* He was planting several agave plants that he must have purchased somewhere earlier that morning. This sight gave me an odd feeling, which shortly turned into an odd pleasure. Gloating, he baptized the agave seedlings with a thick stream of urine, which still had tequila in it from the previous night's drinking. Again I felt odd, as if I had seen a stripeless black-skinned zebra or a chimpanzee in human clothing watering agave plants. The previous day, when I had seen him hanging laundry in front of the house, also naked, I had had a hard time doubting my eyes because he had acted so naturally.

I walked outside and asked him whether he was going to make tequila with the agave plants. He looked at me pityingly and said they were ornamental, that agave plants are a nice thing just to look at. When this naked man who pissed on agave plants looked at me pityingly, I felt pitiful, and I was unsure which one of us was more so. By the time he walked over to me, he had lost the big hard-on I had just seen him with in front of the agave plants, and I thought to no avail about what had caused his penis to get big and then small again. I then mulled on how a penis perpetually gets hard and goes soft. Although his penis had gone soft, it was not small. In fact, every time I looked, his penis seemed to be a different size. I imagined that he kept different-sized penises neatly organized in a hidden drawer so that he could screw one on, like changing a lightbulb, to fit his mood at any given moment.

All the while, I was gazing at his penis, transfixed. He just let me look, not showing any trace of embarrassment, as though his penis was something worth looking at. On second thought, he had no choice. One should not look at a man's penis as he does at his face. I felt a little bit embarrassed, but still I did not look away. Instead, I told him that he had a nice penis, then changed my words and told him that he had a great penis. As in this case, I sometimes say things I do not mean at all, at the same time thinking that my words are not what I mean to say. After uttering such words, I think about how far they are from what I want to say. He did not act proud. Rather, he must have thought that I was being sarcastic. I was being half sarcastic, and half telling the truth. He carried off his penis and began tending to his new agave plants.

His penis made me think about the human penis in general. Of all things in the world, the penis is the thing that triggers the most peculiar feeling in me. Every time I see a penis other than my own, in a communal shower for instance, I feel an indescribable emotion. The penis is so bizarre in its appearance and function. It sports so many different looks: a forlorn, vacant look as it hangs loose in the crotch before suddenly perking up as though with the flash of an idea; a dejected look, an angry look, a proud look, an embarrassed look. Sometimes it looks like the stretched-out head of a turtle, and other times like its withdrawn counterpart. The penis has no choice structurally but to dangle. I consider the penis to be not only the most peculiar part of the human body, but also the most peculiar object in the world. The only other things that trigger this response are the penises of other mammals, such as cows, horses, camels, monkeys, and elephants.

The two testicles are as odd-looking as the penis: together but separate, like two people who appear to be in cahoots but are not actually on the same page. The reason the testicles have separated from the penis and established a distance is unclear.

Testicles may or may not be thought of as independent from the penis, but I consider them to be rather devious. They do not attract much attention, being obscured by the penis, and they are often regarded as mere assistants to the penis. In reality, they might be manipulating the penis from behind the scenes, delegating bothersome as well as pleasurable tasks to the penis, all the while pretending to do little. The testicles, not the penis, might be doing the work that counts. Perhaps the fact that a man has two testicles, not one, has to do with their importance. That way, if something happens to one testicle, the other can step up and take over.

Even as I was contemplating the penis, I made a conscious effort to block any other spontaneous thoughts about it. Looking at the tattoo on the Mexican fellow's arm, I suggested that he get a tattoo on his chest of a tequila bottle with "tequila" written on it, a map of Mexico, and an agave plant. I thought it was a decent idea for a man who appeared to love Mexico to get tattoos of things that symbolize Mexico as a reminder of his heritage. But he just looked pityingly at me again. Then he called me a sissy for looking like a woman. I had long hair. I was shirtless and was wearing sunglasses and a loud floral-print sarong that belonged to my ex-girlfriend. That was how I dressed most of the time. I called him macho for showing off his manliness. In the time we'd known each other, our relationship had become such that we could tease one another. Perhaps it's human nature that two people tease each other when they reach a certain level of closeness. Without the ability to tease each other, two people might not be considered close. I was usually subtle when I ribbed him, but he was often blunt.

That afternoon, as I walked down the hallway, I happened upon the couple having sex with their bedroom door open. I was able to think of a few things I could do if I squeezed in between them. I laughed to myself, thinking that the strong Mexican fellow might shove me away or even kick me off if I did that. When my Mexican friend acknowledged me, calling out "Sister!" before resuming what he was doing, I felt odd. Actually, there was nothing really odd about my feeling. It was only as odd as I made it out to be. As ever, when I remembered that everything that happens happens because it can happen, nothing seemed odd. The only reason that sex seems special is that among all acts during which I think about the meaning of the act, sex makes me think the most.

They looked as though they wanted me to watch them. I thought that if they were putting on a show worth watching, I might stand and watch with folded arms, but I didn't think that they were quite worth watching. Seeing them return to their business, I went and lay in my bed and looked out the window. I felt I could understand the real reason my ex-girlfriend had gotten a house in a vast wilderness. In that house, all one had to do was look out any window to view a barren landscape. Watching the barren landscape, I thought about the couple making love in the next room, and it occurred to me that having sex while viewing a barren landscape would be quite all right.

I continued to look over the landscape, and for lack of anything better to do, I thought of a time when, out of boredom, I looked up and found over 140 euphemisms for penis in English. I recalled the few I had committed to memory: names of people, such as *Jimmy, John, Johnson, John Thomas, Peter, Willy, Little Bob, Little Elvis, Pedro, Percy,* and *Princess Sophia,* as well as descriptive expressions, such as *beaver basher, one-eyed snake,* and *yogurt slinger.* Thinking of the couple in the next room, I imagined Little Elvis slinging yogurt, and a one-eyed snake violating Princess Sophia. Remembering the Latino blood of the fellow, I thought about Pedro bashing a beaver. I felt a sudden urge to throw myself upon them and interrupt, but I resisted, thinking that the beaver might be enjoying herself. I could not help but feel that the one-eyed snake was actually doing Princess Sophia a favor. I couldn't understand why, of all things, one would call a penis Princess Sophia.

I felt that my ex-girlfriend had changed considerably. In the old days, when we were dating, she and I used to have long conversations about nothing in particular. Talking about nothing in particular led to stranger and stranger stories, and this pleased us, so we would talk about things that were stranger still. At those times, I felt that there must be something profound to be found only in incoherent conversations, but I only ever found more incoherent things. She and I no longer had such conversations.

I couldn't remember whether we actually talked about it at the time, but I could picture myself lying in her bed, holding her nipple in my mouth without sucking on it or thinking about sucking on it. I might have lamented, as many men before me have, how unfortunate it is that women don't always produce milk, that it's a crying shame that women evolved so that they do not produce milk at regular times. Although it would have been an insufficient consolation for that sense of loss, a thought might have come to mind that would have comforted me significantly, such as the thought that nothing is as good as a nipple to hold in one's mouth. Judging that this sort of thinking was appropriate while holding a nipple in my mouth, I would have thought about what, other than a woman's nipple, might be so good for holding in one's mouth, and without being able to come up with anything as good as a nipple, I would have concluded that nothing compares to a warm, soft nipple for holding in one's mouth. I might have taken my mouth off her nipple for a moment to share my thoughts, to which she would have responded that there's nothing better than a nipple to let someone hold in his mouth. Once we established that the ability to hold a nipple in one's mouth or let a nipple be held in another's mouth is one of the greatest evolutionary advantages of the human race, she might have let me hold her nipple in my mouth again. Knowing that I like to have my head stroked more than anything else, she would have stroked my head all the while, and I would have been so pleased, thinking that all of these thoughts were possible because she was stroking my head, and that there must not be an animal in the world that does not like to have its head stroked.

I would have resumed holding her nipple in my mouth, and of all things related to nipples, I might have thought about the size of nipples, and that her nipples were the perfect size. I had not seen many women's nipples, but I figured that hers were average-sized. If her nipples were any larger or smaller, I would have thought that they were too big or too small to hold in my mouth, in which case it would likely not have occurred to me that there is nothing as good as a nipple to hold in one's mouth. It was clear to me that men's nipples are too small to hold in the mouth, and this is a sad state of affairs for all the women of the world.

With a nipple still in my mouth, I could have thought about how holding a nipple in my mouth makes me feel that I could wish for nothing more from this world, that everything in the world seems distant, that I have entered a different world, that time has stopped, that I cannot think nor want to think about a world beyond this still, blissful moment, that all problems in the world seem trivial, that I would not mind if this world ended and a new world took its place.

Although there's nothing better than a nipple to hold in one's mouth, and I would have felt as though I could hold her nipple in my mouth indefinitely, it would have been difficult to hold her nipple in my mouth as long as I thought I could. I would have, therefore, started thinking about letting go of her nipple, but I would have continued to hold it in my mouth, thinking that I deserved a bit of challenge when doing such a thing. Holding her nipple in my mouth would have been sufficient, but as though being sufficient wasn't enough, I would have thought that I was missing something and then wondered what things are good for latching on to rather than just holding in my mouth. It would have occurred to me that I did not need to look far because I would have been happy to latch on to the nipple I was holding in my mouth. I would not have asked for her permission, nor felt the need to get permission—as kindhearted as she was, she would have no doubt granted it. I would have decided that I had better not do such a thing, suppressing my urge to latch on, but starting to feel seriously challenged to continue holding the nipple in my mouth, thinking about the nipple in my mouth, the nipples I had held in my mouth, the nipples I had wanted to hold in my mouth but could not, the nipples I would get to hold in my mouth, and other myriad nipples. I would have proceeded to tell her all of my thoughts, and she might have let me latch on to her nipple until she felt a clear satisfaction from my latching on. When we would lie in her bed and think about such things in her dark room, which was great for lying around in, our thoughts probably looked like newly hatched silkworms beginning to crawl.

Thinking about nipples while lying in bed at my ex-girl-friend's place, in the middle of a vast wilderness in California, I stopped feeling like nipples are a nice thing to hold in my mouth. I felt that I would never again think that a nipple or anything else was nice for holding in my mouth while holding it in my mouth. No sooner did I try to stop thinking about nipples than I started thinking again that there's nothing as good as a nipple to hold in one's mouth. One can see this clearly when looking at a baby. A baby knows better than anyone else that there's nothing better than a nipple to hold in one's mouth, and certainly spends much of its time thinking about nipples and about holding them in its mouth, and actually holding one in its mouth. Babies try so hard to get hold of a nipple. A baby not only sucks on a nipple to get milk, but sometimes falls asleep with a nipple in its mouth as well. This shows how much babies love to hold nipples in their mouths, and that they're aware that there's nothing as good as a nipple to hold in one's mouth.

I was engrossed in my thoughts about nipples when the English expression *holy moly* came suddenly to mind. I was sur-prised at how deeply I'd been engrossed in my thoughts about nipples. My surprise was short-lived. My focus shifted to a series of English expressions similar to *holy moly*. In my head, I went through expressions that simultaneously show surprise, scorn, anger, disgust, and frustration, such as *holy Moses, holy cow, holy mackerel, holy smoke, holy crap*, and *holy shit*, and then spoke them out loud one by one. Of these expressions, *holy mackerel* and *holy moly* are my favorites. I thought about the fact that *mackerel* was once a nickname for Catholics, who ate mackerel on Fridays, and that mackerel was considered holy in the seventeenth century because it was sold on Sundays. *Moly* is the name of a medicinal herb that appears in Homer's Odyssey. It has milky-white flowers and black roots. Recalling these facts, I repeated *holy mackerel* and *holy moly* out loud, and I immediately felt good.

Thinking about strange things, lying in bed in a room in my ex-girlfriend's vacation home, I remembered something she'd told me a long time before, when we were together, about a guy she had dated briefly before going out with me. She had told me that when they had started sleeping together, he would massage only one of her breasts at a time, alternating between the left and the right breast every several days. She had thought it strange at first, but had eventually come to enjoy it. She had explained that the enjoyment might have come from the anticipation she felt for the ignored breast, which was to receive a massage in several days' time. Listening to her explanation, I'd understood that the important thing was that the two breasts must feel unfairly treated, that one breast must always be left to feel neglected. I had suspected that she'd made up the story, but I'd done as she instructed and played along. I would often forget the side I had last massaged, but she always seemed to remember clearly; and would offer the breast whose turn it was.

Thinking about the nipples and breasts of my ex-girlfriend, who was having sex in the next room, made the time we'd spent together feel like a lie. Furthermore, the fact that I was thinking about nipples and breasts, lying in a room in my ex-girlfriend's vacation home in a vast wilderness in California, felt like a lie. I thought again about the things we might have talked about. She was clearly not having the kind of conversations we used to have with her Mexican boyfriend. It occurred to me again that she'd changed considerably, and that I hadn't changed much at all. After all those years, I still thought mainly about nonsense, and I usually talked nonsense when I met people.

The couple in the next room finished, and I could hear them snoring in their sweet postcoital nap. I resisted the urge to get a rope and tie them up to show them what might happen while they slept. It had been over twenty years since I'd last slept soundly. I wanted to sleep more than anything. I took a sleeping pill with a shot of tequila, and was able to sleep for a short while. I dreamt a somewhat adolescent dream, in which I was lying in bed with a woman who let me touch her breasts but wouldn't let me look at them.

Every night, we got drunk on tequila. I drank to soothe my deepening hatred of Korea, my ex-girlfriend drank because she was glad her past and current boyfriends were getting along, her boyfriend drank because he really liked tequila. I thought that my reason for getting drunk on tequila was the worst, so I tried to drink for no reason. But when my ex-girlfriend got plastered, she would talk about how Korea's long history of isolation made Koreans the most narrow-minded of mono-ethnic peoples, and how mentally underdeveloped Koreans are. She would mention that the worst thing about Korea is that so much of the country is unnatural, making it difficult for people to exist in their natural state.

Our Mexican friend would listen quietly, lying on the sofa. When he got drunk, he looked like a gangsta one moment and then sort of like a hippie the next. Once, he remarked somewhat out of the blue that hippie culture was huge in Mexico back in the day, and that a festival similar to Woodstock was held in a place called Avándaro. In fact, Mexico had a deep-rooted hippie and bohemian culture. It was too bad that Korea's hippie and bohemian culture did not last, because the lack of such a culture is not unrelated to Korea's lack of a deep-rooted tradition of seeking spiritual freedom. If that tradition could have taken root, perhaps Korea would be a less spiritually oppressive place.

My ex-girlfriend, who had certain bohemian qualities, wasted and slightly off the wall, mentioned that she owed her considerable success to having left me to move to the States, which I interpreted to mean that I should take credit. I thought that we could be good friends because we'd been able to part without bitter resentment toward each other.

One night, I was watching my ex-girlfriend blabber on drunkenly when I began thinking about the time when she was my girlfriend. Of all things, I remembered one rainy night during college, when she and I had been walking to her place after drinking. (She'd been an impressive drinker, and I'd learned to drink from her.) She was suddenly hit with diarrhea. She dropped her panties under her skirt and shat in an alleyway in front of someone's house. There was no toilet paper, so I picked some grape leaves for her from the vines drooping over the fence of the house. She had nearly shat in her clothes. It was definitely better for her to go by the front door of someone's house than in her clothes, and in a way, she'd made a wise decision at a critical moment. I didn't forget to praise her as I watched her empty her bowels. This incident could have been embarrassing for both of us, though it would have been more embarrassing for her. But we had been in such a delightful mood before the incident that this potentially embarrassing event actually made us feel even better. I hoped that we would have such embarrassing yet delightful incidents more often. Since that night, I've considered my having picked grape leaves for a person who had an attack of diarrhea on the street one of my greatest acts of kindness.

This must have happened in the summertime, judging from the size of the grape leaves, which had been as big as my hands. A different summer, we'd had another experience related to grapes. She and I had been traveling from Mokpo to Jeju by boat in a third-class cabin, which was an open room where passengers could sleep anywhere on the floor. I awoke to find someone's leg over my abdomen. The leg belonged to a middle-aged man from Jeju who had a limp from an injury he'd sustained during a battle against the Chinese by the Yalu River some thirty years before. He was returning home from visiting his son, a man about my age who was stationed at a base near the Korean cease-fire line. The man from Jeju apologized sincerely for what his leg had done without his knowledge, and I accepted, forgiving in my heart the culprit leg, which I presumed to be possessed to climb on people's abdomens because it had been injured in battle. The man confirmed that the leg that had climbed onto my stomach was the leg that had been injured in battle against the Chinese. I probably would not have forgiven any other leg so easily, but I was ready to forgive any wrongdoing by a leg that had been injured in battle against the Chinese. The leg looked quite different once I knew that it had been injured in a battle on the Yalu River during the Korean War thirty years before. Although the man's leg was exposed below his shorts, I could not see any visible scars.

I could not guess the reason why the man's leg had climbed onto my abdomen thirty years after being injured in battle against the Chinese during the Korean War, on the man's way home from visiting his son, who must fight the North Koreans if the situation arises, whether he is ready or not. But the thought of that man's injured leg climbing onto my stomach on a boat from Mokpo to Jeju, thirty years after being injured in battle against the Chinese in the Korean War, gave me an odd feeling. I wondered if he'd had a nightmare in which his leg was injured fighting the Chinese. The man didn't know himself why his leg had climbed onto my stomach. I reasoned that it was because we were on a boat, and that a leg climbing onto someone else's stomach is as likely as a boat ending up on top of a mountain. I knew that there were no bridges between Mokpo and Jeju, but I was determined to believe that we had passed under many bridges while we were sleeping, because this would help me understand why someone else's leg had ended up on my abdomen.*

I didn't know how many Chinese soldiers' legs the man had injured in return for his injury, or whether he had damaged more important organs, such as the head or the heart, that would have killed a person. I thought that after a war, statistical research should be conducted on how many legs, heads, and hearts, as well as eyes, noses, mouths, ears, fingers, and toes of a country's citizenry have been impaired, maimed, or paralyzed during that war. That way, if a nation demanded war reparations at an international conference, the country's representative would be able to make an absurd but quite well-founded request for "compensation for our nation's precious assets of 123 testicles, which became impaired or maimed as a result of the war your nation unjustly started. Since they cannot be replaced by anything else, give us 123 healthy testicles from your country."

* Translators' note: In Korean, the words for leg and bridge are homonyms (dari), as are the words for stomach and boat (bae).

As Jeju came into view, the man told us that he'd actually
injured his leg as his unit retreated from the Chinese at the Yalu
River. He said that there had been about a dozen Chinese soldiers at first, then scores, then hundreds. He'd found this very
strange. The Chinese soldiers had hidden away during the day
and rushed in at night, wearing identical winter clothes and hats.
The man said that they'd seemed otherworldly. He turned toward
the Yalu River, far away, and said that the Chinese soldiers had
been elusive, phantasmagoric beings. In the depths of severe winter, his unit had retreated to Changjin Lake and made a narrow
escape through Wonsan Port. He and his comrades had probably
thought that it was impossible to fight phantoms. Most of the
members of his unit had died in combat or had frozen to death.
When he said that injuring his leg might have saved his life, he
appeared to be thanking his leg a little. He said that countless
soldiers in the Korean War had been killed by the cold as well as
by the hand of the enemy.

This encounter led to our staying at the veteran's house for
a few days, picking grapes in his vineyard. I thought about the
strangeness of human relationships while I picked grapes. He
hadn't invited us to his home to put us to work, but we believed
he had. We volunteered to help even though he told us to rest
inside. Picking grapes was as dull as I had imagined it would be,
and more laborious. Fresh-picked grapes were delicious until
they lost their appeal, and we quit picking them after a short
while. The man was uneasy about not being able to do more
for us. I could not tell whether this was because he was always
uneasy or because I reminded him of his son who was serving
in the military, whose picture was hanging in the living room.
The son, who looked nothing like me, was holding a gun in the
picture. He looked poised either to fight if the situation arose or
to drop his gun and run.

One day, the man told us about a number of seldom visited
oreum, Jeju dialect for the ubiquitous parasitic volcano cones
nearby. So we went on a search for one. We were delighted by
the wonderful view from the *oreum*, as well as by an unexpected

event. Lying on top of the *oreum*, we looked far away at other *oreum*, which looked like ancient burial mounds of different heights; closer, at the short grass quivering in the wind; far away again, at the clouds floating in the sky; a little bit closer, at a herd of cattle grazing in a meadow, just far enough away that one had to look closely to make out the shapes of the cows; and up close, at the courting grasshoppers and motionless spiders on the ground. Surrounded by distractions, and talking about how distracting they were, we made love, thinking that all of these things were sharing the moment with us, and perhaps even taking part in our lovemaking. We felt as though all that surrounded us was urging us on, and it was difficult not to make love in that situation.

As we made love, I attributed our lovemaking to the *oreum*, the wind, the grass, the clouds, the herd of cattle, the grasshoppers, and the spiders. The fact that each element had a different physical scale but equal psychological weight added to the feeling that they were all sharing in the moment.

Something else caught my eye as well, and it distracted me more than the *oreum*, the wind, the grass, the clouds, the cattle, the grasshoppers, and the spiders. Two praying mantises were mating in the grass, their bodies overlapping. If they'd been sitting still, I wouldn't have been so distracted. Actually, they were sitting still. The mountain breeze was causing them to move continuously on their long, spindly legs, and I had a hard time taking my eyes off of them, like a baby mesmerized by a mobile. With their small, green eyes, which were relatively large for their bodies, the praying mantises seemed interested in us, cocking their heads from side to side to watch us as they mated.

I thought that the eyes of the praying mantises looked like the stamen of lilies. I'd once looked at the stamens of lilies and thought that they looked like the eyes of praying mantises. Discovering similarities in completely different parts of nature was delightful. I thought about how the image of us making love must look like a mosaic in the eyes of the praying mantises, which perceive objects in mosaic form. Of all insects, praying mantises trigger the most peculiar feeling in me, and so I was delighted that they were sharing our moment.

We assumed a position where we lay facing each other on our sides. I don't know why, but it seemed like an appropriate position for the top of an *oreum*. It allowed us to look beyond each other's faces from time to time at the panorama that surrounded us. Of all the things around us, I liked looking at the clouds the most. I thought that lying down is the only way to look at clouds properly. Later, when we parted ways, I recalled having made love on the *oreum* in Jeju, and hoped that when she moved to America, she would have a chance to make love on a prairie where buffalos roamed. I don't know whether she had that chance.

During intercourse, I looked at the sun between the clouds above her head. A sunbeam pierced my eyes, but I did not care. I liked how blinding it was, and I felt that I was having a blinding day. After we finished, we talked about nothing in particular for a long time. I don't know what we talked about, but I remember sitting on top of the *oreum* and rolling a few pebbles down the slope.

It is one of my hobbies to roll pebbles down slopes, and I do it every chance I get. I developed this habit when I was very young. I started doing it without meaning to make it a hobby, but it became one nonetheless. I used to climb up a hill and roll pebbles down it whenever I was overcome by ambiguous emotions. I would watch the rolling pebbles and fall deeper into my ambiguous emotions. I spent many afternoons on a hill, rolling pebbles down. I started many evenings this way and came back down when darkness fell, feeling as though I had completed my day's routine. It might be a stretch to say that my eyes were opened to many ambiguous emotions while I watched pebbles roll down hills, but I think this was the case.

My ex-girlfriend didn't roll pebbles down hills, but she liked to watch me, and she knew that rolling pebbles down hills is one of my greatest and only hobbies. She would watch, yearning for the pebbles to roll down freely, but they rarely did. They were often too small, or their shape was not round enough. For a pebble to roll freely, the angle of the slope, as well as the size and shape of the pebble, has to be perfect. Even after a pebble got going, seeming determined, mindless, and free, it would often stall as if to show that one should never set his mind at ease, and that nothing ever goes as one wants. There was no special reason for my watching pebbles roll down hills, but it sometimes made me feel mellow. Other times I felt aggressive watching pebbles roll, and sometimes I felt nothing at all.

I remember laughing with my ex-girlfriend on the *oreum* in Jeju, talking about the summer she lost control of her bowels by someone's front door, and I picked grape leaves for her from the vines drooping over the fence. Drunk on tequila at my ex-girlfriend's vacation home, in a vast wilderness in California, I remembered again the night she had diarrhea. I could even remember the tactile sensation of the night's rain. Although the time we had dated seemed so long ago, and I was feeling doubtful that it had actually happened, recalling that particular summer night made our time together seem real again. This made me think that my memory of that night was a gateway I had to pass through in order to feel my way back to the time we'd been lovers. I thought that an act of kindness such as mine could never be forgotten, and that I would remember it even on my deathbed. It was because we shared such a memory that we could remain friends after so many years apart. I also thought that maintaining friendship with ex-lovers, being able to call each other good friends, is one of the most important things in life.

Every time my ex-girlfriend and her boyfriend got drunk, they suggested that I stay with them forever, but they never mentioned it sober. I, too, thought it would be swell to stay with them forever when I was drunk, but I lost all desire when I sobered up. Something about them made staying with them forever seem improbable, and more to the point, it's impossible for me to stay with anyone forever.

Strangely, when I was drunk during the day, I would wish to have the company of a scorpion. I was sure I wouldn't die from a scorpion sting, only suffer great pain. I thought that there was no reason to get stung by a scorpion on purpose, unless I was trying to suffer pain, but if I ended up getting stung, there was nothing I could do to help it. Somewhat aware that I was drunk and not making much sense, I would look around for a scorpion. But whether there were none in the house or they were hiding somewhere out of sight, I never found one. One evening, however, when we were all lying around drunk on the sofa, a scorpion scurried across the living room floor. No one moved to chase it out. Trying to catch a scorpion seemed too involved and too difficult. I wasn't concerned about it stinging me, and I didn't care whether it came when I was asleep and slept beside me. In my drunken state, a scorpion seemed like a nice companion to sleep next to. The next day, we found the scorpion in the bathroom, and we raised a ruckus again chasing it out.

Most of the afternoon, we sat on the porch drinking tequila and talked about infusing tequila with scorpions. We didn't actually try it, though. We didn't think that a scorpion deserved to die in such a manner. On the fourth day, we got bored of drinking tequila and lazing around, so we went in the afternoon to a nearby field surrounded by rolling hills to shoot a pistol. There was nothing else around, so we targeted large cacti, which looked like bundled columns. Our Mexican friend would not specify whether he'd borrowed, bought, found, or stolen the gun, just that he had his means. He, too, was a shady fellow. He'd go out to buy food and other supplies for the house, but he only made his runs when no one was looking. This made everything he brought back seem like goods smuggled across the border from Mexico. I wasn't sure that shooting a gun in the area was legal, but the Mexican fellow insisted that it wasn't a problem. No matter. We never saw a sheriff in the neighborhood or anywhere else in the area. The Mexican fellow seemed eager to show off that he thought little of the law.

I asked whether he had a gun with a larger bore, or a cannon, but he didn't. I would have liked to fire a cannon rather than a small pistol, to see a huge explosion. I felt like blowing up a huge boulder with a cannon without blinking an eye—or rather, I wanted to not blink an eye as I blew up a huge boulder.

Our Mexican friend tried to hit a cactus with every shot, but I tried my best to miss the cacti while aiming toward them. The cacti seemed too blameless for target practice. I didn't want anyone or anything to get hurt, but our friend seemed to think that someone or something had to get hurt whenever a gun was fired. Had there been an eagle around, I would not have liked to shoot at it, but to scare it away with a gunshot. But there was no eagle. There were small birds that would have been scared of an eagle, but I didn't care about the small birds. I wanted an eagle. Besides, I didn't want to scare birds that must already live in constant fear, however slight it may be. When we fired the pistol, we could hear dogs howling like wolves far away. I learned that, in addition to sirens, gunshots make dogs howl like wolves, and I wondered what else makes them howl.

The Mexican fellow and I took turns shooting. Once, when it was my turn, and I was slowly getting ready to shoot, aiming at nothing, I felt the sudden urge to shoot myself in the head. It was similar to the impulse to smash something when holding a club. Actually, the urge stemmed from a persistent hangover headache from drinking tequila the previous night. I imagined the source of my headache to be an ornately patterned glass sphere inside my head, which I could shoot and shatter into a million mosaic pieces. The next moment, for no good reason, I felt the desire to shoot the two people standing beside me. It wasn't a particularly strong desire, but I still had to suppress it. Maybe it was just that there's no target as good as a person. A person is surely a better target than a cactus, which has no reaction at all. Or I might have thought that, unless I did away with the couple, I would end up staying with them forever, drinking tequila and shooting cacti day in and day out. The reason was unclear.

I stood still for a moment as if unable to decide whom I was going to shoot first. I came to a sort of conclusion that the desire to shoot someone is natural for anyone holding a gun. The two of them were talking to each other, smiling, looking in my direction, but that was no reason not to shoot them. Imagining their smiles turning to looks of consternation made me want to shoot them more, and I thought for a moment about which one I would shoot first, and where. It seemed like a good idea to deal with the man first. I would not want to shoot him in the head or chest right away. Remembering that he did three hundred push-ups a day, which was one of the secrets to his sturdy build, I thought that I'd first shoot his legs, making him fall to his knees, and then I'd shoot his two arms.

When I imagined him on his knees, it was as though he'd already fallen, and I thought I would wait for another opportunity. Then I remembered the time when my ex-girlfriend had diarrhea on our walk and I picked grape leaves for her. I remembered feeling content after that act of kindness. I decided to show kindness by letting the couple live, and I felt content. I shot randomly toward some cacti, and the bullet went right through a cactus, leaving a gaping hole. I fired the pistol a couple more times, aiming at the hole, but I missed every time. I fired the last shot toward the scorching sun.

When I handed the gun over, our Mexican friend went to the car to put on a gaucho hat. He impersonated a gaucho, pistol in hand, gesturing as if to shoot a snake or something moving on the ground. Fortunately, there was nothing moving. I recalled what he'd told us about snakes over drinks the previous night. He had told us about how he used to kill and skin venomous snakes and dry them in the sun, hanging them on a line with clothespins. When the flesh became as hard as wood, he would pound it into powder to mix with food. Such was the custom in the rural village in Mexico where he spent his teens. He'd said that many village children emulated adults, killing and skinning snakes. In my drunken state, his story of pinning skinned snakes to a clothesline to dry had sounded strangely poetic.

Using a knife, we cut off a small piece of a cactus that we'd shot to infuse it in tequila. The cactus didn't add any flavor to the tequila. I don't know whether the cactus was edible, but it didn't cause any problems.

Although my ex-girlfriend had changed considerably, one thing hadn't changed: she slept in past noon every day. When her past and current boyfriends, who arose in the morning, had finished a task or two and were looking for something to do, she'd finally get up. She'd tell us the plan for the day, which was usually the same as the previous day. We followed her directives like loyal servants.

We drank tequila for several more nights and went out to the barren field to shoot at cacti in the daytime. This also got old, so we drove out to a place that was also barren but with higher and steeper hills. We climbed up a hill under the intense heat of the sun. Standing at the summit, I looked at the barren land, expecting some dramatic action, as one does. But as though all of the animals were hiding in the shade, resting up for night, all was motionless. The blue sky was deep and vast, and seemed to be indulging in its own depth and vastness. I grimaced at the sky and kicked a few pebbles down the steep hill. Watching the pebbles roll down senselessly, I wanted to do something senseless. I kicked a few more pebbles down the hill. I thought about how many pebbles I had rolled down hills in my lifetime, and figured that if I could collect them all in one place, I could build a small stone tower. Then the Mexican fellow started to copy me. Inexplicably, the pebbles he kicked seemed to travel farther. He was sniggering senselessly, which I guessed was the reason his pebbles traveled so far. My ex-girlfriend just watched us, as though she was going to choose the man whose pebbles traveled farther to be her servant. When I stopped senselessly kicking pebbles, the Mexican fellow also stopped.

The weather was very hot, and we paused as though we'd lost all energy. A small plane appeared from beyond the horizon and flew toward us. This made me feel like we were three people stranded on a barren hill, waiting for rescue. The sky was vast, and the plane was slow. We watched patiently for a long time. The plane finally reached us, but it flew right past as if it had not seen us or meant to leave us to die. Again, we watched patiently for a long time, until the plane disappeared beyond the horizon. I imagined the plane suddenly belching black smoke and making an emergency landing, but no such thing happened. As I watched the plane disappear, I thought it looked like a pterodactyl that had flown in from the Jurassic period. I waited for a flock of pterodactyls to appear in the sky, but no pterodactyls or planes that looked like pterodactyls came. In a silence made heavier by the fading noise, I thought that we would have to give up all hope of rescue and prepare to meet our deaths in silence.

It was too hot to stay on the hill, and we were forced to go down, regretting having hiked up just to kick some pebbles. The way down was as treacherous as the way up. Even the shadow that walked beside me, which looked like my melted skin, seemed exhausted. I thought that if I took my eye off it my exhausted shadow would fall behind, so I kept my eye on my shadow as I walked. On our descent, we saw an eagle perched on a rock on the opposite hill. Beyond that hill were more hills, beyond which were big mountains where coyotes might live.

Driving home, we spotted a broken wheelchair on the side of the road. Our Mexican friend stopped the car, and fired two bullets at the wheelchair, then started off again. I felt sorry for the wheelchair, which once carried people with impaired legs, but which now had become impaired itself. The Mexican fellow was ten years younger than I was and had overflowing energy. I could not fault him for his youth.

I thought that I couldn't stay on with them, drinking tequila, shooting guns, and going up barren hills in the middle of the day. But when I was drunk on tequila, I thought I could continue on indefinitely, and I couldn't think of a better option. Sober, I felt the need to do something different, but there seemed to be nothing else to do. For the next three days we did nothing but drink tequila day and night. Having nothing particular to do, we put off every little thing as long as possible. Something as simple as walking over to fully open a half-open window required determination. I could go on and on, elaborating on how unmotivated we were to do anything. Let it suffice to say that even when we had an itch, we could not be bothered to scratch it. We would just sit there, itching, or ask another to scratch the itch, but we seldom scratched one another's itches.

When something itched, the itch was always accompanied by the annoyance of having to think about the itch, at which point we would scratch the itch, feeling very annoyed.

Tequila bottles piled up in the corner of the living room, but no one bothered to clear them. I thought it was the job of our Mexican friend, but he seemed especially determined to avoid the task. We didn't see any more scorpions inside the house. Nor did we see any scorpions outside the house, so it wasn't an option to herd scorpions into the house so that we could chase them out. One day, we got dressed, got in the car, and started the car as if to go somewhere, but we could not decide where to go. Unable to decide on a destination, we decided it was best that we not go anywhere. So we went back in the house.

On my last day there, I woke up late and went to the kitchen to find my ex-girlfriend doing the dishes in her panties. I approached her without saying anything. I hugged her from behind and grabbed her breasts. They felt like balloons filled with warm water. Just holding them wasn't enough for me to be sure that they were the same breasts I used to fondle long before. I thought that if I saw them, I might be able to tell, but I didn't try to look.

After seven days of drinking tequila, shooting guns, looking down at a barren field from the top of a hill, and chasing scorpions, and another three days of doing nothing at all, I felt as though a hundred days had passed. If I thought that a hundred days had gone by in ten days, it seemed that time had gone by very fast. But if I thought that ten days had gone by in a hundred days, it seemed that time had gone by very slowly. On the eleventh day, we returned to Los Angeles. We went to a Mexican restaurant downtown and ate *birria*, a Mexican goat stew, for lunch. It felt like a celebratory meal after a penance of drinking tequila.

2. Hollywood

WE WENT TO Hollywood because the Mexican fellow had some business there. He went into a nightclub near downtown Hollywood, presumably to meet someone. Seeing him enter the club in the middle of the day with a small bag, I thought again that he looked like a gangsta, a small fry.

As we waited in the car, a car passed by in the opposite direction. In it, a large dog was having the time of its life, its head hanging out the open window, its long hair flying in the wind. Riding in the car with its long hair flying in the wind really suited the dog. I thought the dog looked like a movie star. The dog disappeared from sight and an ecstatic black man, who appeared to be African, specifically Ethiopian, crossed the street, wearing a long, draping, traditional-looking costume, carrying what appeared to be a traditional African percussion instrument. He looked as though he had just heard news of his being nominated to be the next chief of his tribe, and couldn't contain his joy.

After the African chief went away, three women walked by, carrying shopping bags. They looked like porn stars, with enormous breasts filled with silicone. Watching them made me feel that I was in Hollywood for real. The woman in the middle, who had the largest breasts of the three of them, looked like the boss. Her breasts were so large that anyone would sense immediately that she was the boss. I guessed that they decided who the boss was by the size of their breasts. Chewing gum like a boss, the woman blew a huge, breast-like bubble. I imagined her as a comic book character and inserted text in the speech bubble attached to her lips. *What would the world be like without silicone? Would that change our destinies? It's awful to even think about a world without silicone. My dream is to live in a house made of silicone. If I am born again, I want to be silicone.* The other two didn't have speech bubbles because they weren't chewing gum. Speechless, they showed agreement by nodding with their breasts, which were enormous, but not as enormous as the boss's. Their enormous breasts probably had many uses, but I guessed that they were mostly used for nodding.

Next I saw a white dwarf woman hugging a shopping bag with green onion tops sticking out. She was walking side by side with a Latina dwarf who was sucking on a Chupa Chups lollipop. The two women seemed to be a lesbian couple. Both wore grim faces as though they'd just had an argument. The white dwarf woman said something, which made the Latina dwarf snap and scream, hurling her Chupa Chups into the road. I guessed that she would also throw the other woman's shopping bag and walk off, but I was wrong. They were still fighting with raised voices when they disappeared around the corner. The Latina dwarf was sucking on a brand new Chupa Chups. She hurled her Chupa Chups when she was angry, but it seemed that she sucked on a Chupa Chups to control her anger.

I suddenly felt as though I was watching a scene from a David Lynch film. I thought that a Chupa Chups is a nice thing to suck on, but that it is not as nice as a nipple to hold in one's mouth. I thought about the fact that Salvador Dalí designed the logo with the daisy motif on the Chupa Chups wrapper. I wondered what Dalí would have done had he seen the dwarf women, one of them sucking on a Chupa Chups, the logo of which he had designed. He wouldn't have been able to ignore them. He might have tried to court their good graces, and they might have inspired him to paint a surrealist piece, titled *Dwarf Woman Sucking on a Chupa Chups and Her Homosexual Dwarf Lover*.

It was possible that they were bisexual, and one had discovered that the other was cheating on her with a dwarf man. Maybe they were fighting because the white dwarf woman was angry about how much the Latina dwarf loved Chupa Chups; perhaps she loved them more than she loved her lover. It was possible that they fought once a day, and fighting was like a fourth meal of the day. That might have been the one time in the day that the Latina dwarf sucked on a Chupa Chups. Perhaps they went home and ate a dish with green onions made by the Latina dwarf. This might have put them in a good mood, making them forget all about having had an argument, and they might have sucked on a Chupa Chups together. After sucking away the last of their Chupa Chups, they might have been so pleased that they couldn't resist making love. That might just have been their way of being together.

After seeing not just one, but two dwarfs, better still, dwarf women, I was in a very good mood, as if I had seen a twin rainbow. I was reminded of an incident involving a dwarf, which further enhanced my mood. I recalled this incident whenever I spotted a dwarf. I had seen many dwarfs in my lifetime, but only once had I spoken to one. I was walking down an alleyway in Seoul when a dwarf approached me and asked where he could buy paper and watercolors. Unsure which way to direct him, I told him without confidence how to get to the main road. My lack of confidence was partly because I wasn't sure of the way, and partly because I always lose confidence when I face a dwarf. I didn't know what the dwarf man planned to do with paper and watercolors, but I imagined that he might paint himself, his deceased dwarf father, a toad, or a volcano.

I have lost confidence whenever I've faced a dwarf since the time I had an encounter with yet another dwarf. I was lost in an alleyway in Seoul when I saw a dwarf man doing freehand exercises in front of a house, presumably his house. He was moving his body to commands that he was barking out in a disciplined, sonorous voice. I stopped and watched him for a while. I felt slightly threatened, as though I had sensed something dangerous about the man. I felt that the entire street was being helplessly subjugated by his sonorous commands. *Why doesn't he exercise in his house? If he is going to exercise outside, he should at least refrain from shouting commands. Committing two uncouth acts at once? Utterly uncouth!*

To my surprise, he wasn't doing just any old freehand exercises, but was performing from start to finish the "national exercise" routine, which had long ago been forced on every Korean citizen. This routine might have been beneficial for people's health, but my memory of it was not a very fond one, and just watching him follow the routine put me in a sour mood. Few people still performed the exercise routine, but in an era when the entire nation of South Korea strove frantically to escape poverty, it had been performed to commands emanating from loudspeakers in the yards of every school, military base, factory, and company. The dwarf man going through the mass exercise routine in a quiet, narrow alleyway so many years later seemed rather decadent. *Decadence* was probably not the right word, but no other word seemed appropriate because I felt that there was something decadent about what I was seeing. It was probably that same vague sense of decadence that I felt from the totalitarian system, which obsessed over mass exercise, and often employed it to imprint in people's minds the idea that the group is more important than the individual. The dwarf appeared to be soothing his nostalgia for totalitarianism by performing the mass exercise routine.

He seemed to be toying with me. As a child, I had generally stayed put when someone toyed with me. This time, too, I stayed put, thinking, *This dwarf man is toying with me. No one ever toys with me anymore. Toy with me all you want. See if I do anything but stay put.* I thought about running by him, like a Maasai warrior, to disturb his freehand exercises, but I just stood there blankly. I thought that I might watch with interest were he to do apparatus gymnastics instead of freehand exercises. I feel something close to envy for people who are trained in apparatus gymnastics. I could have simply walked away, but for some reason I continued to stand there.

What really scared me was the set of gestures he made after he finished his exercise routine. He stood still for a moment, exhaled slowly as he bent his knees and opened his arms wide, and then moved his hands to his waist. He repeated this several times. He was doing a *chi* exercise. I felt that I was being overwhelmed by some kind of *chi*. He was accumulating *chi*. It seemed that he had accumulated a great deal of *chi*, but was trying to gather more, as though he didn't have enough. I usually turn weak in the heart and docile when I face a dwarf, but this time I became ferocious. The dwarf's hands were shaking, and he was red in the face from exertion. He was consuming *chi* while trying to accumulate *chi*. It looked as if all of his *chi* was going to leave his body. He didn't appear to be accumulating evil energy, nor did he seem to be accumulating good energy. Regardless, for a short while, I was overwhelmed by his *chi*.

He seemed determined to show me how effectively he could dampen another person's spirit when he was determined. Senselessly, I observed his senseless behavior, thinking that he should direct his efforts to dampen another person's spirit toward children, whose spirits are not easily dampened. I didn't try to get a grip on myself, because I thought that doing so would lead to no good result. I considered saying something insincere that he might like to hear, but I refrained from saying anything. I did not tell him, "You intimidate me with your bloodshot eyes and all." He appeared to be playing a trick to drain my energy and boost his morale. I felt that my energy was draining faster than he seemed to be extracting it. His tactic seemed to be to drain my energy little by little. A moment later, my legs went rubbery. As lackadaisical as ever, I stared at him as though looking at a hideous sight, but being observed just seemed to fire him up.

The dwarf man completely failed to notice that I was secretly mocking him, so I made a slightly contemptuous face. He still did not notice, and I became extremely frustrated. I even felt resentment toward the man for failing to notice my contempt. The dwarf seemed rather slow-witted. From his failing so miserably to understand another person's mind, I judged him to be an inattentive person. If I allow myself, I am capable of taking cheap shots under the right circumstances. I wanted to act cheap in front of the dwarf, but I couldn't allow myself to, partly because a thought suddenly came to mind: growing up, he had probably never been told, "You've grown so much since the last time I saw you." While I was entertaining this random thought, he made a sound akin to a battle cry, as though trying to prove that he was not bluffing. This made me think that everything he was doing was a bluff, and I thought to myself, *You are nothing but a bluffer, dwarf man.* I was certain that he was a dwarf, but I was not certain that he was a total bluffer.

Soon he looked fully energized, as if he'd gathered all the

chi he needed. I felt my *chi* blocked and my strength dissipating. I do not know the difference between *chi* and strength, but strength seems more physical. In order to overwhelm him, I needed enough *chi* to dampen his *chi*. As I often did, I imagined how great it would be to dampen another person's energy with my overflowing energy, or defeat an opponent by *chi* alone, without moving a finger. But soon I decided that someone overflowing with energy is not a pretty sight.

Suddenly, the man started throwing hooks like a boxer sparring. I stood still and watched. Instead of disapproving of my staring, he made a face that commanded me to watch him carefully, and threw an air punch in my direction. Like a fool, I stood still, thinking that I could not compete with the dwarf man by standing still, but I couldn't think of anything else to do to compete with him. I wondered what he intended to do with himself, and what he intended to do with me. I was unsure what he was after. He was very aggressive. Despite standing still, I felt as though I was being increasingly put on the defensive, shrinking into a corner. Facing this menacing dwarf, I stood in place, vowing to myself that I would stare him down menacingly rather than retreat. I wondered what he would do next, after performing freehand exercises, accumulating *chi*, and training boxing moves. (I imagined that he'd sit in that alleyway and enter a meditative state, and then go running to finish his important daily task of dampening the energy of passersby through the training of his body and mind. I thought that if his reason for training his body and mind was to dampen the energy of others, then he was no more than a small-minded dwarf.) I fled, thinking that I will never compete with a dwarf. Since then, I have lost confidence every time I have faced a dwarf.

After training his body but not cultivating his mind, I guessed as I pleased that he'd go into his house and eat three raw eggs, exciting his mind rather than calming it, and stare at the ceiling with a smirk, thinking about the unimpressive things he might do that day. Then I thought, *No, I am sure that he is not going to eat raw eggs, but three spoonfuls of honey from a small honey jar. Then he will stare jeeringly at the wall, quietly, like a man who has eaten honey. If there is no honey, he will probably scoop sugar into his mouth. The sweet taste will be helpful for keeping a jeer on his face, which he is likely to do for a good while. There must be a lot of things he can jeer at.* I wished that he would someday be able to jeer at the world from inside his house, calmly playing a broken instrument, such as a trumpet that can no longer make sound, instead of doing bizarre things out in the street.

Soon after the two dwarf women disappeared, I saw a tall, gay-looking, old white man in makeup cross the street. He had no sex appeal, and he looked lonely in the crowd. This made me think that arriving at the age when one loses all sex appeal, to both the same sex and the opposite sex, is possibly one of the saddest things that a person might experience in his lifetime. Sadness seemed to permeate his entire existence. I could feel his loneliness as I visualized the man at home, looking quietly into the mirror, applying makeup. It's possible that he was content with his appearance and loneliness. Regardless, I imagined that the moment he felt the loneliest was when he gazed at his raw face after removing his makeup. The man, too, disappeared, and the Hollywood street suddenly looked like any other street. My ex-girlfriend suggested that I seriously consider settling in California. I told her I would. It seemed like a decent plan, and feasible.

Our gangsta took a long while before coming back out with a large shopping bag in hand. He ignored me when I asked what was in the bag, so I became certain that he was carrying drugs. I pictured myself running away with his goods and sprinkling some in a *koi* pond in some park, bestowing upon the fish an experience of a new world. The carp would lie about at the surface of the water euphorically for about half a day before waking up. The fellow took two bottles of tequila out of the shopping bag, saying that they were of fine quality. In a losing deal, he must have delivered a small amount of drugs and been paid in tequila instead of cash. He could not help but love tequila, having grown up drinking tequila from a young age. He hailed from a town not far from the town of Tequila, Mexico, which is well-known for its tequila production. The fellow never did tell me what he did for a living. My ex-girlfriend didn't give me a clear explanation, either. I don't think that he was involved in anything dishonorable. Rather, he seemed to be trying to appear to be involved in something dishonorable, because he considered doing nothing dishonorable. If that was the case, in my opinion, it would have been honorable of him to just tell it like it was.

3. Inevitable Acts of Senselessness

THAT EVENING, WE traveled north along the Pacific coastline without a clear destination. We stopped and swam at a few beaches. We saw pelicans, seals, and sea lions. We stayed the night at a beachside hotel in Monterey. I wanted to stay the night at a hotel farther up the coast and go to a nude beach near Santa Cruz, but the Mexican fellow opposed this idea, insisting that he could not take off his clothes in public.

The next morning, I was looking out the window of our second-floor hotel room when a white man, who appeared to be in his early twenties, walked out onto the sandy beach. Like a man stranded on a desert island, signaling for help, he wrote something in the sand with his feet in letters large enough to be visible from afar. It was like a scene in a movie. When he was finished, he looked at what he'd written, and I saw that he'd written a name: *Valerie*.

The name *Valerie* reminded me of the poem "The Graveyard by the Sea" by Paul Valéry, but there was, of course, no graveyard by the sea in the vicinity. I wondered why the man had written that name. It seemed probable that he was looking for a woman named Valerie. Perhaps a woman named Valerie watched from her hotel room as the man wrote her name. Valerie might have been punishing the man for something he'd done that deserved punishment, or the man might have been trying to flatter Valerie. The man gazed briefly at the name he had written and, as in a scene in a movie, went off into the distance.

Even more bizarrely, after watching this unfold, I rushed out onto the beach and began erasing the name written in the sand. The man likely had a reason for his action, perhaps to show off for Valerie. If Valerie had made him write her name, it was likely some sort of punishment. For my action, however, there was no reason whatsoever. What I did felt nothing at all like a scene in

36

a movie. Rather, it felt like a scene that must be deleted from a strange novel.

From their hotel window, Valerie and her boyfriend could have watched her name being obliterated mercilessly by the feet of a seemingly mad Asian man. They might have discussed whether that man was sane. The boyfriend, who didn't mind trouble and was fond of causing trouble, could have intended to rush out and confront me, but he'd been dissuaded by Valerie, who did not like to see trouble of any kind. They might have argued briefly over this issue. Perhaps the boyfriend, who could not swallow his anger easily, walked toward the door, telling himself he would not swallow his anger easily this time, either. Valerie might have blocked him, her arms outstretched and her moist eyes looking directly into his glowing eyes, pleading that he control his temper for her sake. Thus Valerie's boyfriend, who liked to deliberately do wrong, might have decided that he would not deliberately do wrong this time.

At any rate, no one was coming toward me. I completely erased the name *Valerie*. I often feel that I am up to some obvious ploy, but I didn't feel that way this time. Actually, I sometimes feel that almost everything I do is some preposterous ploy, but this time I didn't feel at all as though I was up to some preposterous ploy. Looking down at the traces of my action, I gradually became aware of what I'd done, and felt that I needed to do something to remedy the situation. The situation was irreversible, however, and I seemed incapable of remedying it.

Still, out of the blue, an unidentifiable sentiment in the shape of satisfaction arose in me and then dissipated. By the lingering impression of the sentiment that arose but quickly dissipated, I could not be sure whether it was indeed satisfaction. I was almost certain that it was not satisfaction. I noticed that small parts of the letters, which I had thought I had erased completely, remained untouched. I felt a compulsion to remove them, so I erased the remaining parts with my feet. This time, out of the blue, a vague feeling of regret came over me. My emotions seemed to be springing up arbitrarily. I pretended for a moment that I was gently stepping on the feeling of regret that visited me, and a thought occurred, as though awakened by the feeling of regret, a realization that I had done something that could cause trouble, despite my distaste for trouble of any kind. But that feeling of regret also lacked substance, and it dissipated shortly after arising. After that, I didn't feel much of anything.

I thought that I did what I did because I was compelled to rescue Valerie, though I did not know from what. This made no sense. More senseless thoughts flashed inside my head one after another. In vain, I moved sand around with my feet, as if to bury those thoughts. After that, I thought briefly about what else I could do by that sea with no "graveyard by the sea," but I could think of nothing appropriate. I continued to think about what should happen after someone has written the name *Valerie* and I have erased it, as one thinks about the natural progression of events. I felt that I would be just as happy with anything happening as with nothing happening. If something was bound to happen, I thought that it had to be something like my walking into the ocean as if it were no big deal, but the thought remained only a thought. This notion had nothing to do with the fact that I had done something undignified, and that I felt that I needed to do whatever it would take to restore my lost dignity. I didn't believe that walking into the ocean would restore my dignity, which had hit bottom. I nonchalantly lit a cigarette, but this made me feel like the kind of person who acts nonchalant after a gaffe. I stubbed out the cigarette.

I thought, *I don't have anything to do. Should I just freeze in place?* I did not. I just pushed around more sand sheepishly. Then I thought, *I'm feeling mellow. Maybe I'll sing softly.* I didn't do that, either. Next, I thought, *Since I have time, I might walk back and forth on the beach for no reason like a person who cannot make up his mind.* It occurred to me that erasing Valerie's name was probably enough of doing things for no reason. Regardless, I walked back and forth briefly, hoping that doing so would help me make up my mind. By doing so, however, I became even more incapable of making up my mind. I halted and tried to recall whether I knew a woman named Valerie. Regretfully,

I did not. I knew women named Natalie and Teresa, but their names conjured feelings quite different from Valerie's. I thought that I'd been too thorough in erasing the name *Valerie*, that I had done wrong to all the Valeries in the world. I wrote a small *V* in the sand to resurrect the name *Valerie* and left as if fleeing a crime scene.

A little bit later, looking out the window of my hotel room, it occurred to me that I had been overly excited. I thought that the excitement I'd felt seeing the name *Valerie* written in sand and running out to erase it could be likened to the excitement that might arise from capsizing a boat and floundering in the water. But this analogy didn't seem entirely appropriate. Rather, it seemed an appropriate example of an inappropriate analogy. Actually, it didn't even seem appropriate as such. Other equally inappropriate analogies came to mind one after another, but no appropriate ones. I had no choice but to give up trying to find an appropriate analogy, and this tormented me greatly.

The problem then was not what I had done, the incomprehensible act of erasing the name *Valerie*, but the fact that I couldn't find an appropriate analogy for the act, the lack of an analogy. If only I could find an appropriate analogy, I would be able to comprehend and accept the senseless act I'd committed. At that moment, as I do from time to time, I realized yet again how painful it is to be unable to find an appropriate analogy for something. By not finding an appropriate analogy, I realized anew the power of analogy. Had I found an appropriate analogy, I wouldn't have been so tormented. I was on the verge of tearing my hair out, so I tore out some hair, which made me feel like a man experiencing anew some severe emotional turmoil that he thought he had nearly mastered, albeit with much difficulty.

My suffering could be likened to being driven insane looking for an object that one desperately needs, which he knows for certain is in the house but cannot remember where. I decided, however, that these two feelings are clearly different. I realized once again that I almost always use similes when I make analogies. I am not fond of metaphors. I am not sure of the exact reason, but a simile, to me, is like the moisture on the floor where water has

spilled, while a metaphor is like the dry stain that remains after
the water has evaporated.

Having finally given up trying to find an appropriate analogy,
I looked at my footprints scattered across the sandy beach. It
occurred to me that erasing a person's name written in the sand
was one of the most senseless things I'd ever done. I certainly
don't try to commit senseless acts at every opportunity, but I have
committed a fair number nevertheless. This one really stood out.
For some reason, in certain situations, I choose the most senseless option available rather than the most ideal option. In these
situations, the consequences are, naturally, senseless. I generally
consider myself to be rather inane, and from time to time, I
actually consider making an effort to be more inane. I did not,
however, resolve to repeat such an inane act as erasing a person's
name written in the sand if the opportunity presented itself.
Making such a resolution felt like an awfully inane thing to do.

I thought for a moment about how seldom I am motivated
by the sophisticated or sacred causes that lead many people to
action. The causes that motivate me are far from sophisticated or
sacred. I thought briefly about the fact that there are too many
things in the world that one might do without reason, or sometimes cannot avoid doing, and about how these things sometimes
give me great pleasure. I thought about the extent of the pleasure
I had derived from such things, albeit for short periods. I was
encouraged slightly by this fact, and so I thought, *I will commit
another senseless act if the opportunity presents itself.* It was like a
resolution, and I wondered whether it was right to make such
a resolution. I concluded that it didn't matter, because, resolved
or not, I was sure to do a similarly senseless thing again if the
opportunity presented itself. I thought that I might end up doing
such a thing, or I might not. Once again, I recalled the great
pleasure I'd felt after committing senseless acts. I was absurdly
pleased, thinking that few people in the world would resolve to
commit a senseless act if the opportunity presented itself.

In the end, the senseless act that I had committed remained
an incomprehensible event because I couldn't find an appropriate
analogy. Neither Valerie nor the man, who was possibly Valerie's

boyfriend or just someone looking for Valerie, was anywhere to be seen. I was sorry that another man did not come to the beach and write *Valerie* in the sand. I did not know whether I would erase the name again, but it seemed unlikely. Once was enough. I hoped that the couple talked about how they could not possibly deal with every lunatic they met because there were just too many of them. I hoped that they would enjoy themselves wherever they planned to go that day, holding hands lovingly, as though that was the only way they might endure this troubled world and its many lunatics.

As I stood by the window and stared at the letter *V* written in the sand, a fairly comprehensive feeling of embarrassment washed over me. I was compelled to do something about that embarrassment, but I couldn't think of anything appropriate. If I ever feel like someone else, it's when I come up with a wicked idea. At that moment, however, I could not come up with a wicked idea, so I didn't feel like someone else. Looking back, I hadn't had a wicked idea for way too long. On second thought, it felt as though I had never actually come up with a wicked idea. As I was trying to think of something to do, my hands slipped into my underwear without my knowing. I felt my buttocks, which made me think that the situation was beyond all hope.

I had not weighed a lot to begin with, and I had lost a lot of weight from drinking too much tequila and not eating enough. I could feel the back of my hip bones beneath my meager flesh, and it felt as though there was no butt where a butt should be. My butt was like a skeleton model with no flesh. It was real, but I could perceive it as a metaphor for something else. To examine it more closely, I went into the bathroom and dropped my underwear. The butt in the mirror was pathetic to look at. I thought that there is no person more pathetic than a person with a pathetic butt. It was utterly lacking charm, but I told myself that it was at least worth looking at. Actually, it wasn't even worth looking at. I couldn't remember when exactly I had last looked at my butt in the mirror. The last time, it hadn't been so unsightly.

I would have liked to put my underwear back on and move on to something normal, but it suddenly occurred to me that I

must not have let out a respectable fart since my buttocks had
become so unsightly. It seemed only logical that a person with
a nice-looking butt would fart respectably. In order to test this
theory, I tried solemnly to fart, to see what sort of unrespectable fart would come out, but I couldn't break wind. I wished
to release several farts in a row, rather than letting out one lousy
fart, but there was nothing. I was angry at the gas that would
not be released. My failed attempt reaffirmed the fact that trying
to fart on purpose for whatever reason doesn't work. This fact,
too, seemed logical. I was not at all proud that I'd become aware
of two very useless logical facts in a short time. I'm making this
up, actually. From the get-go, I didn't believe I'd be able to fart,
so I did not try.

A thought about the passing of gas wafted past me, but it
didn't captivate my imagination. It was about St. Augustine, who
is alleged to have played an entire song by passing gas. If this is a
true story, he was a magnificent passer of gas. This was perhaps
because he had a magnificent butt. His rear might have looked
like that of a pregnant woman. When he was filled with the Holy
Spirit, he probably passed gas humbly through his rear to play a
hymn, inspiring his audience with the Holy Spirit.

I quit thinking about passing gas and looked at my butt
again. It was so fleshless, I could hardly call it a butt. It almost
looked pathetic to the point of being noble. I christened my
butt "The Incomparably Noble Ass" because my butt deserved
to be ridiculed. I could have just called it a lousy butt. I tried to
find other deserving modifiers for my butt, but I could only find
undeserving modifiers, so I gave up trying to find more modifiers. In any case, I felt that I was being too harsh by insulting
my poor butt.

I became exceedingly embarrassed about having run out
to erase the name *Valerie*, sporting that butt and a matching,
scrawny body. I thought that anyone with a butt like mine must
surely be extremely exhausted, mentally as well as physically. My
butt seemed deserving of punishment, corporal punishment.
Rather than hitting it (since there was so little of it to hit), taking

away its dignity even further and making it more pathetic seemed a more suitable punishment. Let us think about this. Actually, it's a rather simple matter. It wasn't the fault of my butt, but my own fault that my butt had come to look so pathetic. My butt had no fault at all. It was suffering hardship, robbed of its dignity by its terrible master. It was I, not my butt, who deserved punishment. I stroked my butt apologetically, and told myself that I would remember to punish myself later.

Since looking at the reflection of one's butt in the mirror is a rather embarrassing thing to do, I only do it occasionally. Actually, I probably do it at least once a month. There are many more embarrassing things that I do when I am by myself, but I don't intend to discuss them. In fact, looking at the reflection of my butt is not so embarrassing compared to those other things. (It is embarrassing for me to write about extremely personal things, such as my butt and farts, but embarrassingly, I don't have great interest in writing about respectable things.)

The butt in the mirror, which looked as though it had given up all hope, seemed to be telling me to give up hope as well. Pulling my pants up, I concluded that, with my butt the way it was, I was not going to accomplish anything. I wondered, *Where should I place my faith now? What shall I do from now on?* Nothing seemed to be in store for my butt, which made everything feel challenging and embarrassing. It seemed reasonable that a person with such a butt shouldn't even think about the future. Any kind of hope seemed excessive for a butt like that. My butt appeared to be telling me that, with such a sorry butt, I should not even dream of meeting a woman. I thought to myself, *I get it. That's enough.*

I recognized that I was acting rather pitiful. As if looking at the reflection of what could hardly be called a butt in the mirror was not enough, I had moved on to thinking about passing gas and insulting my butt. And as if that still wasn't enough, I'd given up all hope in life. But my pitiful behavior didn't end there. It led to thoughts of acting pitiful. I thought that I should perhaps be in awe of myself, but this was nothing new to me. I often carry things too far, knowingly. Aware that I was acting pitiful, I advanced a makeshift theory about acting pitiful, which can be summarized as follows:

One should act pitiful from time to time, and doing so does no harm. If done well, acting pitiful can be fun and good for mental health, but if done tactlessly, one risks losing face. One must be careful when acting pitiful, because it's easy to take it too far, at which point it could be harmful to the body. One problem with acting pitiful is that it's difficult to do it moderately and well without losing dignity. Acting pitiful can be considered a kind of mental exercise, a desperate mental struggle to fall into the abyss, while at the same time trying not to fall. Acting pitiful can be interpreted as waving the white flag, surrendering to this brutally dull and meaningless world rather than fighting it, while smiling on the inside. Authors such as Kafka and Yi Sang demonstrated this point most effectively. Yi Sang exhibited the essence of pitiful practice when he picked one rather unpleasant day to take a de-worming drug. In my opinion, there is much to learn from the pitiful practices of these two authors. However, one has to have a strong sense of identity when he showcases his pitifulness in order for his pitifulness to shine.

Having arrived at a makeshift theory on acting pitiful, I felt as though I had run out of pitiful acts. My thoughts returned from the conceptual to the concrete: my butt. My butt seemed suited only for lying around idly, so I lay in my bed and stayed there. I imagined a voice inside of me that sounded like a call from the heavens, telling me to give up everything completely. I felt that I was not doing all that I could at that moment, which is how I usually feel when I am lying around doing nothing. Peace of mind, which sometimes comes to a person who has given up everything, did not come to me. There was not even a sign of it coming. The letter *V* written in the sand began to bother me. To me, the letter *V* had come to mean victory, which made my earlier deed seem even more ridiculous. Only after arriving at the conclusion that the person who'd erased the name *Valerie* and replaced it with the letter *V* was out of his mind and should be ignored, was I able to lie still, forgetting about Valerie, my butt, and myself.

At breakfast, I told my ex-girlfriend and her boyfriend about the senseless act I had committed. The Mexican fellow praised me, saying that I'd done the right thing, though he would not have done the same. He added that a man who writes a woman's name in the sand must either be uninhibited or small-minded, or uninhibited and small-minded. He said that if a man cannot be stopped from doing such a thing, his action should at least be rescinded after the fact. The fellow's words sounded either almost senseless or completely senseless.

Still, I thought that if I saw someone else's name written in the sand in the future, I would perhaps end up erasing it. A name didn't seem like something that must not be erased. If it happened, I thought, I might recall the name *Valerie* as I erased the fresh name in the sand. Alternately, I might never erase another name written in the sand, even if I saw one. Once in a lifetime seemed plenty for such an act. Actually, I didn't think I would do it ever again. Once I thought that I wouldn't, it felt like something I shouldn't do. However, my saying that I would never do it again was not a guarantee that I'd not do it. One can decide not to do such a thing, but there is not much one can do if he ends up doing it anyway. What I had done could be a thing that I decided not to do again after doing it once, only to do it again. What is more, committing such an act without a clear motivation gave me a welcome pleasure that I couldn't put my finger on. It was a kind of pleasure that could not be derived from an act with a clear motivation.

I was slowly chewing soft-boiled egg, looking out the window at two children playing in the sand, when it occurred to me that by erasing the name *Valerie* I'd fully demonstrated some hidden talent for doing senseless things. It was a shame that I'd been wasting such a talent rather than utilizing it from time to time. I then thought that my thinking in this way was also senseless. Perhaps, senseless acts are one way of coping with life, which is difficult to endure without them.

After breakfast, we went to downtown Monterey. There were many quaint shops and cafes, but none stood out to me. We were walking down the street when I saw a young woman pushing a baby carriage, inside which a baby girl kept blowing raspberries. *Thbpbpthpt hbpbpthpt thptpth.* It was not a very cold day, but the baby's lips were blue. I suspected that it was from vibrating her lips so hard. She was blond and rather fair. I hold a belief that borders on superstition that babies blowing raspberries means that it's about to rain. I think that babies blow raspberries because they sense rain, like moles predicting an earthquake. I have witnessed numerous such cases. When babies blow raspberries, rain comes almost without fail. It is possible that when a critical mass of babies in an area blow raspberries, it will begin to rain.

Older children, up to a certain age, seem to also have this ability. I vaguely recall that when I was young, I, too, blew raspberries when I sensed rain. I believe that the reason adults try to stop children from blowing raspberries is that they don't want rain. I think that babies have the greatest ability to predict rain before teething, after which their power diminishes gradually. In other words, people lose the power to predict rain as they acquire teeth. As for old people who have lost all their teeth, I believe that they know when rain is coming, but they are too crafty to show their foreknowledge. Perhaps old people do not care whether it rains. This is unlikely, though, because as frail as they may be, elderly people often predict rain by the condition of their neuralgia.

The sky was blue. *Whatever it takes, that blue sky had better cloud up and start raining, or that blue-lipped baby will turn blue in the face and start crying!* I anxiously awaited rain. If it didn't rain, the baby was going to cry, and this had to be prevented. We walked alongside the baby carriage for a short time. The baby in the carriage continued to blow raspberries, announcing repeatedly that rain was certainly coming. She seemed to be warning us to prepare for imminent rain, at the same time pleading with her eyes, begging to be drenched by rain. I reasoned that the baby, having recently left her mother's amniotic fluid, had traits similar to those of an amphibian and enjoyed being soaked to the bone. When I told my companions about my belief, they told me that they, too, had blown raspberries as children, but did not know whether it had been related to rain. I decided that they were very unperceptive adults. I listened with greater attention. The sound the baby was making made me suspect a sun shower.

About half an hour later, we were drinking tea at a cafe. Amazingly, the sky darkened and it started to rain. Watching the steely resolve of the dark clouds shrouding the sky, I had time enough to prepare myself before it poured, but I did nothing. I wanted to face the rain defenselessly. The rain poured down fiercely. Although my prediction of a sun shower proved to be wrong, I was glad that my superstitious belief was not disproven. I was glad it was raining. I imagined that the rain clouds were the accumulation of the breath and saliva of the many babies in the surrounding area, who were exhaling and spitting, vibrating their lips as they blew raspberries.

Since then, on numerous occasions, I have witnessed babies blowing raspberries before rain. Babies are marvelous weather forecasters. When we split off from the baby carriage, the baby had laughed suddenly, making a sound that could only be produced by a baby. She appeared to be laughing from the pleasure of predicting rain, from her certainty of rain. I figured that only sorcerers in a trance and fortune-tellers could laugh in that way, and this made the baby look like a sorcerer or a fortune-teller. If adults paid attention to what babies are trying to say, they would, if nothing else, be able to prepare for rain.

We continued heading north and arrived in San Francisco in the middle of the night. Thick fog shrouded the city. We were unable to read the road signs, and there were no pedestrians to ask for directions. We drove around downtown for a while as though we were drifting in limbo. It felt like a hallucination from which I would never escape. We seemed to drive by places that we'd passed before. I was tickled by our marching in place, and thought that I would not mind staying in that state forever. I imagined that we were an expedition in the Arctic—where nothing is visible save for the endless expanse of snow—running in circles, about to give up all hope. The Mexican fellow, however, tried with all his might to escape from that state, as if to prove that not giving up hope in a desperate situation is as difficult as, or more difficult than, giving up all hope. My ex-girlfriend seemed indifferent. To her, indifference to everything was a sort of philosophy or ideal.

We were lost in the fog for nearly two hours before we managed to finally find our way north, escaping San Francisco via the Golden Gate Bridge. We continued north along the Pacific coastline. We couldn't swim because the water was too cold. Attracted by the name alone, we went all the way to a town called Eureka, which was like any other small town in America. We stayed a night at a hotel in Eureka, and drank tequila. When we were all drunk, my two companions tempted me again to stay with them, but I had decided to resist temptation, and I did. The next day, we drove back south along the Pacific coastline. We arrived in San Francisco at night. The city was again thick with fog, and again we got lost for a while. I had originally planned to go to Los Angeles with them, but I decided to stay in San Francisco for a few days. When they dropped me off in front of the hotel, they told me that San Francisco has one of the highest crime rates in America. They seemed concerned that I would not fare well in the fog. They were used to sunny Los Angeles, and fog made their stomachs turn. But I liked fog. Fog was what kept me in San Francisco. I questioned whether they would manage to escape the fog-engulfed city.

4. American Hobo

THE NEXT DAY, the fog had lifted completely. Gone with the fog was my reason for remaining in San Francisco. I lazed about in my hotel room for a good while before going out. I found myself a San Francisco guide book, but there was nowhere in particular I wished to go. I suddenly thought of Washington Square. At the time, I was rereading *Trout Fishing in America* by Richard Brautigan. On the cover of the book is a photograph of Brautigan and a woman posing in front of the statue of Benjamin Franklin in Washington Square Park.

I went to the park to see the statue of Benjamin Franklin. I stood in front of the statue. I'd never taken special interest in Benjamin Franklin, and standing in front of his statue did nothing to change this. I like to look at statues and indulge in personal emotions as if facing another person, but this statue didn't arouse any significant feelings in me. I thought that perhaps I would become interested in Benjamin Franklin at another time, another chance or opportunity. As I usually do when I observe statues, I carefully examined the hands. Both of Benjamin Franklin's hands are holding objects. I am fond of statues with empty hands. Empty statue hands generally point in a direction, and looking at where they point always leads me to something, interesting or not.

Once, in some park, I went to the place an empty-handed statue was pointing and found a bird's nest in the bushes. In the nest were four newborn chicks waiting for their mother. I watched them for a while. When I left, I waved to the statue that had led me to the chicks. Empty hands generally make statues look awkward. That is perhaps the reason that most statues hold things in their hands. I recalled a statue that I'd seen somewhere and liked immensely. I didn't remember whose statue it was, but I remembered that it had an expression of despair, holding its hands up, maybe down, in what I thought was a gesture

49

of surrender. The statue had seemed to be in a grave state of dejection.

Of all the statues of Benjamin Franklin in the United States, the one in San Francisco's Washington Square Park is unique in that it was donated by a dentist who implanted gold teeth for pioneers of the West during the gold rush. I wondered if the dentist who made his fortune from gold teeth had given Ben Franklin a gold tooth. Smoking a cigarette, I looked up at the statue. There are many notable facts associated with Brautigan, who was a rather eccentric man. For example, he was over 190 centimeters tall. He liked to tell his daughter stories about his childhood, when the family was extremely poor and went hungry for days at a time. He liked to tell her about how his mother used to pick mouse droppings out of the flour, not because the story itself was interesting, but because he found telling the story to his daughter interesting. He wrote *A Confederate General from Big Sur* and *Trout Fishing in America* while camping with his wife and daughter in Idaho in the summer of 1961. He drunkenly fired his rifle in his ranch house in Montana, making bullet holes in the wall. (Perhaps he looked at the bullet holes in his house and the house spotted with bullet holes and was delighted, thinking that his house looked like a beehive.) The beatnik author Lawrence Ferlinghetti said of Brautigan that he was so childish that "he was much more in tune with the trout in America than with people." (It is difficult to say whether his work is also childish, much like it is difficult to say whether a tree or a cloud is childish.) Brautigan lived more like a hippie than anyone else, but he denied being a hippie. He looked down on hippies and mocked them. While he associated with hippies, he tried to distance himself from them. In 1984, at the age of 49, he shot himself, fatally, in his living room, in front of a large window that looked out onto the Pacific Ocean. His house, where his body was found a month later, was in Bolinas, Marin County, which is close to San Francisco. For a period before he committed suicide, he appeared rather cheerful, as if thinking about dying put him in a good mood. His biological father learned of his son's existence only after his death. A certain young couple named their baby Trout Fishing in America. After *Trout Fishing in America* sold millions of copies worldwide, Brautigan only wrote novels that were neglected by readers and critics alike—writing such a piece is an ideal that authors might dream of, but too few authors aspire to this ideal. I did not think about these facts, but about a young Brautigan being carried away to the mental hospital, fighting back his tears, his gaze fixed on a boy sitting in the foyer of an old house with a white cat in his arms.

To a sane person being taken in a car to the mental hospital, even a person walking by with a fishing rod, logs in the back of a truck, a raven on a tree branch, the yellow line marking the center of the road, and haystacks would have appeared melancholy, let alone a boy sitting in the foyer of an old house with a white cat in his arms. I didn't offer a silent tribute to Brautigan, who spent his hardly normal adult life in San Francisco, except for the time he spent in Tokyo and Montana. I didn't think that he would have wanted people to offer silent tributes. More than that, actually, I hoped that he would not have wanted people to offer silent tributes, even after his death.

I was immersed in thoughts about Brautigan being carried to the mental hospital when a man approached and interrupted me. He was about 190 centimeters tall, so I was momentarily under the illusion that Brautigan had appeared in front of me. He had seen me smoking and had come over to bum a cigarette. I still felt as though he was Brautigan, and I was sort of glad to see him. We naturally began conversing, sharing my cigarettes. Upon studying him more closely, I decided that he looked more like Jesus than Brautigan, with sunken eyes and a bushy beard. I eventually became certain that this man was Jesus resurrected. I observed the smoking man in light of this new revelation, thinking that he was Jesus immediately after his Second Advent, smoking a cigarette before he did anything else.

He was a hobo. *Hobo* is a name some people call drifters in good humor. A hobo is easily distinguished from a beggar. This man was too energetic to be a beggar. He had a stench from not washing often, but it was not as dizzying as the stench of most beggars, which causes a temporary coma. It was a stench that I would expect to smell on a bear that had hibernated too long, sleeping right through spring until summer because of some disruption in its biorhythms.

The hobo told me that he was from New York City, and that he used to serve on submarines in the Navy. As soon as I heard him say the word *submarine*, words like *nuclear-powered submarine* and *intercontinental ballistic missile* flashed in my mind. I asked whether he'd served on nuclear-powered submarines, but he said that they were regular submarines, which disappointed me slightly. He talked as though he could disclose no further information. I pictured the man detecting ships and other submarines with sonar. I laughed under my breath because submarine crewman seemed a strangely fitting job for resurrected Jesus to have had in his youth.

He had roamed across America for nearly a year. He'd worked as an almond picker in California. He told me that he planned to travel north along the Pacific coast, through Canada to Alaska, and board a crab-fishing boat—his words made the entirety of Canada seem no more than a no-man's land that one must trek through on the way to Alaska. I imagined that he was planning to make disciples of the crabbers, and this made him seem more like Jesus. Unlike the old Jesus, who imparted teachings to the fishermen of Galilee, this new Jesus seemed determined to hide the fact that he was resurrected Jesus and live as a hobo to the end, quietly catching crabs and picking almonds. I was starting to like this man. A small tattoo of a cross on the back of his hand was the only evidence that he was Jesus. I think that he was hiding the fact that he was Jesus, but not completely, revealing his identity only to people who could recognize his tattoo. Hearing that he was going to Alaska to catch crabs, I imagined a place with countless crabs preparing for a crabbing boat to capsize so that they can feast on drowned crewmembers. I hoped that the hobo's life wouldn't be terminated in Alaska by crabs of all things.

He told me this and that about hobos. The world has its share of people who talk without being asked, and he seemed to be one of them. He told me that drifters are people who roam from one place to the next, and that drifters can be divided into tramps, who only work when absolutely necessary; bums, who never work and are not so different from beggars; and hobos, who find work as they roam. He said that hobos have held an annual American hobo convention since 1900, and that hobos have their own code of ethics, which prescribes that they must help other hobos in difficult situations, and have control over their own lives. Hobo culture is a weighty subject matter in American literature. Many authors, including Jack Kerouac, Jack London, Eugene O'Neill, and John Steinbeck, lived as hobos and wrote about hobos, coining numerous new terms, such as *possum belly*, a term that describes free-riders lying flat on their bellies on the roof of a train car so as not to be swept away by the wind. The hobo added that San Francisco is like a holy ground for hobos. These were all things I'd read about hobos. I listened carefully and quietly to catch inaccurate information, but everything he said checked out. It was as if he had memorized the content of some hobo manual.

Emphasizing that helping one another is the most important thing to hobos, he kept asking for my cigarettes, as though I was a fellow hobo, and what I could do to help him as a fellow hobo was to keep supplying him with cigarettes. Although I had made up my mind to not give him cigarettes before he asked, and not give him any even if he asked, I ended up handing him one cigarette after another. He looked me up and down as if gauging whether I was man enough to live as a hobo in America, and gave me a few tips in case I became a hobo. He said that a cross painted on the wall signifies that food will be provided for hobos after a party, that a cat picture means that a kind woman lives inside, and that a horizontal zigzag means that there is a fierce dog on the other side, which were all things I didn't know. When I asked about a vertical zigzag, he said that there was no such thing. I thought that I would mark myself with a vertical zigzag if I became something similar to a hobo. A vertical zigzag could become the mark of a pretend hobo.

The hobo must have thought that I was moved by his story and wanted to move me further. He stressed that hobos were the true drifters, and that they were clearly different from bums in that they had self-respect. It appeared that he'd been snaked by a bum and was holding a grudge against all bums. I thought that his stories were ridiculous, so I gave him another cigarette. Unsuspecting, he smoked it in all seriousness and exhaled a long trail of smoke as if to exhibit some newfound pride. He kept on telling utterly uninteresting stories about his experiences as a hobo, mostly about helping other hobos in difficult situations. He did not tell stories I expected to hear, about being chased by the police or being arrested and incarcerated; attempting to steal a chicken or a watermelon and being chased away by an aggressive dog, getting bitten on the leg or the butt; swimming across a river at night, clutching the stolen chicken or watermelon in his arms; or about limping for a while after falling from a wall he had attempted to climb over. He lacked such experiences. He was, at best, a dull hobo. Still, he put on airs and tried to impart his knowledge as a senior hobo, having determined that I was on the verge of becoming a hobo, too.

He was missing one top front tooth and one bottom front tooth. I hoped that he would at least tell me an interesting story about his missing teeth, but he didn't. He wasn't old enough for his teeth to have fallen out, so I asked, at the risk of offending a stranger. The story behind his missing teeth could not have been more unimpressive. In my opinion, a person missing two front teeth needed to at least have a meritorious story. It turned out that the two teeth had been knocked out in the dullest possible incident, when he fell down drunk in a bar and his face landed on something hard. There hadn't even been a fistfight, as one might expect of a hobo. As they were falling out, and for evermore, his two teeth must have felt wronged that they'd been lost in such a dull incident. Surely, the remaining teeth had nothing to do with the loss of his two front teeth, but when he opened his mouth, the remaining teeth looked as though they were showing off and expressing glee, and I began to believe that the remaining teeth had hatefully removed the two missing teeth, because this seemed less dull than the real story.

I was beginning to lose interest not only in the hobo who looked like Jesus, but also in hobo life in general. I thought that if I were to become a drifter, I wouldn't be a hobo, but an unpresentable bum who never worked and lived a life hardly distinguishable from a beggar's, having let go of a hobo's self-respect, of all self-respect, knowing no self-respect.

Like a drunkard repeating himself, the hobo told me again that he was going to go to Alaska and catch crabs. He sounded not as though he was about to catch all the crabs in Alaska, or as though the fate of all the crabs in Alaska was in his hands, but as though his fate was up to the Alaskan crabs. Although I listened half-heartedly, I heard everything he said. I must not have done a good job of listening half-heartedly.

I could sense that he was as bored as I was. Even though I knew that my companion was bored, I didn't care. I wanted to bore him some more. But then he asked me what I do for a living. I told him that I'd never been a hobo, but that my life was not unlike a hobo's. I told him that I hadn't been far from being a hobo even in my youth. What I said sounded true, and I felt as though I was more of a hobo than any actual hobo. He regarded me with suspicion, as if I were a con man posing as a hobo. I doubted that any non-hobo in his right mind would pose as a hobo, but I thought that some hobos-turned-bums who have a hard time accepting that they have degenerated into bums might pose as hobos.

I told the hobo that I translate books from English to Korean, and we talked about books. Somehow we got to talking about the American author Raymond Carver. I told him that I do not particularly like Carver, though I have translated one of his books. Carver is a good example of authors whom I used to think well of but who I now believe have joined the ranks of mediocrity. There are so many such authors and artists. The hobo, who'd never heard of Carver, asked how I could translate a book written by an author I didn't like. I told him that I hadn't had a choice. I added that I had translated about fifty books, all of them out of necessity. He responded, sympathetically, that he had no choice but to live as a hobo, though he hoped to be an author one day. I questioned whether the hobo in front of me could really become an author, but considering that there are people who become authors after living as hobos, and you never know what might happen to a person, and there was nothing keeping him from becoming an author, I felt that it was possible for him to become an author. Then I thought that if he actually became an author, it would only be because you never know what might happen to a person, because there was nothing keeping him from becoming an author, and because there are people who become authors after living as hobos. I did not tell him that I'm a writer.

I changed the subject and asked whether he had met a real American Indian. After much consideration, he said that he hadn't. Regretfully, I hadn't met a real American Indian during my time in America. Of course, I would have been able to meet a real American Indian who was drunk or on drugs had I gone to an Indian reservation with a casino.

The reason I mentioned American Indians was a sudden thought I had about Jim Morrison. I thought not about the fact that he was born the son of a naval officer, that he dropped out of UCLA, or that he spent a lot of time on the roof of his house. (I am unsure whether I read this somewhere or made it up.) Rather, my thought was related to Morrison, four years old, witnessing an auto accident in which an American Indian family could have been injured or killed. He referenced this event repeatedly, in his songs "Dawn's Highway," "Peace Frog," and "Ghost Song," in his poems, and in interviews. He believed that this incident had been the biggest influence on his life. His father recalled the family driving past the site of an auto accident on an Indian reservation, and how it upset his son very much, even though they had passed only a few American Indians. The incident left a powerful impression on young Jim's mind, and he thought constantly about crying American Indians. Like some primal memory, the image of Indians scattered across the highway, bleeding to death, continued to haunt him.

I thought that it wouldn't be bad to have such an image of dying Indians, or some similar image, as a primal memory, or to consider it as a primal memory. When I visualized Indians, they were sometimes standing or sitting expressionless on a rock in the wilderness, like wooden statues or totem poles, gazing at their confiscated land. Other times, I visualized drunk or doped out Indians, sprawled out or crawling across the wilderness like Galapagos tortoises. At those times, I thought that they were like Galapagos tortoises banished from the Galapagos.

I was thinking about Indians who reminded me of Galapagos tortoises when the hobo beside me startled me by stretching his hand out toward me as though he was about to hit me. The thought flashed, *This hobo is trying to hit me, as if being dull is not enough. He is a wicked hobo who hits people for no reason.* He was not trying to hit me, actually. He was catching a fly. In an instant, a fly that was flying between us ended up in the hobo's hand. It was as though he had performed some kind of magic, a dull magic.

I expected that he would amazingly toss the fly into his mouth, but he let it go as a fishing hobbyist lets go of his catch. I thought that he did this to catch it again if he had the chance. He seemed masterful at catching flies with his bare hands, and this was likely what he was best at. I complimented him on his fly-catching skill. He said that he'd been catching flies with his bare hands since he was seven years old. He was forty, which means that he'd been catching flies with his bare hands for thirty-three years, which is likely the longest he had spent on anything. It was rather pitiful that such extensive experience was good for nothing more than catching flies, but considering that his years of experience made him particularly good at catching flies, it was not so pitiful.

With his hand raised, as though he was about to hit me if need be, he looked around as though waiting for the same fly to return. Perhaps the hobo failed to spark its interest. The fly flew away and didn't return. The hobo gazed at the sky and waited, as if waiting for a lover who'd left him, but his lover never returned. The fly seemed to have gone off to seek other foul-smelling hobos or beggars, fragrant young women, or foods that smelled either good or bad.

The hobo waited, willing to settle for a different fly or any flying insect, but no fly or flying insect was willing to fly over. He seemed quite wistful, and this I could understand fully. He had not been given the opportunity to show off his greatest skill.

I thought I might be on my way, but I didn't get up for a while, because there was nothing in particular I wanted to do after parting with the hobo. I could have just started walking, but I lingered. I got lost in complex thoughts about what I would or would not do. I know how to make simple things difficult, and I am particularly good at it.

I was feeling at a loss when the hobo gave me a reason to go. He began scratching his head, which made me suspect he had head lice. He scratched all over, front and back, left and right, so I thought that there were at least four lice living on his head. He continued to scratch his head, now with both hands, without constraint, so it seemed that there were as few as four and as many as a hundred lice nested in his hair. His head seemed rather small for a hundred lice, so I imagined that they might be pushing one another away, trying to shove one another off his head, and that they were trying with all their might not to fall off. I was okay with most things, but I had no desire to get lice from a dull hobo, so I got up. If indeed there were about a hundred lice on his head, I thought the hobo might hope to give several of them to me, having nothing but lice to offer anyone.

Looking down at the hobo scratching away, I imagined that on other parts of his body lived fleas, who did not care to face the lice on the hobo's head. I thought that the lice and fleas must live in a precarious peace, their non-aggression pact being breached from time to time, causing bloody battles that lasted until they retreated to their respective territories. I felt a little bit pathetic, thinking about how I'd been lured by the fog to stay in San Francisco, and had ended up in a park, thinking about head lice and fleas. This was not so extraordinary for me, however. Quite often, I entertain one trifling thought after another. The more trifling the thoughts, the more they drag on. At times, I become absorbed in troublesome thoughts as if looking for trouble in my thoughts, and these thoughts torment me.

This time, too, in torment, I continued to entertain troublesome thoughts, for instance, that the hobo might, when bored, take off his shirt, pick from his body five of the freshest-looking fleas, and place them on his belly to hold a high jump competition. The champion would be specially allowed to suck blood from his nipple, and the flea that came in last would be quarantined until it could be handed off to another person so that it could start a new life on more fertile ground. A flea high jump competition could be a good thing to do to while away the time for a hobo who has to agonize over what to do with all the time on his hands. Perhaps he might bet against another hobo on a flea high jump competition, and the loser of the bet would have to steal a chicken from a farm. Maybe the bet would stipulate that the winner steal a chicken and the loser steal something far more difficult to steal. I didn't share my thoughts with the hobo, however, because I hoped for him to come up with his own ways of spending his time enjoyably, if not wisely. I hoped that he would get along with the fleas and the lice, which love hobos and have probably accompanied hobos throughout American history, since the pioneer era of the American West, or even before that, possibly exhausting them further but lessening their loneliness to a degree when they were exhausted and lonely.

The hobo, who'd smoked my cigarettes to his heart's content, told me that he didn't know how to thank me for my generosity, or whether he should. I told him that he didn't need to thank me. Then I gave the thankless fellow the rest of my cigarettes. By doing so, I was able to say that I'd lost all of my cigarettes to a dull American hobo. He seemed quite experienced in mooching cigarettes from people. Showing his true colors, the hobo delighted, as though he had approached me with the intention of taking all of my cigarettes, and had achieved all he'd desired. The hobo, whose family name was Fitzjames, said he was ready for a nap. I parted, wishing him a good sleep, and told him to be wary of crabs. According to the hobo, *Fitz* means so-and-so's son. Fitzjames was the name given to the bastard son of England's King James II, so the hobo was related to James II, however distantly.

The hobo, who might have been the descendant of a royal bastard, fell asleep as soon as we said our good-byes. Watching him, it occurred to me that although Jesus existed long before the appearance of today's American hobos, he was a kind of hobo.

Perhaps Jesus roamed the Arabian Peninsula as a hobo, picking olives and dates, and collecting salt from the Dead Sea. Perhaps something shocked him, leading to his singular determination to save humanity, which Jesus himself might have thought was perfectly nonsensical. Was he compelled to try because it was nonsensical? Was he, at the same time, convinced that it was a splendid idea? Did this lead him to proclaim himself to be the son of God and go down a path of no return? There was no knowing, but I suspected that Jesus not only lived as a hobo, but also as a hippie for a period. I realized that it was a real hippie that I wanted to meet, not a hobo. Continuing to think that Jesus had been a hobo long before today's hobos came into being, I mused that if I went back further in hobo history, all of early mankind, who for some reason gave up their possibly cozy cave-dwelling lifestyle, could in fact be considered hobos.

I was making my way slowly toward the hotel, having thought of nothing to do, when it occurred to me that the hobo I'd just met might be tolerating an itchy head because he was raising the lice on his head, and considered them friends. I imagined that when the hobo lay down in the grass to rest, the lice frolicked in the grass, and when the hobo stood up, they hopped back onto his head to accompany him to the next place. Perhaps, because the lice had tickled his head pleasurably for so long, he felt that something was missing when they were not there tickling him, as one might feel when he loses two perfectly good teeth. Then I wondered whether the lice that drifted with the hobo could also be considered hobos. They were settled on his head in a way, but the head itself drifted constantly. Head lice that settle on the head of a drifting hobo can probably be considered hobos of a kind.

Back at the hotel, lying on the bed, I resumed the thought that had been interrupted by the hobo. I'd been thinking about Brautigan, who lived as a hobo for a phase of his life. He was locked up in a psychiatric ward after he was arrested for throwing a rock through a police station window. One theory is that he was so poor that he was trying to get himself incarcerated to avoid starving. Another theory is that when his girlfriend criticized the poems he showed her, he was so dejected that he went straight to the police station and demanded to be arrested. But the police told him that they could not arrest him if he hadn't broken the law, so he went outside and threw a rock.

At the psychiatric ward, Brautigan underwent twelve sessions of electroconvulsive therapy, which is now used mainly for the treatment of patients with severe depression. There he began writing a very short novel titled *The God of the Martians* (I had not had the opportunity to read this piece of writing, but I was sure of its strangeness). The treatments literally shocked the wits out of him, which might have made a totally eccentric character out of an already eccentric person. I couldn't imagine what it feels like to undergo electroconvulsive therapy. (Perhaps I would not feel anything since I would be anesthetized.) I thought that if I suffered serious depression and were given electroconvulsive therapy, I would have my convulsing self videotaped so that I might watch the tape alone whenever I had the chance, or watch it with a woman I fell in love with, or show it to my young child when he became an adult. The moment of convulsion might be beyond my memory, but when I saw myself convulsing like an electroshocked frog, my body would remember the moment of convulsion and shudder. I might feel a deep sorrow, which might soon turn into immense pleasure. Of course, the pleasure might not last, throwing me back into deep sorrow, but after that, my feelings could become serene, as though I'd watched a video of a waterfall.

I thought about Ezra Pound, who was arrested for treason after praising Mussolini and Hitler. He was incarcerated in a cage with metal bars for three weeks, after which he became unhinged. (If I remember correctly, he was locked up not in a prison, but in a cage for animals.) I recalled a very old, ground-less theory of mine that I became slightly unhinged after hitting my tailbone against a dead branch when I fell from a tree I had climbed to pick persimmons.

For some time, I've thought that I'm destined to live an unhinged life because I became unhinged after hitting my tail-bone against a branch. Truly, one autumn, when I was about seven, I fell from high up in the persimmon tree in our court-yard, which I'd climbed to pick persimmons. I passed out for a moment, and even after I came to my senses, I couldn't move for a long while. Lying under the persimmon tree, feeling excru-ciating pain in my tailbone, looking up at the tree I'd climbed and the persimmons that I had failed to pick, I thought not that there are things in this world that I cannot pick, but that this is a world in which one might die picking persimmons. I then became engrossed in peculiar thoughts, and they were interesting to me. I decided to think like that more often. Thus I came to think that it was due to this event that I became naturally drawn to unnatural thoughts and emotions, and became unhinged.

In truth, there is no knowing whether this is true, and it is more likely untrue, but I came to believe it, and the event became fixed as the point at which I became unhinged. In fact, a person probably doesn't become unhinged just from falling out of a persimmon tree and hitting his tailbone on something. It's more probable that I was born with the potential to become unhinged. But I stuck to my belief anyway. Since then, I have come to think that anything pristine is uninteresting. Falling out of a persimmon tree and growing up an unhinged individual might have made it possible many years later for me to rush out onto the sand at a beachfront hotel in Monterey and erase the name *Valerie,* which someone had just written.

I came to believe that I became unhinged after falling out of a persimmon tree and hitting my tailbone, but the reason I climbed the tree in the first place is unclear. The most obvious reason is to pick persimmons, but there are possibly other rea-sons. I could have climbed the persimmon tree just because I wanted to be in a high place, or to sit quietly on a tree branch like a bird. I lean toward this reason. In my childhood, I climbed many kinds of trees, including persimmon trees, and sat quietly on their branches like a bird, making the birds sitting in other trees curious what a human was doing in their domain.

5. Things I Consider Fun

FIVE YEARS LATER, when I returned to the United States, I didn't contact my ex-girlfriend, because I thought that we would only spend time drinking tequila and shooting guns if we met again. Of course, that wasn't a terrible way to spend time, but I didn't want to repeat what we had done. I was, however, curious about the agave plants her Mexican boyfriend had planted. I did not want to contact her just to find out about them. The agave plants were either dead, or alive and still being showered with urine by our Mexican friend, which might make them the only agave plants in the world to be showered regularly with human urine. In that case, those agave plants could be considered somewhat ill-fated, having to drink the urine of a person who had drunk alcohol distilled from their cousins. I thought that if I had another chance to return to the United States, I might contact my ex-girlfriend.

For several days after I arrived in San Francisco, I stayed at a hotel and looked for an apartment to rent. The whole time, the city was shrouded in fog. Prior to my return, I often thought about San Francisco, and fog was always the first thing that came to mind. Like a true fog city, San Francisco had so many foggy days that it was impossible to think about the city separate from fog. There was something special about the fog there. It often covered an enormous stretch of the California coast, sometimes reaching as far as Vancouver Harbor. It reigned along the coast-line, like a colossal, conscious being. Like a large army form-ing up for a march, it would remain stationary before advanc-ing slowly and decisively toward land, occupying it, and then retreating.

For those few days, I strolled along the foggy streets of down-town San Francisco and the city beach, or brought the chair to the hotel window and sat watching the fog for a very long time. To me, the fog was not a backdrop I could easily tire of, but a primal substance that filled the void. Like rain, fog, which is water in a different state, seems to have certain abstract properties. This is perhaps because water in all of its various forms, and all liquids, have inherent elements that are perfectly abstract. It seems to me that while one might easily grow tired of looking at concrete forms, abstract things possess something in them that prevents people from losing interest.

The fog made me think that I might write something, whether about fog or unrelated to fog. In fact, a significant part of this novel was conceived while looking out the window at the fog and walking in the fog. Without the fog of San Francisco, this text would still have been written, but it might have turned out quite differently. Actually, I had received an invitation from UC Berkeley, so I thought about getting a place in Berkeley, which is about half an hour away from San Francisco. But I felt as though the fog of San Francisco was pulling me, so I found an apartment in San Francisco. Across the Bay from San Francisco, Berkeley's weather patterns are starkly different, and Berkeley doesn't have as many foggy days.

The whole time I was writing this piece, as always, I felt quite bored and blue. I wrote this piece to assuage my boredom and gloom, but doing so did nothing to diminish my boredom and gloom. Even though San Francisco has much charm for a city, possibly more charm than any other city, I couldn't help but feel bored and blue, as I do in other cities. In order to get away from my boredom and gloom for a bit, I tried to immerse myself in playful thoughts. I think that the mind possesses a tenacious desire for play, and this piece of writing is, in a way, a play on that desire.

I originally intended to title this novel *My Idea of Fun*, but I saw another not-so-interesting novel with the exact same title, written by an English author, so I gave up that title. He attempted to write about his idea of fun, finding other people's ideas of fun rather dull, but he seemed to have failed. Finding his book dull, I was able to read no more than a few pages. The book I am writing now might not offer any enjoyment whatsoever to some people, or many. That said, this book will be largely about my idea of fun.

Before I begin to list the things that I think are fun, I would like to take a moment to list the things that I do not consider fun: noises of all kinds, nearly every kind of music, violent things, depression, conventional works of fiction, fiction that reflects the times, novels that discuss scars, consolation and healing, novels in which characters' actions weigh more than their thoughts, grandiose novels, touching novels (perhaps speaking of the dull nature of the critics who fawn over such novels could be somewhat fun, but not really, so let us just say that the reason for their behavior is that they either have no talent as critics or have no self-esteem as human beings, or both), growth novels, all-too-serious novels, novels that don't exude an excess of self-consciousness, proverbial poems, things explained by common sense, obvious ploys (and those responsible for them), flawless people, people with nothing peculiar about them, people whose entire beings exude authority, people who are diligent and eager, people who want to contribute to society, people who have no interest in clouds, simple folk, talkative people, overly greedy people, people who know jokes but are without humor, unspeakably dull people who make me speechless (they are really dull), racial chauvinists, self-conscious women who act coy while pretending to be nonchalant (such women can be found everywhere in the world, but more so in Korea than anywhere else; since there has never been formal research, their exact number is unknown, but it is certainly more than the number of a certain species of near-extinct penguin in the South Pole), men who show off their strength and manliness (such men also exist in large numbers in South Korea; among them are those who tense up and crack their bulked-up necks noisily and walk with an exaggerated swagger; such a man might be a good match for a self-conscious woman who acts coy while pretending to be nonchalant), conservatives, and economic issues. I could probably add to this list endlessly. (Adding endlessly to this list is sometimes fun and sometimes dull.)

What I consider fun includes shadows, clouds, wind, fog, all of the world's fish that jump into the air for whatever reason, all animals that dig tunnels underground, animals that get frisky in mating season, the weather, trees, drunkards (they are sometimes fun and sometimes dull), mischievous children and adults who still have mischievous qualities, unselfish people (although there are many dull people among them), beggars who are not especially interested in begging, children whose dreams are not overly ambitious, nudists, memories of dumping or being dumped by women, certain thoughts on revenge, plays on words, works of poetry and fiction that say very little, illnesses that are not agonizingly painful, poverty (while wealth might enable one to do many fun things, it is not fun in itself; on the other hand, fun can be had from poverty because it forces one to act pitiful), loafing, attaining mastery in playing with words, groundless or weakly founded ideas, forming a theory on something trivial, quietly scoffing at and badmouthing this and that about the world with no one listening, and thinking about something until I cannot think anymore. I could probably add to this list endlessly. (It's fun to add endlessly to this list.) Many things that I consider fun I also happen to like, but I do not necessarily like everything I consider fun. For example, I consider apparatus gymnastics, boxing, sky diving, synchronized swimming, and the circus fun, but I do not especially like them. Among the things I consider fun, there are many that are difficult to explain. Below are a few examples.

A few days after I arrived in San Francisco, I read in the event listings of a local weekly newspaper that there had been a bacon-themed gathering somewhere downtown several days prior. For a small fee, anyone could attend the event, at which the participants made their own bacon, discussed bacon, and sampled bacon. There was also time set aside for a session with a bacon expert, who talked about all things bacon. I do not know whether I would have participated had I known about the meeting, but having missed the chance was regretful, because a bacon-themed meeting is as interesting to me as a Saturn-themed meeting.

The two meetings could be combined to make a more interesting meeting, where people eat bacon while talking about Saturn. I think that Saturn's rings look like a gargantuan strip of bacon wrapped around the planet, and I naturally think of Saturn's rings whenever I eat bacon. Sometimes I imagine that I am eating the rings of Saturn and think that Saturn's rings taste salty and rich. Similarly, whenever I eat baked or boiled whole potatoes, I think that they are like asteroids, and I think that civilization as we know it might be obliterated by a gargantuan potato-like asteroid crashing into the Earth. Perhaps, people who can find similarities between bacon and Saturn's rings can, by eating bacon that resembles Saturn's rings, bring the otherwise distant-feeling Saturn closer to their hearts. Along with bacon and Saturn, participants of this new meeting could discuss the artist Francis Bacon.

Once, I was strolling along the marina near AT&T Park, the home of the San Francisco Giants, when I saw a baseball hat floating in the water. It was in motion despite the fact that there was no wind and the water was calm. I watched, finding this remarkable, though it is not impossible for a hat to move on its own in calm water. I soon discovered that a seal was tapping the hat from below the water's surface. It was a Giants hat, and the seal was undoubtedly an avid Giants fan. It seemed natural that one would see a seal that was an avid Giants fan in the ocean right outside the Giants' stadium. As if to demonstrate what a fan he was, the seal nudged his head into the hat, jumped slightly out of the water wearing the hat, and then dove under water and swam away. There was no game that day, but I could imagine that on the days that the Giants played home games, countless seals of the San Francisco Bay Area would gather, wearing their team hats, to cheer for their team.

One fine day, lying in a park, I felt again that the mind possesses a tenacious desire for play, and that there's something rather mischievous about this desire. Lying in the grass, feeling the strong sunlight penetrating my closed eyes, I felt an indescribable pain in my head, so I waited with my eyes closed for the headache to subside, trying hard to feel the headache as something different. This led me to envision a park with marble statues suffering indescribable headaches. I imagined that the marble statues could feel my headache. The statues didn't especially look as though they were suffering headaches, but all of their eyes were closed. I alone knew the location of the park, which opened only in the wee hours of the night after other parks had closed. I imagined that strolling in the park in the middle of the night cleared my head. Whenever I passed the marble statues, they suddenly opened their eyes, as though their headaches had disappeared. This thought did not magically cure my headache, but it lessened the pain a little.

To be exact, my indescribably terrible headache subsided at least to the degree that it was merely difficult to describe, and I continued in my head to invent a park with marble statues with knee pain, a park with marble statues grimacing from toothaches, a park with marble statues that had stomach ulcers, a park with marble statues suffering backaches, supporting their backs with their hands, a park with marble statues suffering from acute migraines, a park with marble statues suffering from ringing in their ears, a park with fainting marble statues (I was to develop a special feeling for these particular statues: three years ago, I fainted after feeling extremely dizzy; fainting did not feel bad at all, but I didn't start fainting whenever I felt like it; often, I'm so bored that I feel like fainting, but, regretfully, I cannot will myself to faint), a park with marble statues of patients who have undergone brain surgery, a park with marble statues that had their limbs amputated due to frostbite, and a park with somnambulistic marble statues that stepped down from their pedestal each night and wandered around the park. Before I knew it, my headache had disappeared.

These are examples of things I consider somewhat fun, but not very fun. A lot of people do not know what is fun about these things, but the few who know what fun is would consider these things fun. If there were more people who knew what fun is, the world might become a more fun place.

6. Catfish and Cat

I TRIED AT FIRST to get a room in the Haight-Ashbury District, which is known for having been the home of hippies and followers of the Grateful Dead, or the Castro District with its gay communities, but there were no rooms available for short-term rent, so I ended up with an apartment in the Marina District on the northern shore. The neighborhood was clean and safe but with few points of interest. My apartment was fully furnished but lacked character. The walls were painted white, reminiscent of a large hospital room. The view out the window was nothing spectacular, but when I opened the blinds in the morning, I could see, about as big as rats' tails, a few upper connector cables of the Golden Gate Bridge.

In the afternoon on the day after finding my apartment, I went back to Washington Square Park, where I had met a hobo five years earlier. This time I met a different hobo. I was in the company of a dragonfly. I was lying in the grass with my hand on the ground when a dragonfly landed on the back of my hand and started eating its lunch. First, it ate the body of the smaller insect, and then the spindly legs. I lay still and observed the dragonfly taking its meal. When it was done, it used a leg to wipe its mouth clean, lowered its wings, and relaxed on the comfortable haven of my hand. Looking closely, I saw that the dragonfly's lower left wing was damaged slightly, but not enough to hamper flight. A moment later, the dragonfly moved to my arm and rested facing me. Then, as though it had found a better place to sit, it moved up to my forehead and rested there for a long time. I remained motionless so as not to disturb the dragonfly's rest. We stayed in that state for a long while, and I thought that I would never tire of the dragonfly's company.

The hobo approached me after watching in amazement as I passed the time with the dragonfly. Surprised by his arrival, the dragonfly flew away, and I resented the hobo for making my dragonfly fly away. This hobo, who came to accompany me in place of the dragonfly, was from Oklahoma. He had not been a hobo for long. I doubted that the hobo had any idea what it means to be a hobo, but he did have some idea. With some idea of what it means to be a hobo, he'd decided to become a hobo, but he didn't seem sure himself whether he was a hobo. I told him a few things I knew about hobos, but he said he had never heard any of it. He seemed more of an ordinary drifter than a hobo.

As we smoked my cigarettes, I felt as though my encounter with a hobo in that park five years prior was being reenacted. I asked the hobo whether he had met a real American Indian. He had not. He asked the reason I was asking, and I told him about Jim Morrison's story of American Indians. He seemed slightly soft in the head, and did not appear to understand what I was saying. He might have been disinterested in my words and been lost in his own thoughts. We talked about this and that without a thread. When he told me that he did not know what he would do with his life as a hobo, I felt that he was a true drifter. This true drifter from Oklahoma did not have a lot to say about hobos, but he seemed to have a lot to say about other things. Before he left, he told me excitedly about how he used to catch catfish with his bare hands when he was young. Based on his story, I later came to write this piece, which could be titled "Catfish and Cat." It's a somewhat dreadful, somewhat tragic, somewhat melancholy, and somewhat farcical account of catfish.

The word *noodle* generally refers to a type of food, but used as a verb it refers to fishing without a fishing pole or other equipment, especially for catfish. It is unclear whether American noodling originated with American Indians, but it's practiced mainly in Oklahoma and along the Mississippi River in southern states such as Mississippi, Tennessee, and Missouri. People dive into a muddy river where nothing is visible and feel around inside mud holes along the bank, under rocks, and under brush to find fish. The hand is sometimes used as a kind of bait. When a noodler finds a catfish, he thrusts his hand inside the fish's mouth and grasps its lower jaw.

Noodling is best done in summer, during the spawning season, when catfish are rather aggressive. Catfish can grow as large as 75 pounds, nearly the size of a sturgeon. Some noodlers wear gloves and socks to minimize injury, but self-proclaimed purists often mock them, insisting on barehanded fishing, and even deriving pleasure from receiving wounds. The sharp teeth of the catfish often lacerate the hands and arms, sometimes causing serious injury. A noodler might get a deep cut or lose a finger from infection. There is also the danger of drowning. More dangerous than the catfish are the snakes, turtles, alligators, muskrats, alligator snappers, and beavers that live in the catfish holes after the catfish have left. Most noodlers wear nothing but a pair of shorts because of the danger of getting their shirts caught on rocks and roots.

Noodling is presently enjoyed by many people as a sport or hobby, but it was originally practiced by laborers along the Mississippi River, who did it for food or for a living. Noodling, one of the most American of activities, has been rediscovered as a result of the fever in America for things that are quintessentially American, the same way Americans have rediscovered bluegrass, which has roots in the music of England, Scotland, and Ireland, and is influenced by jazz and the blues. The most famous noodler is Jerry Rider. He went on the David Letterman Show in 1989, and traveled as far as India to demonstrate noodling to a massive crowd of curious Indians. He even appeared on MTV. After a short period of living in extravagance in California, he confessed that appearing on television did not make him happy. A true Southern country bumpkin, he felt uncomfortable with a life of extravagance and convenience. Rider was interested in nothing but catching catfish, or so he professed. Perhaps he couldn't imagine a life without catching catfish. The shrewd Californians might have offered to build him a huge aquarium or dig him a small river with catfish in it so that he could catch catfish and continue living in California, to which he might have said no.

He might have told them that he would also need snakes, turtles, alligators, muskrats, alligator snappers, and beavers. Finding his request unfeasible, they might have instead promised to put plastic snakes, turtles, alligators, muskrats, alligator snappers, and beavers in the water, causing him to return home disappointed.

Noodling contests sprang up after the release of the 2001 documentary *Okie Noodling* by Bradley Beesley. Bass and trout fishing contests have a long tradition in America and contest prizes had grown quite large, but noodling had attracted little attention from the general public. Dissatisfied by noodling's lack of popularity, noodlers decided that they needed to do something, so they started noodling contests. The first noodling contest was held in Oklahoma to a tremendous reception. The contest evolved into an event broadcast live on ESPN and other networks nationwide. The most famous noodling contest is held in Pauls Valley, Oklahoma. Noodling is legal in eleven states in the United States. The largest catfish ever caught were caught in rivers in Thailand and Italy.

In a documentary about noodling, I saw catfish that had been fished out of the water. Their heads were the size of a cat's head. The fish were lying on their bellies, opening and closing their mouths, gasping. They looked rather unhappy. The people around the unhappy catfish acted very happy. The people's joy and the catfish's sorrow were in stark contrast. Soon the catfish were beheaded, and only the heads of the catfish were left gasping for breath. While the fish were literally about to die, the people observing them looked as though they might be amused to death. The people were extremely rude and didn't show the least bit of due respect to the dying. Those dying catfish were not allowed quiet deaths. Actually, one might consider their deaths to have been relatively quiet since they were lacking bodies with which to struggle. All they could manage was to open and close their mouths repeatedly. They had no way of expressing their displeasure with what the people had done to them. The catfish continued to open and close their mouths until they stopped breathing. In this scene, to say that the catfish were tongue-tied would not do justice to their astonishment at what was happening to them. The catfish didn't even have tongues to be tied.

The most memorable scene is the one of people feeding catfish to a cat, which eats the catfish with relish. The catfish is named after the cat because of its whiskers, which resemble those of a cat. But their whiskers are the extent of the similarities between the two, which makes me think that both sides might feel wronged if they found out that the catfish is named for the cat. Actually, the catfish would probably feel much more wronged. Those people might have fed catfish to a cat because they found a certain irony in feeding catfish to a cat. The cat did not know such irony, and ate the catfish like a special treat. After learning the taste of catfish, cats might go down to the riverside to while away their time watching the river where the catfish live whenever they think of the unforgettable taste of catfish. In this little drama featuring the people, the catfish, and the cat, there was a family, one member of which was a girl with a shy smile, clad in country garb, whose name might have been Maggie, which sounds like *megi*, which means catfish in Korean. She might later watch this footage and reminisce about catfish, recalling that joyful time with her family on the day the catfish died.

Some time later, I ordered catfish at a Vietnamese restaurant in San Francisco's Chinatown. I couldn't find out whether the catfish had been born and raised in the Mississippi River, or had come from some river in Vietnam or China. Like much of the catfish that appears on tables, it was highly probable that it had come from a farm. Wherever it had come from, I had no trouble eating the catfish that appeared on my table at the Vietnamese restaurant in Chinatown. Luckily, the catfish had been prepared without the head, and the body had been chopped, so it did not remind me too much of the catfish that died miserably after being caught by the noodlers of the Mississippi River Valley. Had the head been intact, I would still have been able to eat it, but I would have had some trouble.

The thing is, noodling, which Americans take pride in as one of the most American of activities, is not at all special, or uniquely American. People living by rivers all over the world practice noodling. I remembered that I, too, was once a noodler. Growing up in a country village, I used to go to the nearby river and catch catfish with my bare hands. The fish I caught were not large, but I occasionally got bitten or stung while fishing. Going back in my memory, what I recalled most was the feeling of the slippery catfish sliding through my fingers. Recalling the slippery texture on my fingers, I put a piece of fish in my mouth, but it did not take me back to childhood as a madeleine cake does. That period felt impossibly distant, almost as distant as a past life. I thought about countless children living by rivers and catching catfish around the world, some of whom might eat catfish at a restaurant in a foreign country years later, and reminisce about catching catfish in their childhood.

I mentioned noodling to several Americans I met thereafter, but no one had heard of noodling. I thought that this might have something to do with the United States being such a large country. Having never heard of noodling, they found it interesting. I found talking with Americans about noodling as interesting as noodling, which is considered one of the most American of activities. It was as interesting as the time I heard stories about the famed admiral Yi Sun-shin of the Joseon Dynasty and his Turtle Ship for the first time from an American. The American, whose profession had nothing to do with ships, had near expert knowledge of the history of battleships.

7. The Eccentric and the Deranged of San Francisco

SAN FRANCISCO HAS as many eccentrics as it does hobos and beggars. It is not difficult to spot eccentrics; they can be identified as eccentrics upon first glance. Some afternoons at Washington Square Park, one can find a man sitting alone in the grass, silently eating cherries from a large plastic bag. He eats cherries, looking at nothing but the cherries he is eating, as though he is harboring a deep, bitter grudge against cherries, as though he had been pestered by cherries all through the night—though it is difficult to imagine what harm cherries could inflict on people. Watching the man, one might wonder how he came to harbor such a deep and bitter grudge against cherries to eat cherries in such a way.

In the way he eats cherries, there is an element that makes everything around him seem inconsequential, and this makes him appear as though he is looking for the answer to an unsolvable riddle that he came up with. It also makes his cherries seem extraordinary, even something other than cherries, perhaps a riddle in themselves.

It is impossible to know why the old Asian man silently eats cherries in Washington Square Park, but after he has left, one can find a heap of cherry pits that scream of some gruesome revenge. The following day, however, the cherry pits are nowhere to be found. I imagine that the squirrels of the park take them all, collecting the cherry pits to build a tower in a secret location. I suppose that the squirrels do this in their free time, as a hobby, with a rather strange, genuine, and special passion. My theory assumes that it is not unreasonable for squirrels to have hobbies, and this theory can be understood by looking at Coit Tower on Telegraph Hill, close to Washington Square Park.

Coit Tower is one of the only symbols of San Francisco that I like. What I like isn't the tower itself, but the anecdotes related to an eccentric woman with deep connections to San Francisco, who's responsible for the existence of the tower. The Art Deco tower, like many towers in the world, was born of somebody's rather strange, genuine, and special passion, and shows that one's rather strange, genuine, and special passion can be most effectively realized by building a tower. To some extent, Coit Tower fits my idea of a true tower, soaring to the sky without any actual function.

Coit Tower was constructed in memory of a woman named Lillie Hitchcock Coit. A rather eccentric character, she often dressed like a man, and shaved her head so that her wigs would fit better. From the age of fifteen, when she witnessed firemen suppressing a fire, she jumped to extinguish any fire she saw, and felt a special attachment to fire hydrants. Ultimately, she came to be regarded as a legendary character of San Francisco, an honorary firefighter, and a guardian saint to the city's firefighters. Perhaps, as a young girl, she liked playing with hoses, and was the happiest when she was spraying water.

Lying in Washington Square Park, looking at Coit Tower, I was reminded of a woman in Korea. One winter, when she was a young girl, she saw a fire engine near her house. Excited by the prospect of seeing a fire, she followed the vehicle. But her excitement soon turned into surprise. The house at which the fire engine stopped was none other than her own. Before her eyes, her house burned down completely and finally collapsed. Under normal circumstances, this would have shocked her, but she felt more embarrassed than shocked, because what her parents saved from the house was not something of sentimental value, such as a family photo album, but a color television set, which was extremely precious at the time. She expressed her regret to me that she'd been unable to watch the news of her house burning on that television set.

For a few months after the incident, she spent a happy period in a temporary residence while her house was being restored. The summer after the restoration was completed, the house flooded, and she had to spend another several weeks in a temporary residence, which she also recalled as a happy period. She said that she kept her valued photo albums, journals, and dolls inside her rectangular Boston bag in preparation for suddenly having to evacuate the house again for whatever reason. The two disasters, although they did not serve as opportunities for her to look at the world differently, afforded her a happy childhood. Telling her story, she asserted that happiness, especially in childhood, comes from unexpected places, in unexpected ways.

She was fairly eccentric, but she claimed that her eccentricities had nothing to do with living through two disasters as a child. She was forced by her parents to take piano lessons, and one night after the fire, she dreamt of a fire in a music shop, where pianos and string instruments burned, billowing black smoke. This, she said, was one of the best dreams she had ever dreamt. She remarked that had she been a composer, she would have written a kind of requiem for the burning instruments.

Other than hobos, beggars, and eccentrics, San Francisco also has many people who have passed the point of eccentricity, who are slightly off, halfway gone, nearly deranged, or completely deranged. There are so many deranged people in the city that unless a person did something seriously weird, people might just say, "No one would consider that weird," or "You don't even come close to being a weirdo."

A middle-aged Caucasian woman takes a walk at a regular hour in the afternoon in a park near the apartment where I stayed. She dresses in Gothic style from head to toe, as if she believes that she is still living in the Middle Ages. Her complexion is fair to the point of being pale, and her black outfit is adorned with various metal ornaments. The large black dog that accompanies her on her walks in the park wears a leather collar with pointy studs. She wears a similar collar around her neck, which makes me wonder whether they switch collars sometimes. Watching her, I naturally imagined various scenarios. Perhaps she has various gothic garments on display in glass cases in her basement. Maybe she has constructed a prison cell with bars, in which she sleeps every night, with her dog standing guard. She might want more than anything in life to live like a corpse: pale, with no color whatsoever. She seems slightly off, but appears likely to become halfway gone in the near future.

At the nearby library that I frequented, I often saw an old Caucasian lady who was always wearing a long black dress, as if she was on her way to or returning from a masquerade. Every time I saw her, she was wearing either roses or daisies of various colors on her black bonnet, or a small flower in her hair. She looked as though she had walked out of an old romantic poem: half asleep after a long nap, combing her disheveled hair with her fingers to shed sleep. Looking at the woman, I imagined that, stubbornly rejecting the notion that flowers must root in soil, she had come up with a unique and ingenious way of sowing and watering seeds to germinate them in her hair. This brilliant woman, who knows how to make flowers bloom on her head, might sow different seeds each season.

The woman reminded me of "San Francisco," the most well-known song among over a thousand songs about San Francisco that were sung like hymns during the hippie movement. The song, by Scott McKenzie, begins with the phrase, "If you're going to San Francisco, be sure to wear some flowers in your hair." (This song is often referred to as "San Francisco (Be Sure to Wear Flowers in Your Hair)" to distinguish it from the countless other songs about San Francisco.) She might be an original hippie, still living in San Francisco after arriving with flowers in her hair, one of many hippies who came from all over with hearts buoyed by the ideals of freedom, love, peace, harmony, and community. At that time, thousands of hippies came to San Francisco from all over the world, singing "San Francisco," handing out flowers with flowers in their hair. In addition to attracting so many people to San Francisco, the song became a hymn of freedom among the Czechs, who were resisting occupation by the Soviet Union during the Prague Spring in 1968. She appeared more than halfway gone.

San Francisco has no lack of deranged people. There are so many of them that it is a wonder that there is no mention of them in San Francisco guidebooks. It is probably untrue, but I feel as though these people came to the city with flowers in their hair, after losing their minds, in a different wave from the hippies, who flocked to the city en masse before them. Even if this is untrue, imagining their wave, I can sense a gentle tremor in my heart.

It is also possible that a great number of hippies who came to the city a long time ago remained there after losing their minds completely. There are some deranged people who, lost in their own thoughts, mumble quietly with a slight movement of their lips. Others shout out their thoughts. It seems obvious that deranged people become engrossed in their own thoughts, but why do some of them shout? I had always been curious whenever I saw deranged people talking to themselves out loud. Observing them, I'd tried and failed to fathom the reason. Seeing them in San Francisco and really deliberating on the issue, however, I felt as if I could get to the bottom of it. There are, of course, those who curse vehemently at the world or at somebody. Excluding these cases, however, people who say out loud what need not necessarily be said out loud could ultimately be talking to themselves, for the benefit of none other than themselves. One could say that people speak out loud purposely, despite being able to hear themselves think, because it is incomparably more effective for hammering in their own thoughts than thinking or mumbling to themselves. Quite possibly, people speak out loud so that their words are engraved clearly in their own heads, so that their meaning will not leave their heads, so that their heads are filled with those same thoughts. All of their thoughts converge into several distinct thoughts, which they mumble like mantras, casting some sort of spell on themselves.

Once, on a bus, I saw an old African American lady who counted continuously in a loud voice: "7 ounces! 9 ounces! 13 ounces . . . !" She seemed to be weighing something, clearly occupied by a certain thought about weight. Perhaps she had previously held a job that involved weighing things, and she continued, even after losing her mind, to feel obliged to do that job. I have also seen a man on the street, who repeatedly shouted, "Look for the door!" and a mad middle-aged woman who roamed the park, giggling, all the while saying, "It's not funny anymore."

I have also seen a well-aged Caucasian woman who made mosquito noises as she walked. I walked alongside the woman for a while and listened to her mosquito, which had a striking resemblance to the real thing, and I felt as though I was walking with a humongous mosquito. It was unclear whether she thought she was a mosquito, she was trying to threaten people or keep them away by making mosquito noises, or she was trying to summon a swarm of mosquitos to attack people.

Many people who have lost their minds appear to have unmistakably distinct individuality, which might be attained only after people lose their minds. In a way, the mind has a will to head toward the extreme, and when it reaches the farthest possible point, a person might be said to have entered a state of having lost his mind. Perhaps it is when a person loses his mind that his true self is revealed.

In many ways, San Francisco seems a decent place for the deranged to live. There are already plenty of deranged people there, and they make up a natural part of the city. I don't know whether psychopathological research has been conducted on mental patients who are in a sort of natural, unregulated environment rather than confined to a facility, but I think that San Francisco would be an ideal place to conduct such research.

Sometimes I think about the possibility of losing my mind. Of course, no amount of effort might be sufficient to attain derangement, and derangement might not be attained by effort alone. Nothing seems to be keeping me from becoming deranged, considering that I have always lived in a world of distorted reality, that I'm often trapped in uncontrollable emotions from which I cannot easily escape or absorbed in my ideas (especially nonsensical or morbid ideas, because thinking only seems meaningful when excessive), that I seek refuge in those ideas, that I'm writing a novel that reeks of a deranged person's memoir, and that I sometimes talk to myself.

I might lose all judgment at any moment and become deranged. A person might expect this to happen, and this expectation would not be unrealistic if he is without any sort of hopes and dreams, unable to draw happiness from small and simple things as people commonly prescribe, and therefore unable to treasure such things, not because he has passed the stage of being able to, but because he never had the ability.

I might be walking down the street one rainy day and hallucinate all the open umbrellas on the street spinning like tops as they rise into the sky, and realize that I, too, am being lifted by the umbrella I'm holding. Or I might hallucinate the Aurora on a clear day. One such moment could mark the official beginning of my new life.

If I become deranged, I hope to goodness that I will talk to myself quietly rather than becoming aggressive, making a scene, or causing others harm. Once in a while, I tell myself in a tiny voice, *It's all useless.* If I become completely deranged one day, I wonder what I will mumble to myself in a tiny voice then. At that point, I might not know what I am saying to myself, but it will not matter. Perhaps meaningless letters will fill my head and flow out through my lips like air bubbles.

I might become lost in thoughts about springs, screws, or insect wings and talk about such things. That would not be terrible, but I'd prefer that I talk only about floating clouds, or lightly rippling or calmly flowing water. I hope that my thoughts about those things would put a broad smile on my face, if not cause me to tremble with delight. Clouds and water are the kinds of things that I can gaze at, quietly immersing myself in thoughts about them or other things, the kinds of things that I can gaze at, immersing myself in thoughts about them and then gradually clearing my thoughts, the kinds of things that, when nothing comes to mind, I can be contented to mindlessly watch as they gradually change shape, the kinds of things that I can gaze at when feeling helpless and feel my helplessness become infinitely softer, if not diminish or disappear, the kinds of things that I can engage in endless conversation about without any language at all. Therefore, even though I would not perceive that everything is like a dream if I were deranged, I still hope that I would live in a dreamy state, living in a house with walls and windows and a roof made of clouds, furnished with tables and a bed made of clouds, wearing clothes made of clouds, eating food made of clouds, thinking and behaving like clouds, imagining that all that is not clouds is clouds, making it impossible to think about anything other than clouds, thus thinking and talking only about clouds.

8. The First Monkey to Ever Reach the North Pole

I BOUGHT A black jacket one day at a clothing shop on Hayes Street. I put the jacket on in front of the mirror at home, and I thought, just as I had when I bought it, that it looked very much like a stage costume. The garment had long lapels that would look good on a long-necked bird. I felt, just as I had when I bought it, that I would hesitate to wear it out on an ordinary day. So I confined the jacket in the closet as though caging an animal, and took it out only occasionally to wear it at home while I drank coffee, wrote on the computer, or sat on the sofa watching television—when I did this, the jacket appeared to rejoice over its liberation. At those times, I felt like an actor affecting coffee drinking, writing on the computer, or sitting on the sofa watching television. Everything I did wearing the jacket felt like an affectation. Looking in the mirror felt like an affectation of looking in the mirror, and lying in bed felt like an affectation of lying in bed. Even drinking a glass of water felt like an affectation of drinking a glass of water.

I put the jacket on one night, and looking at my reflection in the window, I put on a sorrowful expression, like an actor playing a sorrowful scene. I looked like a talentless actor. So, like an actor who has no talent but is determined to become a great actor through desperate effort, I looked out into the street on the other side of the closed window, raised my arms, and spoke in a loud voice as though reading the lines of a play to a faraway pedestrian. But the sole member of my audience did not show any reaction, which made me feel like an actor who can never become great, no matter how much he tries. I lowered my arms dejectedly, as though putting all ambition aside, and gazed at the glass. I looked like a person who had abandoned the last thread of hope.

A few nights later, I was sitting quietly by the window again, wearing a very old, frayed, black turtleneck sweater inside my jacket. The wind outside was fierce, and the window shook as though some invisible being was pounding on it. Sitting motionless like an audience member waiting for an actor to appear on stage, I thought suddenly of an anecdote about the artist Francis Bacon. The story goes that Bacon nonchalantly greeted a man who broke into his apartment, and invited him to bed, marking the beginning of a homosexual relationship between the two men. The burglar became one of the most important figures in Bacon's life, and the subject of many of his paintings. I felt that if a stranger visited, or broke into my apartment at that moment, I'd naturally be able to spend the night talking to that stranger, whoever that person might be, like an actor in a ham performance. But no one came.

Out the window, I could see pedestrians struggling to walk against the wind, and felt an impulse to join the procession of pedestrians who were struggling to walk. It seemed a fine night to struggle to walk against the wind. I had an urge to trudge through the street. I resolved to walk to the Golden Gate Bridge, which was about two and a half miles away, and beyond, not stopping until the end of the night. I left my apartment, dressing the part, the collar of my theatrical jacket turned up, hands in my pockets. In the end, I was stymied by the wind and forced to turn back. The wind was so strong that I felt I would be able to fly gently were I to grow small wings. All I needed to fly were small wings and willpower. My inability to fly was due to my lack of wings, not my lack of willpower.

I sat by the yacht docks, clutching the seat of the bench. The yachts groaned miserably, as if they could not bear being tethered. I felt strangely uplifted by the sound. I was watching the yachts, which appeared to be about to crumble from the wind, when a thought came to me, as if delivered by the wind, about one particular monkey. I don't know why I suddenly thought of that monkey, but it might have been that the rocking boats sounded like a large troop of playing monkeys.

On nights with heavy winds, when most boats do not dare set sail, a phantom ship is said to enter the San Francisco Marina.

Aboard the ship is a monkey from Java, Indonesia, who died in Africa at the age of ninety-nine, which is young for a monkey. He was legendary not only among people but also among monkeys, thanks to a rumor that he was the first monkey to ever reach the North Pole, and his screw was turned loose by the Aurora. He lost his mind, but he led a happy life because of it. He always carried a coconut under one arm, either to remind himself of the place he had left, or to perpetuate the feeling that he was not alone.

The monkey had always been a loner. As a young monkey, he had liked to spend time alone in a cave on a deserted island. The coconut had been with him since his youth. With the coconut in his arms, the young monkey had watched boats sailing across the ocean, the sun setting over the horizon, the stars in the night sky, and a number of comets darting through space. The monkey had always thought that he would spend his final years, after losing his sight, living with the coconut in a cave on a deserted island, reading Braille books until he died. The coconut would watch over his dead body. The coconut was the monkey's favorite thing in the world. He was a serious monkey, but he also liked to play games. As long as he had the coconut, he could play endlessly without ever getting bored. He found playing in the light dull, and played only in complete darkness. In the dark, merely placing the coconut between his knees and remaining still with his mouth ajar or his arms raised, or making a disgruntled face and then actually becoming disgruntled, became extreme games. Such were his usual games.

Little is known about how the monkey occupied himself in the Arctic. There are no facts, only rumors. There was nothing sweet in the Arctic, and the monkey grew nostalgic for his birthplace when he craved sweet things, especially tropical fruit. At those times, he would lick balled-up snow, which provided only a cold taste that numbed the inside of his mouth. He was sent home by the first human expedition to reach the North Pole, only to set out again on a wandering journey. He roamed the world until he was killed by an endemic disease in Africa. Rumor had it that anyone who encountered the monkey's ghost would go mad and return to sanity, go mad again and return to sanity.

Recalling the story about the monkey from Java by the docks of the San Francisco Marina, I imagined that the story might have originated with a person who believed that he was the monkey, perhaps a long-time sailor who had been admitted to a mental institution, or a man who was a seasoned sailor in his delusions despite having never been to sea and having spent his entire adulthood in a mental institution. When my thoughts arrived at a person who had never been to sea but believed that he was a monkey from Java who reached the North Pole, I returned home somewhat excited, putting the phantasmagoric rocking vessels behind me.

I sat quietly by the shaking window. It occurred to me that I could write a play about the man who'd never been to sea but believed himself to be a Javanese monkey that reached the North Pole, a man who'd been released from a mental institution after a long time in confinement and was writing a play based on his story but refused to interact with the world. The man was not all there, being old, bald, toothless, and hairless—I thought that he could not possibly be of sound mind, having lost all his teeth and hair. Looking like a toothless lion, he composed on his typewriter, but he was incapable of typing more than twenty words a day. His composition was practically a list of words. The subject of his writing was his thoughts on such objects as a bowling ball that inexplicably ended up in his room, an empty birdcage, a flamingo figurine, a coconut, a model ship . . . anything that triggered his fancy.

I thought that while writing the play, I could wear my theatrical jacket, and perhaps wear the expression of a person who's been writing for too long: forlorn, grim, too enervated to be bothered with life. That wouldn't have been difficult for me to achieve. I always look that way when I write. I reckoned that it wouldn't be long before I turned into the character in my play who'd never been to sea but believed he was a Javanese monkey who reached the North Pole and wrote a play based on his life story after being released from a mental institution. I thought that when that time came, I might wear a strange conical hat while writing. It would not matter if I looked hideous. I felt that I needed to dress the part when writing such a composition, looking miserable or unsightly. My appearance would be pathetic, but that would be in keeping with the objective of the attire.

After that, I came to believe that in order to write the play, I needed a complete outfit to match my theatrical jacket. So I went on a search of San Francisco's shoe stores for a pair of boots. I didn't have a clear idea of the precise shape of the boots I was looking for, but I believed that I would recognize them when I found them. The search was fruitless, and I blamed my failure to write the play on not having acquired the necessary outfit. Months later, when I left San Francisco, what I most regretted was having failed to write the play because I'd been unable to find the right boots.

A few nights after I bought the theatrical jacket, I fell asleep wearing the jacket and dreamt that I was lost in a Costa Rican jungle, looking for an orchid that had yet to be discovered. I found a pair of boots that were hardly recognizable, looking at least a couple hundred years old. I guessed that they had belonged to one of the first Spanish conquistadors to arrive there. Not far from the boots were some phalanges, which likely belonged to the boots' owner. Based on the fact that no other set of phalanges was visible, the man seemed to have died alone, lost in the jungle. I put on the Spanish conquistador's boots, put his phalanges in my jacket pocket, and walked deeper into the jungle. I saw monkeys making bird calls from treetops (I had seen similar monkeys in a jungle in Southeast Asia) and then I heard parrots making nearly identical noises from nearby trees. The parrot calls were indistinguishable from the monkey calls. Deep in the forest, I discovered what looked like ancient Aztec ruins with hovering towers. The towers were incomplete and were being constructed by flat-nosed, Tibetan-looking monkeys climbing up and down ladders. The monkeys were peculiar in appearance, comical but with deep gazes, their heads shaped as though they were wearing bizarre conical hats that one might expect to see on Tibetan monks. I was watching the monkeys move busily about like worker ants as they carefully constructed the hovering towers, when I awoke from my sleep. The towers were crumbling as quickly as they were being erected.

Some time later, I bought a pair of green socks at a sock shop on Dolores Street in the Mission District, which had become one of my favorite spots in San Francisco. I thought the socks were a good match for my stage costume. I also happened to be in the market for socks because two of the five pairs of socks I owned had developed a hole on one sock. A sock typically develops a hole at the big toe—or it could be the little toe since socks have no left and right—but the holes in both my pairs were on the edge of the foot. Come to think of it, my socks usually develop holes on the edge of the foot, perhaps because I walk a little funny.

The green socks were rather attractive. I left the sock store and went to a cafe, sat at a curbside table and ordered coffee. I examined the socks closely, and sure enough, they were women's socks. "No wonder you are so attractive," I said indignantly to the socks. I mused on why everything worn by men has to be made so obviously and significantly less attractive, or at least a little bit less attractive, than everything worn by women. This is a huge issue for me. It seems totally unfair, considering that in some ways . . . no, in every way, women are created more attractive than men. If men's clothing were made a little bit more attractive, men who became more attractive by wearing it could at least be gentler, if not more charming. In a way, I thought that men dressing less attractively than women might be a self-ish behavior on the part of men, to help them gravitate away from one another and toward women, who are more attractive.

I thought that women who wear socks that fit me must have fairly big feet. The green socks were knee-high. I imagined that a person who wants to do nothing special on a special day, perhaps his birthday, might wear such socks all day. Such socks could be a good birthday gift for that person to give himself. When feeling lonely, not overly but bearably so, or when overcome with sad but identifiable emotions, one might sit on the sofa and gaze at his socked feet, sinking quietly into loneliness and sorrow rather than trying to dispel them. The important thing was that the socks would look good with my theatrical jacket. All I needed was a shirt, a pair of pants, a pair of shoes, and a hat to go with them. I felt as though I could become lost in "colorless green ideas [that] sleep furiously" just by wearing my theatrical jacket with my green socks and a matching shirt, pants, and hat. With that outfit, I'd be able to distance myself from everything in the world when I wanted to, or to believe that I was doing so. The problem was, I didn't know where to find the missing parts.

I decided to postpone finding those parts, and watched the passing people. After I saw one redheaded woman, I began to count the passing redheads for no reason. Like a person with a mission, I tried to do a faithful job, and I counted redheads as though counting the number of puffins with beautiful beaks in the Arctic. Counting is a hobby of mine, like rolling pebbles down hills. These could be said to be my only hobbies. In a way, it is regretful that I am unable to find something productive to do that makes use of my hobbies, which sort of make use of certain talents of mine.

In addition to the many countable things, there are many things that are unsuitable for counting, clouds and wind being prime examples. Nevertheless, I am capable of counting them, thinking, *Thirteen frowning clouds passed by*, or *Thirteen winds went by, failing to conceal their shock*. Some things are even more difficult to count than clouds and wind, including raindrops and bubbles in boiling water. I need to focus in order to count them, and I invariably become confused before long. Still, I've counted over a hundred bubbles, which I christened *bubbles of unconcealable joy*, as I boiled water for tea.

Counting things unsuitable for counting is perplexing and enjoyable at the same time. I came across large flocks of sheep in the countryside in the USA, France, and Turkey. Counting the number of sheep was as difficult as it was fun. The sheep were not concerned with being counted. They didn't wait for me to count, but continued moving, which made counting accurately very challenging. On countless sleepless nights I have counted sheep in my head. On nights after counting real sheep in the countryside in the USA, France, and Turkey, I was able to sleep only after counting a mixed flock of the sheep I had seen that day and imaginary sheep—they included blue sheep, purple sheep, and invisible sheep, as well as others I inserted sneakily, such as a sheep in wolf's clothing and something that seemed furthest from a sheep, but which was unidentifiable, and therefore unknowable. If I ever have the chance to go to Africa or South America and I come across a flock of sheep, I will probably count them as though it was my purpose for going there, feel challenged doing it, and feel that I am really in Africa or South America.

I show a strange obsession when I count things. I often think that it is natural to show a strange obsession, and that certain things are difficult to count without showing a strange obsession. Once, when I was walking down a small street in Seoul, a small dog inside the gate of a house suddenly started barking ferociously and startled me. I stopped walking and, with the gate between us, I counted the number of times the dog barked, looking down at my watch. For whatever reason, the dog barked at me intently, showing tremendous animosity. There must be some dogs that usually bark for no reason, and every dog must sometimes bark for no reason, but this dog was not barking for no reason. There was desperation in its barking, and the dog did not appear to be doing something desperately for no reason. Clearly it didn't feel good about me, as it showed blunt antagonism by exposing all of its teeth. I generally have no specific position on things, but I have a stern position on trivial issues such as ways to deal with the various dogs of the world. My position, which is stern and almost resolute, is that people and dogs must maintain an appropriate distance and avoid offending each other. So I stood some distance away and stared at the dog, which barked frantically like a mad dog, without even pausing to breathe.

I wasn't sure whether I was making the dog bark. I suspected that barking so frantically is painful for a dog, unless it is barking out of joy—it must be painful even if it is barking out of joy. The dog endured the pain and kept barking. I tried in vain to think of a reason the dog would bark so, despite the pain it was suffering. The dog was literally foaming at the mouth. I thought the dog might faint if it continued barking like that, foaming at the mouth. The barking was very loud, and I listened with my hands over my ears. I worried that the dog might lose its voice barking, but it didn't lose its voice. A passerby gave a puzzled look at the dog and me, but we were not concerned, and concentrated on our respective tasks.

In one minute, the dog barked nearly a hundred times with hardly a break. After a minute, the dog looked extremely exhausted. It felt as though we'd taken turns hitting each other a hundred times, the dog hitting my chest, and me hitting the dog's flank. I had a headache, and I thought the dog's legs must feel weak. I wanted to punish the poor dog some more for being antagonistic for no reason and barking itself to exhaustion. I had the sudden revelation that the best way to punish a dog is to bite its nose until it hurts a little. I considered biting the dog's nose, but the gate was in the way. I also knew that the dog was more likely to bite my nose if I tried. The embarrassment of being bitten by a dog on the nose for trying to bite a dog on the nose would haunt me for a long time. It seemed that no one was home. The dog's owner must have gone out after ordering the dog to bark at passing people and foam at the mouth. I thought about timing the dog for another minute and wearing out the dog completely, but I decided not to and went on my way. I hoped that the dog would stop barking, which was causing it pain, and find something else to do. I thought that if there was nothing else to do, the dog had no choice but to resort to barking. Perhaps the dog felt refreshed after barking that way. I thought later about my idea that the best way to punish a dog is to bite its nose until it hurts a little, but the notion felt wrong in every way.

Redheads weren't common in San Francisco, and I counted six in about two hours. I waited with the unfounded belief that seeing seven redheads in a day would bring me luck, but the seventh redhead never appeared. It was regretful that I could not count seven as I wished. One of the six redheads was a man, and two of the five women seemed to have dyed their hair. Before going home, I walked around for a while to get to seven, but I never found the seventh, as everything seems to disappear when you decide to look for it. Still, when I got home, I thought that the day had been rather fruitful.

It occurs to me that there is another thing that I do as a hobby: writing. I can tell that I write as a hobby just by the fact that I write with the same mindset I have when I roll pebbles or count things. I roll pebbles and count things with unusual persistence and tenacity rather than love, as if committing an indecent act out of desperation. Such persistence and tenacity, which are immensely unpleasant to consider, have kept me writing to this day.

9. The Fruit That Did Not Roam the Pacific Ocean Because of My Complete Lack of Motivation

THERE WERE MANY new days I loathed to greet because of my complete lack of motivation. Upon waking, I would sense that a very challenging day was ahead of me. My energy would be dampened the moment I opened my eyes. I would be overcome by fatigue just thinking about getting up and starting the day, so I would lie back down for a long while before getting up again.

Usually, I could foresee almost everything I was going to do in the course of the day, and almost everything happened as predicted. I knew how I'd feel if I did something, what I would talk about if I met someone (though I spent most days alone without meeting anyone), what I would not talk about (I couldn't talk about certain topics with certain people), what I would think about, and what I would eat. My predictions were rarely off. I felt weighed down by the helplessness that arose from the thought of spending another day that was practically the same as the previous day. Living the rest of my life knowing that the days to come would hardly be distinguishable from the countless days I had already lived could be likened to spending every day reading books or watching movies with almost identical plots. This was the truly hapless component of my life, which was largely without haplessness.

On such days, I continued to think negative thoughts as if to demonstrate to myself how difficult it is to think positively in an impaired state of complete lethargy. My thoughts would race as though my brain had become more active. At some point, the fact that I felt no heartfelt desire to do anything had become the biggest real challenge in my life, one that I faced all the time. This might be a strange way to describe my condition, but I had come to do everything reluctantly.

I learned to do certain things without any motivation whatsoever, but doing those things drained my energy. In most cases I was better off doing nothing, so I generally did nothing. Doing nothing was what I did best, but I also felt spent after doing nothing all day, many times more so than after having done something.

In the end, I would usually get up again with the small but seemingly grand hope of spending the day working on a meaningless and disembodied piece of writing, which felt rather unpleasant. It was rare that I was able to write, and even if I managed to, the end result was disappointing, and I ended up scrapping it most of the time.

When I had no motivation, I also lacked appetite, which was natural and inevitable. Having appetite when there was no motivation was neither logical nor becoming, but rather extremely cumbersome. If I had no motivation or appetite for several days in a row, I'd spend hours not knowing what to do, between feeling that doing anything other than satiating my hunger didn't make sense and feeling that doing anything including satiating my hunger didn't make sense. When the situation got out of control, I'd feel as though I ought to refrain from doing anything at all.

As I grappled with hunger because I couldn't be bothered to eat, I sometimes had vivid sensations of something that existed in hunger that was more real than anything else in life, which could be called the realism of hunger. This seemed to be the one benefit of hunger. Other benefits were difficult to find. If possible, I wanted only to lie motionless and think, fighting with hunger without eating or going to the bathroom. But hunger could not be left alone. Even if I had no desire to eat anything, I had to fill my stomach in the end. Even after deciding to eat something, there remained the difficult challenge of deciding what to eat. Some days I spent easily two or three hours crippled by indecision. After finally giving in and eating something, I would often feel wretched or guilty, even if I had taken only a few bites.

When eating rice or bread felt like too much trouble, because they require chewing before swallowing, I usually went to an Asian restaurant to eat noodles, which I could eat with minimal chewing, and rather absentmindedly. One day, I couldn't even be bothered to go to a restaurant, so I somewhat halfheartedly made Thai noodles at home, using whatever ingredients were at hand. Although I was thinking of Thai noodles as I cooked, the result was a dish of indeterminate nationality, made with Vietnamese rice noodles, Thai spices, and vegetables probably produced in the USA. I thought that my noodles were the kind of food that a stateless person must eat from time to time in order to remind himself of his statelessness.

I topped the noodles with a few leaves of spinach, which I had started to wash two days prior to make salad. The spinach, which had been sitting in water, had swollen remarkably but not unrecognizably—actually, I almost did not recognize it. The leftover spinach filling the bowl of water did not look like water hyacinth covering a pond, but it reminded me of water hyacinth. It looked somehow ominous, even slightly frightening. Looking at the spinach, I thought that I had never in my dreams imagined that spinach could seem ominous and frightening. It was a good thing that the spinach was missing its roots, because it might have grown even more enormous with roots. (I left the remaining spinach in the water to see how much bigger it would get, but it must have reached its largest size, because it began to spoil and I had to throw it out in the end.)

The spinach had nearly doubled in size, but it seemed to have lost more than half of its original spinach taste. It tasted strange, as if it were not spinach. It seemed to be retaliating against the person who'd treated it so unfairly. The noodles, cooked by a maladroit cook, were surely perverse. The meal looked sad and tasted sad, and I became sad the moment I started eating it. In a way that would have probably made any onlookers lose their appetites, with an uneasy feeling as if doing something that cannot be accomplished without uneasiness, with a face showing much discontent, like a person holding a grudge against noodles for unspeakable reasons, in fact, almost holding a grudge against noodles, with my heart steeled, almost desperately, I picked at the noodles with my chopsticks and felt very pitiful. I thought that eating so pitifully would result in indigestion or stomach ache, so I stopped eating after a few bites. I thought about throwing my chopsticks, but instead put them down gently. Not only was acting pitiful never good for one's body, but it seemed to me that one could never act pitiful in a dignified manner.

There was another reason that I stopped eating after a few bites of noodles. For three days, I'd been afraid to go to the bathroom because of hemorrhoids, and was therefore afraid to eat. Hemorrhoids gave me a heavy heart, and in those three days of suffering, I had many thoughts triggered by hemorrhoids, all of them rather pitiful. I believe that there are two sides to everything, so I tried to see the good side of hemorrhoids. I tried to believe that the mind and energy of a person can be distracted by hemorrhoids, mitigating the whirling of his mind slightly, but it did not seem true. Hemorrhoids seemed to aggravate the whirling.

I had bought suppositories two days prior. After inserting one into my rectum, I felt a strange pleasure, but I was unsure whether it was derived from the act of insertion or from having something inside my rectum. Thinking that the two possibilities might be completely different, I thought about each separately, and both seemed equally good. The suppository, however, soon melted away from body heat, and the feeling of having it inside dissipated. With the suppository, the pleasure, either from inserting the suppository or having it inside, disappeared. The pain of my hemorrhoids swept over me once again. Actually, I am just kidding about using suppositories for hemorrhoids. I was dealing with the unmitigated pain of hemorrhoids because I couldn't be bothered to go purchase medication. What I've written here are thoughts that occurred to me when I used suppositories for hemorrhoids in the past.

After I quit eating noodles, recalling the thoughts that had occurred to me in the past while suffering from hemorrhoids, I simultaneously felt self-pity and misery. Self-pity and misery are similar yet with subtle differences. Misery seems slightly more emotionally charged, and thus more plaintive. Upon further musing, however, it seemed rather unlikely that one would wallow in self-pity and not in misery. In addition to wallowing in self-pity and misery, I seemed to also be wallowing in senselessness and foolishness. It would have been nice if I could have put a stop to all this, but for whatever reason, as though I was trying to see how far I could take it, I thought about what else I could wallow in. I considered wallowing in frivolousness and agitation, but this was redundant because I already seemed to be frivolous and agitated. For some reason, I do not care about being frivolous. In certain situations, I readily show double standards, but I'm consistently agitated by my wallowing in agitation. I thought to stop wallowing in agitation, but thinking was easier than doing. Even after deciding to stop wallowing in agitation, I continued to feel agitated, though to a lesser degree, like an aftershock. For whatever reason, I thought of pain as something else I could wallow in, and I wanted to wallow in pretend pain. But the pain of my hemorrhoids was real, and my hunger remained unsatiated, so I was technically unable to wallow in pretend pain, which was a bizarre situation. I was overcome by a sense of abhorrence, directed toward none other than myself.

When my thoughts reached that point, I mused that I could venture to call myself a pity monger, as a person who likes to daydream is called a daydreamer. As I was wallowing in self-pity, suffering from hemorrhoids and fighting hunger, a thought that comes to me without fail whenever I am wallowing in self-pity flashed through my mind: *How unrespectable and flawed as a human being I must be to wallow in self-pity in such a way!* My character flaw seemed to be the source of my ability to wallow in self-pity. Thinking that it would be difficult to wallow in self-pity to such a degree were I not so diffident and twisted, I felt something akin to satisfaction and smiled a little—thinking that all of this was possible because I was at the age least likely to know moderation, aware of the excess of my self-consciousness, thinking that one had to have a strong sense of identity in order to properly wallow in self-pity—because it occurred to me that the world of a frighteningly pitiful and diffident person is a hilarious yet frightening world. I know that contemptible and profane world all too well, but being inside that place, which is like a narrow room, was disconcerting.

Even though nothing was stopping me from wallowing in self-pity, I didn't have to take it so far, and I could have chosen not to wallow in self-pity. Wallowing in self-pity didn't give me any kind of relief, nor did I become keenly aware of being alive—which happens once in a while—or feel that the countless hours I had spent thinking about numerous things while wallowing in self-pity were very precious. I felt rather foul, because there is a human aspect to self-pity, and I felt as though I had displayed my humanity by wallowing in self-pity. This made me feel bitter and proud at the same time. The thoughts I immersed myself in as I wallowed in self-pity gave me no energy, but rather drained what little energy I had. I felt as though I'd gone through a rather intense ordeal, so I decided to call it a day. (The reason I'm telling such a pitiful story, which clearly shows my diffidence and small-mindedness, is that the story fits this novel, which is an attempt to write as an exercise in extremely trivial, useless, and hollow contemplation. Nevertheless, telling a story that is beyond small-minded, bordering on pathetic, makes me rethink how I came to be this way.)

The next day I went to a Vietnamese restaurant in Chinatown. The time was around three in the afternoon, which is normally a relatively quiet hour, but the restaurant was almost full. After being seated, I looked around and saw a group of around twenty kids and several adults. Judging by their attire and accent, they had come on a tour from rural Texas, or they were on a group outing from an orphanage or something. The younger children were being boisterous, and the ones who appeared to be in their teens looked sullen, wearing expressions that would be awkward on anyone who is not a teenager, as though nothing was to their satisfaction. I was eating my noodles when I noticed a baby Caucasian girl staring up at me from a stroller parked beside me. No one in her group was paying any heed to her. The baby was so homely that my heart ached looking at her face, and I let it do so. At a certain point, a heavy sigh came out of my mouth. She stared rather amazedly at me, and did not turn her head away when I stared back. Even as my heart was aching uncontrollably, I was almost touched by her very homely face, and I was overcome by the strange emotions stirred by that face.

I always felt that the sight of a person chewing food vigorously, diligently working his lower jaw, is rather unattractive. That unattractive sight can be appreciated best when looking at a face in profile. Conscious of the baby's gaze, I ate moving my lower jaw as little as possible, taking care to look less unattractive. Yet I still felt self-conscious. I tried to convince myself that the baby didn't think that I was moving my lower jaw in an unattractive manner. Chances are, however, that the baby thought me to be very unattractive. She just couldn't talk. Anyway, rather than thinking about such things, the baby seemed to be discovering the wonders of humanity by watching me eat noodles. She didn't take her eyes off of me until I had cleaned my bowl. Only after I had put my chopsticks down did she look away as if she had seen enough. I felt weird having been watched by someone through an entire meal. I had merely eaten a bowl of noodles, but as soon as I put my chopsticks down, I felt as though it was all up for me.

To her, the sight of many strands of long, thin, white things continuously disappearing into my mouth must have been marvelous, almost magical. Although she may not remember later in life, this event could possibly remain permanently in her unconscious or subconscious mind as one of her first impressive and important memories. All the while, the woman who appeared to be the baby's mother or guardian did not pay any attention to the baby. She was too busy ordering food and talking to her companions, and was therefore oblivious to the fact that her baby was experiencing what was to become one of her first impressive and important memories. The baby was now watching a person eating noodles at a different table. Even as her mother fed her noodles, she didn't take her eyes off that person. I was unsure whether she was amazed by noodles or the person eating noodles.

I didn't want to go home straightaway after my meal, so I sat at the restaurant for a while longer and thought about what to do next. I glanced at the television in the corner of the room, which was showing a program showcasing funny videos. One video featured a woman and her dog lying side by side on their stomachs, reading together with a blanket over them. The dog was reading a news magazine and appeared to have great interest in current affairs. The dog seemed much more interested in current affairs than I am. I actually have no interest in current events. Leaving current affairs to the dog and any interested people, I went to Pier 39, the most popular tourist site in San Francisco. One time, I almost made it to the pier, but lost my nerve and turned back after seeing the hordes of tourists.

I had a particular reason for going there. The dog whose head was poking out from under the blanket reminded me of a seal. I was not trying to spot seals, though. From Pier 39, I'd seen night swimmers in the ocean. They looked like seals upon first sighting, but they had arms and legs, and it became clear that they were people when they came out of the water. Because the water was very cold, they swam in wetsuits, which made them look very much like seals from afar. If I turned my eyes away from what first appeared to be seals and then back, I gradually saw them as people. I didn't want to see seals, but swimmers that look like seals. This time, however, they were nowhere in sight. Instead, I saw a few real seals, but they weren't what I was after, so I gave them little regard.

I was waiting to take a tram home when I saw, sitting on a bench, a young white woman who was very fat and a young black woman who looked very peculiar, just like a moon bear cub. The white woman's face was bright red, and the black woman's face was half covered with hair. The black woman was decisively more impressive. She looked really strange, yet she had a very cute side to her, like a moon bear cub. I like faces that remind me of animals, but regretfully, my face does not resemble that of any animal, though this is only my opinion. Actually, from time to time I think that I'm growing to resemble a jocular llama. The two women appeared to be the best of best friends. I suddenly realized that I didn't have a best friend. It's possible that someone considered me his best friend, but there was no one to my knowledge. I thought that I was fine without one. I sat next to the women, and for a moment, I tried to eavesdrop on their conversation, but they seldom exchanged words, and were barely comprehensible. They were mostly watching the passing tourists. Both women seemed a little weak in the head. I thought that they might be on a brief outing from a shelter.

On the tram I saw a dwarf man, who was very small even for a dwarf. I wondered how he ate his meals at home. Did he sit on a long-legged chair for young children? I visualized the man eating alone at home, properly using a fork and knife, a white napkin around his neck. Was all of his furniture custom-fit to match his height? Or did he have normal furniture and have to sit up tall in his chairs? I had always wanted to be invited to a dwarf's house. While I am slightly intimidated by every dwarf I see, I have often fancied having a dwarf for a friend.

When I transferred to the bus, I saw a very old woman who looked to be in her late eighties. She was reading what must have been a new release by John Grisham. Apologies to John Grisham, but I thought that I cannot be friends with people who read John Grisham. I also thought, without feeling sorry for the old woman who could not be my friend, that she'd lived to nearly ninety just to read John Grisham. She seemed to have led a rather peculiar life. I got off the bus and was walking toward home when I passed a young black man with a large boom box on his shoulder, dancing to the beat. It had been a long time since I had danced to music, and it seemed unlikely that I would do so in the future. This made me a little bit sad. I imagined getting up from my deathbed and dancing a little, assuming that I would have enough energy, before lying back down to die. That wouldn't be bad. I didn't think, however, that I would feel at all like dancing just before dying. Perhaps I would be able to visualize dancing with my eyes closed, gasping for my last breath. I'd been dancing in my room one day when I stopped for no reason and told myself that I would not dance again until the day I die. I had not danced since.

Once I got home, I closed the door behind me and lay in bed. Everything I had seen that day—the baby who stared at people eating noodles, the seals, the white woman and the black woman who looked like the best of best friends, the dwarf man, the old woman who was reading what appeared to be John Grisham's new release, the young black man who danced as he walked—felt so far away, like the pictures in storybooks I read a long time ago. I tried desperately to hold on to their impressions, but they faded gradually until they were completely gone. I had no feelings left at all. I tried in vain to be moved by something. It was as though my emotions had been powered off. My face felt like an expressionless wooden mask that I was wearing over my real face.

The next morning, I couldn't imagine cooking anything or going out to eat noodles, so I went to a nearby store and bought large quantities of grapes, peaches, bananas, and pears, and filled my stomach with fruit. The fruit gave me heartburn. I meant to savor the pain that I had brought upon myself, but the pain was bitter. Nevertheless, I went back to the store that night and bought apples, blueberries, avocados, and mangos—like some kind of fruit collector, as if I were hoarding canned foods and batteries for an emergency. The next day, too, I ate only fruit. I had soured on eating fruit, but that didn't stop me from eating more fruit. I thought that it was quite natural to sour on fruit after having eaten fruit until it gave me a sour stomach. One of the reasons I continued eating fruit was to punish myself for refusing to eat a proper meal. I punish myself whenever I feel that I need punishing.

I put some fruit out on the table and stared fiercely at it for a good while before finally eating it. When I picked up a piece of fruit and ate it from my hand, I felt like a person feeding fruit to a monkey and like the monkey being fed at the same time. After eating, however, I felt like a monkey who'd eaten a piece of fruit he'd stolen. Once, after eating an avocado and a peach like a playful monkey, I softened my expression, and with an air of optimism, I ate one piece of slightly wilted spinach from the refrigerator as dessert. Spinach seemed a most inadequate dessert after fruit. In the end, my face hardened and I felt like a rather pessimistic person. I felt that the spinach had instantly turned me from an optimist to a pessimist, so I ate another piece of spinach as if to take revenge, which made me feel like a pessimistic goat.

In the middle of the night, I was unable to bear my hunger. I took some food out of the refrigerator, only to put it back like a fasting person who will not give in to temptation. Then I remembered the honey in the cupboard, and, failing to resist that temptation, I ate a few spoonfuls of honey. I often eat honey when I am in a difficult situation or am in agony. Eating honey does not change anything, but honey is a good thing to eat when I am in a poor state and have no appetite, because even after eating it, I cannot exactly say that I have eaten something. Honey is also a good thing to eat absentmindedly when I feel like I am losing my mind.

I couldn't bring myself to eat any more fruit the next day, so I decided not to touch fruit for a while. I agonized over ways to discard the leftover fruit, and finally thought of a way. It was stormy that night, but I went out into the storm, found a park, and discarded the fruit piece by piece under various trees. I was carrying an umbrella that had lost a spoke in the fierce rainstorm that had hit San Francisco a few days prior. I was getting drenched, but I didn't mind.

Once I considered it a task, disposing of the fruit became almost pleasurable. There are some things that I derive pleasure from doing, even if doing them makes no difference, and this was one of those things. As I discarded the fruit, I ate one peach, in order to reinforce my resolution not to touch fruit for a while. I wanted to believe that the peach I ate under the umbrella while disposing of the fruit in the rain because I could not subsist on fruit alone any longer was sweet to the point of being bitter, but in actuality it was merely sweet. Like a rigid man of principle who takes procedures seriously even when procedures are unimportant, I discarded each kind of fruit under a different kind of tree. This is how mangoes ended up under poplar trees, avocados under pine trees, peaches under eucalyptus trees, and melons under elm trees. I told myself that a curious event had occurred that night in San Francisco: a strange terrorist had appeared and thrown fruit under trees.

It was one of those days when I'm in a particularly good mood because of the bad weather. On such days, the bad weather seems to heighten my mood considerably. It continued to rain through the night, so I inevitably stayed in a good mood. At one point after returning home, I felt sorry for the fruit I'd discarded, as if I were an animal that had had no choice but to dispose of its newborns. But my mood, heightened by the bad weather, was irrepressible, so I had no choice but to stay high. Having no choice but to stay in an elevated mood could be an unpleasant way to be, but I didn't feel that way, which makes me suspect that I was under a manic spell, which happens so rarely. Twenty or so years ago, when I started writing novels, I'd fallen into a bad mood and had been perpetually in a bad mood ever since, as if writing itself gave me a negative vibe. That night, I felt almost uncomfortable with the way my unrelenting high clung to me with unshakeable force. The next day, there was still fruit left over, and I wanted it to meet a more brilliant end than the other fruit had, so I came up with another way to dispose of fruit. Driven by a spontaneous thought, I packed mangoes, avocados, peaches, and a melon in a shopping bag, and that night I walked all the way to the Golden Gate Bridge. I stood in the middle of the bridge and began dropping fruit piece by piece into the Pacific Ocean. The fruit floated under the Golden Gate Bridge, which I feel belongs to the Chinese because many Chinese immigrant workers died during its construction. I found an onion in the shopping bag. I made a face to express my having no clue how it ended up there with the fruit. The onion appeared puzzled by the whole thing. I dropped it off the Golden Gate Bridge. The onion might have felt wronged for having been dragged into this strange and secretive ritual of dumping fruit into the Pacific Ocean, but I hoped that, despite feeling wronged, the onion would fare well, drifting across the Pacific Ocean. I hoped that the tidal currents would take the onion across the national border to Canada or Mexico. Better yet, I wanted the onion, which had dropped off the Golden Gate

Bridge, which I feel belongs to deceased Chinese men, to cross the Pacific Ocean to China, but that seemed far-fetched.

I had driven across the Golden Gate Bridge a few times, but I'd never walked across it. I'd watched people walking across the bridge from afar, and thought that they were strange. Walking across the bridge myself, it indeed felt strange. When I first saw the Golden Gate Bridge in its entirety, I did not like the look of it, but it grew on me once I saw it shrouded in fog. I liked the bridge most when it was covered completely in fog save for the tips of its towers. I was certain that no one comes to the bridge in order to dump fruit and an onion into the Pacific Ocean. I thought that although people probably don't know it, the Golden Gate Bridge is the perfect bridge from which to drop fruit and cast it adrift.

The Golden Gate Bridge is also a place from which countless drowned bodies of people who have committed suicide are swept away. The Golden Gate Bridge is the most popular place for suicides, not only in America, but in the world. It is followed by Aokigahara Forest, which lies at the base of Mount Fuji. I regard the Golden Gate Bridge as the bridge of dead Chinese men, the bridge of drifting drowned bodies, and Aokigahara Forest as the forest of corpses hanging from branches. I do not know how most people meet their deaths in Aokigahara Forest, but whenever I think of the forest, I picture dead bodies with ropes around their necks, swinging gently in the breeze. In my imagination, on moonlit nights, the dead bodies smile mysterious purple smiles at the gratifying stroke of the moonlight on their bodies. There's one thing about people who hang themselves from trees that I've always found curious: they have to struggle, perhaps groaning a little, to climb the tree before hanging themselves. It must be fundamentally more difficult for people who cannot climb trees to hang themselves from trees. On the other hand, the people who hang themselves from trees might be people who are good at climbing trees. Perhaps there are people who consider climbing a tree before dying to be a bit silly, and so use a small ladder. Otherwise, they risk a particular embarrassment from their rather comical effort in the resolute moment before facing death.

Having dropped fruit and an onion from the bridge, it occurred to me that many people from all over America and the world come to San Francisco with grand hopes of jumping from the Golden Gate Bridge. San Francisco suddenly felt like a somewhat special place, but not the city's symbolic Golden Gate Bridge. No other city in the world has so many people arrive with grand hopes of jumping to their deaths. I had not considered the city to be that special, even though, of all the cities in the United States, San Francisco is the most open, culturally diverse, and above all, natural place—a place where hobos, beggars, eccentrics, old hippies, and deranged people make up natural parts of the city. When I thought that San Francisco is not only a place that people seek to jump to their deaths, but also where many hippies came with flowers in their hair, and where a different group of countless deranged people might have descended, the city suddenly felt quite special, though not exceptional. San Francisco is not an exceptional city, but it is a fine place to live, which might be the true sign of a fine, possibly even exceptional, city. I thought some more about it, but the city still didn't seem exceptional. No place in the world is that exceptional.

People who come to San Francisco with grand hopes of jumping to their deaths must take a bus or taxi to get to the Golden Gate Bridge, which is in the northwest corner of the city, stand on the bridge and hesitate for a moment, or jump off the bridge without hesitation, and enjoy the short final flight before plunging into the cold ocean. I wondered if some people become elated in their final moments, thinking that their dead bodies will drift across the Pacific Ocean. The success rate of suicide by jumping from the Golden Gate Bridge is 98 percent, owing to the height of the bridge and the low water temperature. Among the very unlucky survivors are those who fight the strong currents and swim out of the water. Survivors must believe that a miracle has occurred. I wondered whether there are people who jump off the Golden Gate Bridge for a second time.

Once, a mechanical engineer installed a motion sensor

camera under the Golden Gate Bridge. It is said to have captured seventeen people jumping off the bridge in three months. Her project was later included in the Whitney Biennial. I have not seen the video, but I imagine it to be like a nature documentary, like those that explore the lives of hummingbirds. I fancied writing a poem about a person throwing himself off the bridge, but I didn't write a poem since I'm not a poet. Still, I decided to believe that if I were a poet, I would have written a beautiful poem about a person throwing himself off a bridge, as though writing about a flower falling from a branch.

One day, I was looking up at the Golden Gate Bridge from a distance, imagining people jumping off the bridge, when I recalled the fact that Einstein developed his theory of gravity and acceleration based on a random thought that he had while sitting at his desk at the patent office in Bern, Switzerland. He wrote in 1907, "Suddenly, the thought struck me: if a man falls freely, he does not feel his own weight. I was taken aback. This simple thought experiment made a deep impression on me." From his imagining a free-falling person, Einstein developed a theory that would change the course of physics. I am unsure whether my dropping fruit and an onion from the Golden Gate Bridge was based on my imagining people throwing themselves from the bridge, but it is clear that I was unable to develop any theory through the experience, which is regrettable.

After dropping all of the leftover fruit, I thought that perhaps some of the fruit might sink rather than float. The fruit that sank to the bottom might roll slowly along the ocean floor, as if rolling down the hallway of a building. Although I had not assigned it any mission, the fruit was on a mission to roam the Pacific Ocean while gradually disintegrating. I imagined the fruit roaming the Pacific Ocean, and thought that its fate had been brought about by my complete lack of motivation.

But none of this is true. In actuality, I had known that pedestrian traffic was banned on the Golden Gate Bridge after a certain hour at night in order to prevent people from committing suicide by jumping. Therefore, I was unable to drop fruit from

the suicide-tarnished Golden Gate Bridge at night and allow it
to roam the Pacific Ocean. What I couldn't figure out was what
good such a measure was, when people who are determined to
die are willing to die by any means and will eventually find a
way. Among the people who come from all over America and
the world to jump from the Golden Gate Bridge, oblivious to
the fact that walking on the bridge is banned after hours, there
are perhaps people who postpone or give up suicide by jumping,
feeling irked by their inability to die at the time and place they
had in mind. Perhaps that was the effect the city officials were
after when they banned pedestrians on the Golden Gate Bridge
at night. However, a person who has carefully considered all
aspects before deciding on the time and place of his suicide could
be hugely disappointed when his plan falls through, and that
disappointment could in turn make the person wish again to die.

The real reason that I was unable to take a bag of fruit and
an onion to the Golden Gate Bridge and drop them into the
Pacific Ocean to drift was that I didn't have the motivation to
do so, and all of this happened in my head as I lay quietly in bed
without any motivation whatsoever. In the end, the fruit ended
up not roaming the Pacific Ocean thanks to my complete lack
of motivation. Therefore, this piece of writing, which was originally meant to be about the fruit that roamed the Pacific Ocean
because of my complete lack of motivation, ended up being
about the fruit that did not roam the Pacific Ocean because of
my complete lack of motivation.

What I wanted that night was to remain still and be lost in
my thoughts. What I wanted even more was to not think at all.
Due to my complete lack of motivation, I spend a lot of time
feeling lethargic and doing nothing. For me, the realism of lethargy is as enormous a challenge in life as the realism of hunger,
and this challenge felt especially formidable that night.

At some point in the night, despite completely lacking motivation and feeling melancholy, I suddenly felt the urge to write,
as if lethargy was the source of my writing power. I put on my
green socks and theatrical jacket and sat at my desk to write the
play I'd drawn up. I failed, however, and was unable to write a

single sentence. So I gave up and started watching public pro-
gramming on television. The program was about euthanasia. It
showed the process of a patient with a terminal illness killing
himself at a private hospital in Zurich, Switzerland. The entire
process had been taped as proof to the police. It felt like a theatrical performance. The patient drank apple juice, then pentobarbital sodium, which is a type of sedative, and then more
apple juice. A couple of minutes later, he died quietly, as if falling
asleep. Because a high dose of pentobarbital can cause vomiting,
the patient had taken an anti-nausea drug thirty minutes prior.

After the program, I learned through Internet research that
pentobarbital is often used for euthanasia in the state of Oregon,
and that taking the drug is considered to be the most peaceful method of suicide. Pentobarbital is widely known by the
brand name Nembutal. The cause of Marilyn Monroe's death was
Nembutal overdose, according to the coroner's report. Monroe
supposedly swallowed forty-seven capsules. When over nine hundred cult members committed suicide in Guyana, a large amount
of pentobarbital was found in the body of the cult leader, Jim
Jones. Nembutal was circulated in the 1960s under the street
name Yellow Submarine, borrowing from the title of a Beatles
song. I imagined that some of those who took Yellow Submarine
might have thought that they were in a yellow submarine on a
path of no return.

After watching actual footage of a person committing suicide, still wearing my green socks and theatrical jacket, I was
overcome with great sadness, which I labored to make smaller.
But as my sadness shrank in size, my gloom only grew larger. I
couldn't fall asleep easily because of my annoying fit of gloom,
and in the end I placed a total of seven multi-colored sleeping
pills and sleep aids in a blue glass bowl that I had bought a few
days earlier. (It felt like a dog bowl to me. I ate many things out
of it, including yogurt and fruit, and I even drank coffee from
it.) I ate them with chopsticks, like snacks, and drank wine.
Even after sleeping pills and wine, I couldn't fall asleep. The pain
of sleeplessness might be compared to the suffering of people
who are not granted eternal rest after death, but the former is

probably nothing compared to the latter. I thought that the pain of sleeplessness can only be understood by those who suffer it.

For whatever reason, I felt that I was going to have a very strange dream in full color. If I could, I wanted to have a decent nightmare for a change. Based on nothing at all, I felt as though eating a raw onion might help me have a pleasant nightmare. Tearing from the spiciness, I ate a raw onion, and then thought about the nightmare I might have, which might or might not feature an onion. I didn't know what kind of nightmare features an onion, but regardless of the context and the onion's role in the dream, I thought that some dreams can easily turn into nightmares by the appearance of an onion alone. What is more, the appearance of an onion is probably enough to make for a decent nightmare.

One time I had a nightmare that featured sardines that I cannot exactly call decent. Teddy bears also appeared in that dream. I don't remember how the entire dream went, but in the middle, three male teddy bears appeared and bullied me into the dead end of a dark alley. They were thugs, not hulking but stout. I could tell that they were thugs before they did anything. Each of them was covered in disgusting brown fur, and wore a tight-fitting vest for no clear reason, with the top two buttons unbuttoned to look more thuggish. As if that were not enough, they chewed gum audibly, and constantly spat into the distance, showing off their masculinity, as if the act was awakening, or magnifying, their masculine nature. They were acting as though spitting far was proof that they were not ordinary bears, but I could tell upon first glance that they were ordinary, and before long I became certain of it.

The teddy bears looked old for their age, as though misbehaving fervently had aged them prematurely. In an attempt to look adorable, they twinkled their eyes, which had gone murky, or I should say they kept blinking their eyes, which were too murky to twinkle, but they were the opposite of adorable. I have always been terrified by people spitting on the ground. I was terrified out of my wits and was unable to move my legs, which seemed paralyzed as if I had polio. I imagined that if I

had matches, I would light one and ignite their fur so as to see
teddy bears on fire. I was dismayed that the thugs appeared in
the form of teddy bears, toward whom I had no personal hard
feelings. I recalled the fact that the teddy bear was named after
US President "Teddy" Roosevelt after an incident on a bear-
hunting trip, and my situation felt ironical. I imagined the bears
with cigarettes in their mouths and thought that the image suited
them, because smoking would allow them to hawk up phlegmy
balls of spit. By the look of them, however, they had quit smoking for their health.

The teddy bear thugs began taking things out of their bulging
vest pockets and throwing them at me. The things turned out
to be sardines. The sardines reeked of decay and were mangled
almost beyond recognition, as though they had been partially
digested and thrown up by a shark and then partially digested
again and thrown up by a seal. When the odor hit me, I remembered hearing about the infamous teddy bear gang that went
around throwing foul sardines at people. They seemed to be
enjoying what they were doing. It was probably natural that
they enjoyed thuggish acts, being thugs and all, and thuggish
acts probably excited them more than anything. Living up to the
infamy they'd gained from throwing foul sardines at people, the
teddy bears were now throwing foul sardines at me. The innards
of the sardines were exposed, and stuck to my body everywhere
like leeches. (A few days prior, I had dreamt that I was lying
in bed when the ceiling suddenly swelled up like the belly of
a gigantic cow and cracked, spilling cow's entrails all over me.
Entrails appearing in a dream seemed related to having an upset
stomach.)

In the nightmare that featured misbehaving teddy bears that
threw sardines at people, what pained me more than the foul
sardines they threw was the sound of them chewing gum and
their spitting. I noticed that one of the bears spat farther than
the others, and I presumed that he was the boss. He appeared
quite relaxed as he spat. I pleaded with them to do anything but
spit, but it was no use, because I was only shouting in my head,
unable to open my mouth. I could not even plead for my life. I

endured the humiliation, thinking that those who have not been humiliated by thuggish teddy bears cannot speak of humiliation. I hoped that those teddy bears would go to hell. I prayed from the bottom of my heart that they would be made to flounder forever in a viscous pool of the Devil's saliva, chewing gum until their jawbones caved in every day.

After running out of sardines to throw and having spat to their satisfaction, the teddy bears went away leisurely, continuing to chew gum. I was in Korea when I had that dream. It was after a man walking toward me spat and it nearly landed on my pants. (In Korea, there are so many people who spit on the street. This information should really be included in Korea guidebooks. Korea is second only to China in the number of spitters. Collecting all of the saliva from people spitting on the street for a year would yield enough saliva to make a recreational lake. The guidebooks should warn tourists who come to Korea to be supremely careful of spitters, who are as nasty as they appear. They should be warned that in that barbaric country of people with no consideration for others, it's almost impossible to take a quiet stroll because of the spitters and honking cars, and that Koreans have an implicit understanding that the loudest voice wins, which makes it difficult to even eat alone quietly at a restaurant.)

This piece, which I wrote while hating with all my heart people who spit on the street and plotting revenge on them, is also dedicated to them. I'd been fond of teddy bears and sardines, but since teddy bears appeared in my dream as thugs with sardines as their weapon of choice, they have become causes of dread to me. Like teddy bears and sardines, anything can be nightmare material. I continued to eat sardines, but I began to feel nervous whenever I saw teddy bears. The bright-eyed, cute teddy bears in stores or in people's arms looked poised to spit at any time.

The night I intended to have a nightmare featuring an onion, I finally fell asleep after the sleeping pills kicked in, only to wake up shortly after dreaming a dream I could not remember. I only fell asleep again after finishing the bottle of wine. When I woke up in the morning, I again could not remember my dream. I could only compare it to a red flower, wilted and lackluster and as pallid as a dying flame. My fingers were sore, as if I had pulverized a dried red peony between my fingers. The dream was not a nightmare, nor did it feature an onion. The inside of my mouth felt tender when I woke up, as if I had talked determinedly throughout my dream. Looking into the mirror, I saw that my lips had gone blue, like the baby I once saw, who continuously blew raspberries, forecasting rain, until her lips turned blue. It did not rain that day.

10. Mendocino

I MET A married couple in San Francisco through a friend who was from San Francisco but was living in Seoul, where he was researching the Korean poet Yi Sang. The husband, an Irish Caucasian man named Richard, originally studied oboe but was now repairing cellos for a living. His wife was from Japan and had also studied music. She had no relation to the Japanese royalty, but there was something quite princessly about her. It is not easy to like a woman with princess-like qualities who has no relation to royalty, but she was rather charming. On the first evening that we met, we ate at an Ethiopian restaurant in the Mission District. Using the thin spongy bread to wrap curried chicken was difficult to do elegantly, but she appeared determined to eat like a princess. On one wall of the restaurant was a painted portrait of an old man who looked like a king. Despite the solemn air he was exuding, he looked as though he was barely managing to keep from bursting out laughing.

A few days later, I visited Richard's workplace. The three-story building had no sign and had the appearance of an unlicensed business, but the company, which was owned by an old Swiss man, was well-known among musicians on the west coast. Advertising was unnecessary to attract a great number of customers whose string instruments needed fixing. In the building, there was a room that looked like a morgue for cellos, filled with cased cellos waiting to be repaired. I was drawn to that room, and when I told Richard, he told me that he liked the instruments, of course, yet he sometimes felt the urge to execute every instrument in the world.

That same weekend, the couple invited me to their house in the Dolores Park area of the Mission District. Like me, Richard was into Schoenberg, Kafka, and Beckett. We discussed Beckett in Richard's library while we listened to Schoenberg's *Pierrot Lunaire*. We then talked about foreigners who spent a phase of their lives in California, and about what it would have been like had Kafka or Beckett lived in California. It was difficult to imagine Kafka by the California shore, but we figured that Beckett would have fit right in. He excelled at sports in his youth, showing talent in rowing and rugby, and was probably a good swimmer. They would perhaps have been depressed, nihilistic, and weary wherever they were, California or anywhere else. All the things people consider blessings of California might not have been able to eliminate their gloom, despair, and weariness. They might have done anything to find reason for gloom, despair, and weariness. To them, gloom, despair, and weariness probably had nothing to do with the situation they were in, but rather were properties of existence, derived not from something in life, but from the impossibility of life itself. This is probably because gloom, despair, and weariness lurk in the farthest corners of the mind, and because the ability to command gloom, despair, and weariness is the true core of man's intellect.

On one wall of Richard's library was a photograph of Allen Ginsberg, one of the leading figures of the Beat Generation. The photograph was taken in Ginsberg's apartment by his friend. On the day the picture was taken, Ginsberg served coffee in a metal bowl and waited anxiously for the friend to finish the coffee. The friend supposedly learned later that the bowl, which looked like a dog bowl, was the only bowl in the apartment, and Ginsberg was waiting for the bowl to become available so that he could eat cereal. Looking at the photograph, we laughed and talked about the laughter sometimes presented by poverty. Meanwhile, Beckett was looking down at us from a photograph on the wall. This particular photograph happened to be my favorite portrait of Beckett, taken by John Minihan, who is well-known for the many photographs he took of Beckett. In the picture, Beckett looks as though he has been lying dead in a coffin for many days.

We also talked about Beckett's novels. Richard spoke particularly of the main character of *Molloy*, who is obsessed with bicycle bells, and has the urge to ring a bicycle bell whenever he sees one on the street. Richard said that he, too, felt the urge to ring the bells of bicycles he saw on the street, and so did I. Later we went for a stroll in Dolores Park. He asked whether I wanted to ride his bicycle, and I told him that I did. I rode his Mini Velo bicycle, pedaling slowly, feeling as though I were riding a foal. Richard told me that there are many bicycle thieves in San Francisco, and that everyone has to a have a heavy-duty lock on his bicycle. According to Richard, when a thief cannot steal a bicycle, he often steals the bicycle seat. I imagined the interior of a bicycle thief's home with a large collection of bicycle seats on display. Looking at his bicycle seat collection might calm the thief or it might trigger distinctive emotions.

As I rode, I sounded the bicycle's bell a few times for no reason. It made a very pleasant sound, similar to that of a tuning fork. When I told Richard that I was quite fond of the sound, he told me that he had another bicycle bell that made a similar sound, and that he would like to give it to me. After spending some time at the park, we went back to his house and he handed me the bell, which made a clear ringing sound. This made me very happy, partly because I thought that it was the kind of gift that truly makes people happy, but also because I thought that the bell would be useful to a zookeeper for announcing snack time and waking orphaned baby raccoons from their naps. Then the baby raccoons, awakened by the bell, would wonder, *Is it time already? It must be late since I feel hungry. Time goes by so fast.* They would yawn and then make happy faces in anticipation of their snacks. I kept the bell on my kitchen table and sounded it before starting my meals.

Richard and his wife invited me to spend the next weekend at their cabin in a forest in Mendocino, about three hours away from San Francisco. Mendocino County, like Provincetown in Massachusetts, is well-known for its artist colonies. The town of Mendocino is on top of a mesa on the Pacific Coast. It's very small, yet brimming with galleries and artist studios.

Along California's long coastline, abalone are abundant, especially along the coast of Mendocino. Each year several people die diving in rough waters for abalone. Wherever one goes, there are always risk takers, and among them there are always those who end up losing their lives. When I went to Mendocino, people were risking their lives diving for abalone. The majority of the divers were Asians, who are culturally partial to abalone. They were not fishermen, but tourists who had come from elsewhere to pick abalone. If one of them died, what would the widow say to her children, I wondered. Rather than telling them that their father had died fighting the wild sea to pick abalone, perhaps she would tell them that he had been attacked by a shark that he was trying to catch, while fighting the wild sea, which is abundant with abalone. Nowhere did I see a gravestone honoring the people who had died picking abalone. When I visit places, I like to see gravestones honoring people who have died there. When I think that people must have died in a place, but I do not see a gravestone, I often erect one for them in my mind. On the Mendocino coast, I erected a gravestone in my mind, honoring those who had died picking abalone on the Mendocino coast, as well as one for the abalone that died at the hands of men.

Mendocino County is a place where many hippies settled after the hippie era. Richard told me that an old hippie lived in a house in the woods about a hundred meters from his cabin. For months and even years at a time, the driveway to the house was overgrown with weeds, as if used only by animals. Richard suspected that it was mainly used by the deer that lived in the woods. When I expressed that I would like to have a conversation with the hippie, Richard told me that I should be wary of him, that he'd lived alone for a very long time and didn't know how to contain his excitement when he saw people. Once he started talking, he did not know when to stop. The night that I arrived, the lights in the old hippie's house remained lit past three o'clock in the morning. I thought about going over to talk to the man all night long, but decided against it in the end, because I found it truly challenging to listen to a garrulous person talk. Normally I speak few words, but on rare occasions I don't mind blabbing on about anything and everything to someone, usually when I am in a desultory mood. However, I do mind someone else blabbing on about anything and everything to me. Actually, I don't like when I blab on about anything and everything to someone else, either. I often feel as though my soul is escaping my body when

I talk to a garrulous person. People who talk too much usually don't know that talking too much is an enormous character flaw. Richard said that he tried to avoid bumping into the old hippie if he could, but when he did bump into the man, they inevitably ended up talking, and he felt delirious.

I am often bewildered by where I find certain things, such as the red door that was leaning on a tree in the middle of the old hippie's driveway. There was nothing wrong with the door, which had been taken off its frame, though it had little decorative value if any. Perhaps it was functioning as a signboard marking the beginning of his territory. The problem was, if anyone chose to knock on the door, the old hippie could not hear the sound from inside the house. He might have set up a mechanism that allowed him to hear knocking. In the end I decided that none of this mattered anyway, because it was difficult to imagine anyone visiting his house and knocking on the door. Perhaps the door's function was to challenge people to walk past the door to the house of the old hippie who could not control himself when he saw people, and usually tormented people by talking endlessly. Red seemed to be the old man's favorite color. His roof was red, and a red flag flew over his roof, which made me suspect that he was a communist or an anarchist.

That night, Richard showed me a trick for building a fire in the fireplace, which was to stack the logs to form a square rather than a triangle. We watched the flames in the fireplace as we talked. Richard told me that there were many eccentrics living in Mendocino, and that one of the enormous mansions on the shore once belonged to a drug dealer who made a fortune producing and selling mass quantities of cocaine. The drug dealer built his own wharf to import raw materials, mostly from South America. Richard was not sure whether the drug dealer was in jail or living elsewhere doing illegal business. According to Richard, an eccentric man published a rather unusual weekly newspaper in a region called Anderson Valley in Mendocino County. The man was notorious for his scathing criticisms of everything, which was probably what attracted the fairly large readership the newspaper enjoyed. Perhaps the eccentric publisher of the newspaper criticized the rivers that run through the region and the fish underwater, the fields and the blooming flowers, the seemingly inappropriate slope of the roof of his house, the chimney drawing smoke properly, the constant clear weather that made him lose his desire to do anything. Perhaps he lived for the joy of slandering things, while finding his uncontrollably acerbic reaction toward everything unbearable.

According to Richard, forest fires became frequent in California after eucalyptus trees, which were brought from Australia, multiplied rapidly. This is because eucalyptus oil is highly flammable and is prone to spontaneous combustion. There are known cases of ignited trees exploding. On warm days in Australia, vaporized eucalyptus oil is said to form a thin blue mist in the woodlands. Richard also informed me of the ticks found in American forests that live on deer blood. He said that infection from deer ticks can lead to anemia and Lyme disease, which can cause a person to sleep constantly. Perpetually deprived of sleep and willing to do anything to sleep soundly, I imagined myself searching the forest for deer ticks, which would give me Lyme disease and help me sleep for a very long time. But Richard told me that not everyone with Lyme disease sleeps constantly, that not everyone bitten by a tick gets Lyme disease, and that going into a wild forest does not guarantee that one will be bitten by a tick. Just like that, the glimmer of hope I'd found in ticks vanished.

Through the window, we could see the lit house of the old hippie. Richard told me about a hippie from Pennsylvania that he used to know. For a phase of his life, the hippie did nothing for a living and was so poor that he was always starving. He would bring home raccoons and deer that had been hit by cars on the quiet road some distance away to make stews and soups to sustain himself. Richard had long been out of touch with the hippie and had no idea what he might be up to, whether he was still living on dead raccoons and deer or had left this world.

Lying in bed alone that night, I couldn't stop thinking about the hippie who used to scavenge dead raccoons and deer and did nothing for a living. Despite the fact that he was a complete stranger to me, and that I had never lived his lifestyle, that hippie felt so close and familiar to me. This is perhaps because I understand hunger so well, having spent many days hungry, albeit for a different reason than the hippie—usually for lack of appetite or motivation.

The hippie in Richard's story matched one of several images I had of hippies, and that night, I lost myself in a rather ferocious contemplation, and made up a rather nonsensical story about the hippie (with the intention of making up a rather nonsensical story). In the hippie's way of life, I saw the lifestyle that I'd been seeking. I added details as I pleased to the story of the hippie who spent a phase of his life doing nothing for a living and eating raccoons and deer killed on the road. The following is the story I made up. (I am digressing again, but this is because I am fine with this novel heading in any direction, and because this novel has no message to convey. What I want in a novel is for new stories to emerge and break away from the original story, and eventually for all of the stories to become jumbled and confused.)

The hippie intended to do nothing, although doing nothing inevitably made him poor. Every day was the greatest day to do nothing, and, luckily for him, those days continued. He was always hungry, however, despite having done nothing. He was constantly grumpy about always being hungry, because he had done nothing strenuous. Still, he didn't wish to make the mistake of blaming someone else for his hunger, so he blamed his stomach, which always reminded him of his hunger. Twice a day he walked over to the road to scavenge for raccoons and deer killed on the road. The man had little else to do, and this was one of his only daily routines, and the most important.

From time to time, the hippie brought home raccoons and deer that had been flattened by cars that ran over them after they'd already died. The hippie was fond of food with broth, so he usually cooked stews and soups. Flattened food didn't taste different. It tasted like raccoon or deer meat, and didn't taste flat, whatever that means. The hippie shared the raccoon and deer meat with the old dog that lived with him. The dog had to accompany its master in his poverty, with no choice but to join its master in satiating its hunger with the meat of raccoons and deer killed on the road. The hippie was very lazy. Once he learned the pleasure of laziness, in which one can indulge infinitely, he tried to remain indulged. He had become so accustomed to hunger that he was unaffected by even the fiercest hunger. It was the dog that moved the hippie's heart and made him leave the house in search of something to eat. The hippie felt that he ought not to starve his dog, though he might starve himself. In human years, the dog was older than the hippie, so the hippie believed that it was his responsibility to support both of them. Once, he got fed up with eating raccoon and deer, so he fished out a dead but fresh-looking frog that was floating in a nearby pond. He took a bite of the frog, but the dog would not touch it. After some deliberation, he concluded that the dog would not eat frog meat because it did not know the taste of frog. He did everything in his power to feed the dog frog meat, which he found delicious, and teach the dog the taste of frog, but the dog did everything in its power to avoid eating it.

The hippie spent most afternoons sitting in a chair on his porch, listening for a car to make a sudden stop, but the road was too far away to hear very well. His dog usually sat still by his side, without the energy to do much else, and waited for its master to give it something to eat. Dogs are supposed to have better hearing than people, but the old dog was hard of hearing and was no help to the man. The dog, sitting at the man's side, perked its ears up from time to time, not because it heard something, but to see if it could hear something, or to see if it had misheard something. Regardless, the pair listened carefully whenever they sat on the porch, but they heard everything but a car screeching to a stop. Having nothing else to do, the hippie spent long days watching the weeds taking over his property, feeling that they were inconsiderate, even ungrateful, rather than commendable, to grow so vigorously with no help at all from him.

When the hippie sat on his porch, his gaze was always fixed beyond the overgrown weeds, on a broken fence. Once he fixed his gaze, he almost never turned his eyes away. He was often dazed looking at the broken fence, his eyes out of focus. Fed up with watching the man watch the fence and desperate for attention, the dog would bark, reminding its master that there were other things to look at. The hippie would move his gaze slowly to look at the dog, and then go right back to watching the fence, or a bird's nest on a tree branch in the forest beyond the fence, as if he had begun a new mission. There was no telling what he thought about while watching the fence or a bird's nest. Perhaps he entertained only tenuous thoughts, and marveled at his ability to do so. He might not have felt that he led a more satisfactory life than anyone else, but he might have felt that he would not exchange his life for anyone else's.

No animals migrated seasonally to that region, which meant that seasonal changes did not bring different species of roadkill. Raccoons and deer were the only animals being killed on the road in any season. Thus the hippie was unable to sense the change of seasons through the kinds of animals killed on the road. However, he had his own unique way of knowing the season. Once every other month in spring and fall, once a month in summer, and once in winter, he took a bath. In other words, he kept track of the seasons by changing the number of times he bathed each season. Even on very cold winter days, although he couldn't say that being cold was nothing compared to being hungry, he couldn't be bothered to start a fire to heat the house. Instead, he used his marvelous adaptation skills and trained his body to adapt to the cold.

When he became sick and tired of raccoon and deer meat, he took his dog to a nearby orchard and sought permission from the owner to pick up fallen fruit. The orchardist disliked hippies, idle people, and idle dogs, and hippies wandering in his orchard displeased him, but not enough for him to mind idle hippies bringing their idle dogs to pick up fallen fruit in his orchard. As far as the orchardist was concerned, the fallen fruit was wasted, so he saw no reason not to give it away to the idle poor, or rather, he was probably giving it away gladly. Perhaps he thought of hippies as nothing more than animals scavenging fruit on his orchard grounds.

Most of the fallen fruit was bruised or partially rotten, but the hippie thought that it was more delicious than wholly intact fruit.

He was picky, even though he was not in a position to be picky, because there was nothing to stop him from being picky. Thinking this way, he did not touch the fruit hanging from the branches, even though he had the chance. When he found a worm in an apple he was eating, he would eat the worm, asking himself, *When was the last time I saw a worm in an apple?* (The answer was usually a couple of days prior.) The fruit on the ground had certainly fallen from the sky. In a way, raccoons and deer killed on the road, and dead frogs floating in ponds could also be considered to have fallen from the sky. It could be said, the hippie wanted nothing to do with anything that had not fallen from the sky.

Close to the hippie's house was a river, which was abundant with fish ready and willing to be caught. He could have fished to sustain himself, but he considered himself a kind of farmer, and was careful not to covet the job of fishermen. In any case, fish had to be fished out of the water and could not be considered to have fallen from the sky. Occasionally, he brought things that fell from the sky as gifts to his poor, indolent hippie friends. There were several nearby hippies who did nothing for a living. When they got together, they ate fruit and raccoon and deer meat, and talked endlessly about what they had to eat and whatever else.

Once, after starving for several days because its master couldn't find any roadkill, the old dog, unable to take hunger anymore, took it upon himself to go out hunting. He brought back a live field mouse and shared it with his master. The dog could surely scare a field mouse, but it was more likely that an old or injured mouse had fallen into the dog's lap than that the languid dog had caught a healthy, nimble mouse. Perhaps the dog, which still had enough energy to bark, had intimidated a snake that had caught a field mouse, exposing a few unhealthy teeth, though it felt slightly scared of the snake, making the snake drop the field mouse from between its teeth and slither away grudgingly. The hippie thought the mouse was especially delicious after having eaten only raccoon and deer meat for so long, so he sent his dog out several times to get more field mice, but the dog came back empty-handed each time, leaving its master, as well as itself, to contend with hunger while longing for field mice. The hippie tried in vain to teach the dog to hunt small animals like field mice. The dog was too old to learn a new trick, let alone hunting.

The indolent hippie, who ate a frog and a field mouse on two rare occasions but mostly ate raccoon and deer meat, sometimes prayed to God for the chance to eat things other than raccoons and deer, such as pheasants and wild turkeys killed on the road, promising that he would work to earn a living if his wish were granted. He didn't promise, however, that he would work hard. He promised only to work hard enough to eke out a living. God once felt compelled to rain down manna to deliver his chosen people, but he is indifferent to some people, and he didn't hear the hippie's prayer. The hippie, whose indolence was unmatched, prayed to God that his dog would not go hungry, even if he starved. God didn't hear that prayer, either. The hippie thought that doing anything diligently not only looked bad, but was also bad for him, so he prayed only halfheartedly.

The hippie continued to live that phase of his life, eating raccoon and deer meat, which he no longer desired to eat or even to think about, resenting God's indifference, encouraging his dog to resent God's indifference. (The dog expressed its resentment toward God's indifference by barking at the sky.) The hippie had had close friends in the past. He was unsure whether he missed them or not, but he chose not to stay in touch with them for fear that they would be delighted to hear from him. He suspected that all of his friends would delight in his pitiful situation, and he didn't wish to allow his friends, whom he didn't miss, to delight in his pitiful situation. Consequently, none of them ever heard any news of the hippie.

After thinking ferociously about a ludicrous hippie who lived a phase of his life being poor, living on raccoons and deer, I finally took some sleeping pills and went to bed at the crack of dawn. Still unable to fall asleep, I listened attentively to the frogs that had been croaking all night. All of the frogs sounded the same. I could not tell them apart because I was not a frog. Studying the frogs croaking in unison or one after another, I counted a total of four frogs. Of course it's possible that there were frogs that were not making noise, intimidated by the croaking of the other frogs, or for some other reason. Counting only the croaking frogs, I guessed there were between three and five of them, but this was only a guess. There could have been dozens of frogs croaking in perfect harmony, or only two frogs making various sounds to achieve the effect of many more frogs.

I named the frogs Richard I, Richard II, Richard III, and so on, because I felt that Richard was the reason I was hearing those frogs croaking. As I listened, the croaking frogs began to sound like historical kings of England who had failed to attain eternal rest and turned into frogs every night. I listened carefully to discern the words of the restless kings of England, but I couldn't make out any of it. I imagined that they were speaking in Old English. I thought that, had I been drunk, I would have set out into the forest in search of the late kings of England who had turned into frogs. However, I had not had a drink that day. Still, as if I were drunk, I thought that frogs would be a good thing to search for when inebriated.

I was curious to know whether frogs have their mouths open when they croak. My guess was that they keep their mouths closed. I remembered seeing frogs croaking while inflating and deflating their throat sacs, but I couldn't remember whether their mouths were open. Most frogs stop croaking when a person approaches, and resume croaking when the person disappears. I thought that they probably keep their mouths closed when they croak because it must be difficult to inflate the throat sac with the mouth open, though this didn't seem like a convincing argument.

The croaking frogs were a perfect distance away, and as the sleeping pills kicked in, the sound faded in and out. When the sound faded in, it was crystal clear, as though it were an auditory hallucination. I finally fell asleep, feeling as though I were sinking slowly into a pond. It felt as though the frogs were taking me to a pond of slumber. I believed that what ultimately put me to sleep that night was the frogs. I slept soundly for the first time in nearly two decades. When I awoke in the morning, I felt so refreshed that, although I didn't get up from bed and dance, I smiled, and I felt that it was the first honest smile I'd smiled in nearly two decades.

11. A Contrived World

I TOLD RICHARD about the frogs at breakfast on the patio. Richard told me that they were Pacific tree frogs, which are indigenous to the region. He added that the population of indigenous frogs had shrunk due to a rapid increase in the population of bullfrogs, which originated from the southeastern United States. It seemed that bullfrogs were usurping environments in many parts of the world. I told Richard that in Korea, too, bullfrogs were a headache. A few years back, Richard had bought a small crossbow to shoot bullfrogs at the pond. He had placed the frogs on a rock in front of his cabin like an offering to the crows. Ever since, he had been offering bullfrogs to the crows at every opportunity.

We could hear no frogs croaking. Two deer came into the garden in Richard's front yard and began eating apples that had fallen from the apple trees. I recalled the hippie whom I had thought up the previous night, who mostly ate dead raccoons and deer, but sometimes scavenged fallen fruit in orchards. I thought that his situation might be worse than that of the deer in front of us. After eating apples to their heart's content, the deer watched us eat, and we threw them a couple of grapes. After eating the grapes for dessert, the deer disappeared into the forest.

After our meal, Richard brought out a chainsaw from the shed and began to cut down the shrubbery around his cabin. He said that he could be fined if he didn't cut down the shrubs within a certain distance from the building, because they can cause a fire to spread from the woods to the building. I watched, but did not help or think about helping, because he had told me that he didn't need my help when I asked. I liked watching others work without thinking about helping. Richard came to his cabin often, and there wasn't much that needed cutting. He had been cutting shrubs for a long time and was good at it, so he didn't appear to need my help. What is more, he seemed to be working extra hard because I was watching. I sat on a middle rung of a ladder leaning on one side of the cabin and watched as though supervising a hired worker. There didn't seem to be anything I needed to concern myself with, but I did feel the urge to tell him to please stop working so hard.

I had never used a chainsaw to cut wood, and it crossed my mind that I might like to try it, but I couldn't be bothered to get up. I thought that I might want to try it if Richard were using the chainsaw to cut down a large tree rather than prune branches. I thought that if I cut down a huge tree, I might feel the satisfaction of knocking down something huge, but this seemed too selfish an idea.

Richard suggested that I go check out a small pond nearby, saying that I might see frogs if I was lucky. He must have thought, *This guy is not very useful. If I asked him to do something, he'd probably do a shoddy job. I'd better not ask for his help, so I'll send him away. I'll send him to the pond so he can watch the frogs.* Still, I didn't budge, thinking, *What would I do at the pond?* I like frogs, and seeing them is always nice, but I could not be bothered to look at frogs at that moment. Then I thought, *I don't need a reason to go to a pond any more than a rabbit needs a reason to go to a pond.* On second consideration, I thought that every rabbit that goes to a pond must have a reason, so I could not go to the pond like a rabbit without a reason.

A moment later, however, I came down from the ladder as if I had tired of watching the shrubs being cut. The real reason was that the chainsaw was too loud. The noise was painful to bear. It was slicing my brain in half. I walked into the woods, toward the pond that Richard had mentioned. Without a reason, I went to the pond, where I was told I might find frogs. I thought I might find a rabbit that had come to the pond with a reason. I walked stealthily in hopes that if I saw a rabbit, it wouldn't run away immediately, but exercise some vigilance and finish what it was doing. Although I didn't know what I would say to a rabbit if I saw one, I was mentally prepared to meet a rabbit, and felt that mental preparedness was all the preparation I needed to meet one. I recalled a fact about rabbits: they must grind their teeth on wood or other hard materials throughout their entire lives because their front teeth never stop growing, and they might die otherwise. This is every rabbit's destiny, and I thought that I might be reminded of this if I faced a rabbit. Thinking it would be a good rib, I thought to tell a rabbit about this if I met one. However, it seemed more likely that we would stare at each other without saying anything, which I imagined to be a trite yet respectful way for a human and a rabbit to treat each other.

I went deeper into the forest, led by my thoughts about rabbits, but I couldn't find the pond that was supposedly nearby. I was lost, but I kept going anyway. I found a shallow, waterless pit covered with weeds, which might have once been a pond, though there was no evidence of that. Perhaps the pit turned into a pond temporarily after heavy rains, maybe for only a few days a year. It was difficult to call such a thing a pond, but it was equally difficult to say that it was not a pond.

Not far from there, I stood still in the dense forest for a moment, thinking that I'd come quite far, too far to go any farther. According to Richard, the forest was inhabited by owls, moles, deer, and even small bears, but they were nowhere in sight. Instead of a real bear, I thought that a person clad in a bearskin, who might be mistaken for a bear, might appear, but no such person appeared. I imagined that in the depth of the vast Mendocino forest, there was a person living the life of a bear, denying himself a civilized life. In the presence of no one, I wanted to do something that I could do in the presence of no one, something that no one would ever find out, but nothing special came to my mind.

Of all of the animals that lived in the forest, I wanted to see a bear, so I waited for the chance to face a bear. It seemed unlikely, however, that with its heightened sense of smell, a bear would come toward me unless it wanted to prey on me. Waiting for a bear seemed a foolish effort, but I wanted to consciously make a foolish effort. A bird that had been sitting on a branch suddenly began to chirp noisily as if to tell me that it was fruitless to wait for a bear where I was. I waited for a moment, but nothing happened. The bird continued to chirp, now as if to egg me on to keep on waiting in vain so that I could waste more effort. I was suspicious that the bird was mocking me, and soon I was convinced. Mock me all you want, I muttered. I waited a while longer, but still nothing happened. Waiting turned out to be fruitless in the end, so I thought about leaving that place like a person who is burned-out from waiting, but I decided not to. Something in the forest seemed to be holding me there, though I didn't know what.

Just then, I spied a bounty of red fruit in the bushes. It looked like wild strawberries. Pushing through the shrubbery, I walked over to the bushes, thinking that a bear might come to eat the wild strawberries. I wondered, *If a bear appears, will I have to yield to it despite having arrived first? There is an order to these matters. Shouldn't the bear wait its turn since I came first? Will the bear have a differing opinion and think that I have invaded its territory and try to kick me out? If it's alright with the bear, perhaps we can graze on the berries side by side.* Grazing on wild strawberries side by side with a bear was far from realistic, but it pleased me to imagine it, and I sincerely hoped that it would happen. Such an event, which I not only hoped for but dreamt of, would be unforgettable. If such an event actually happened, and I told the story to someone, he might refuse to believe me and think that I was a liar, and I would go on and tell the story to someone else.

Perhaps the bear and I would forget about each other, frantically devouring the wild strawberries, and then look at each other with red all over our hands and mouths. I hoped that neither of us would have to get red in the face or bring out our claws over wild strawberries, but there would be nothing I could do about it if it happened. I hoped that we wouldn't end up fighting over wild strawberries. I thought I wouldn't mind being forced to run away, being chased by the bear, which was determined to have all the strawberries to itself.

I remembered one time I was standing in a forest in Seoul when a magpie flew over with some red fruit in its mouth and landed on a branch above my head. I yelped, startling the magpie, which dropped the fruit and flew away. I picked up the fruit from the ground and learned that it was a cherry. I considered what I might do with the cherry that I had unintentionally taken from the magpie. I didn't eat it. I waited in vain with the cherry on my palm for the magpie or any other bird to come and snatch it away. In the end, I threw the cherry on the ground and left, thinking that the cherry, previously owned by a magpie, could be eaten by anyone that eats cherries.

When I got up close, I realized that what had looked like wild strawberries were actually some hard, red fruit. I picked one and bit into it, but it didn't taste like much. Actually, it tasted strange, so I decided I'd better not eat it. I did not eat it, but I thought that a bear might. I considered eating a few pieces to see what would happen. I imagined that my eyes would become bloodshot and I would do strange things. I sort of wanted that to happen, but I restrained myself. After being expectant and excited about eating wild strawberries, I was feeling defeated. Then I noticed a beehive hanging on a nearby tree branch. Bees were flying in and out of the small beehive. Counting objects is one of my hobbies, and I do it whenever given the opportunity. Concentrating as if solving a difficult math problem, I began to count the bees. It was not easy to concentrate persistently, and I began to count halfheartedly and hesitantly at thirty. At any rate, I counted to fifty-five. That number, however, didn't include the bees that remained inside the beehive. I felt frustrated by the inaccuracy of my bee count, and thought that counting objects might be an unhealthy hobby. I suddenly felt an incomprehensible urge to cause a scene by touching the beehive and running away from the bees as they tried to sting me. My mind was not a complete shambles like a stirred-up beehive, but rather calm. I felt strangely balanced, as though it was impossible to be carried away in any direction, but I also knew that this feeling could not be trusted. At any moment, such balance of mind can be shattered completely, and I can be carried away by any single emotion.

I recalled that I once narrowly escaped from a bee that chased me even though I had not touched its beehive. Unrelated to that experience, I decided that touching a beehive is never a good idea. Being careful not to aggravate the bees, I walked back to where I had been standing a moment before. I recalled thinking once about keeping bees for a living, deep inside a forest. I cannot remember why, but I had thought that I'd be able to live amongst bees day after day, mesmerized by their charm and fascinating dances. When I thought about it, it seemed that keeping bees for a living was the last thing that I had aspired to, however vaguely, and never since had I had an aspiration. My aspiration to become a beekeeper, which I had harbored without any seriousness, seemed to be the last aspiration in my life.

I returned to the spot where I had seen the bird perched on the branch. A second bird of the same kind flew over and perched on the same branch. Perched side by side, the two birds made quite a racket. I couldn't identify the birds, so I had no choice but to call them by their common noun, *birds*, and I thought of them as common birds. The common birds were probably communicating their needs, but I imagined that they were also talking about me, because I felt that they were watching me. Once, I was passing in front of a monkey cage at a zoo, when I sensed that the monkeys were watching me and screeching and making gestures to speak to one another about me. To my chagrin, they seemed to be speaking negatively of me, judging by the way that they were exchanging remarks rapidly with slight excitement. Perhaps monkeys, like people, know the joy of slandering someone or something. I imagined that they mainly slander one another, but from time to time they slander other things, such as the humans who cage them and observe them and point at them. Perhaps slandering is what all animals with some intellect do to pass the time.

The birds perched on the tree branch seemed to be talking about themselves, and they flew away a moment later. I watched the branch gradually become still after being shaken by the birds' departure, and waited for a different kind of bird that I would not be able to identify and would also have to call a common bird. I thought about what I should do next, but nothing suitable came to mind. The sound of Richard's chainsaw hadn't stopped. I suddenly remembered a story about a person who defeated a grizzly bear in Alaska by clouting it on the nose, and thought that if I met a bear, I would punch its nose so hard that my fist would hurt. I reasoned that if the story was true, the nose must be the bear's weak point, and this must be true for all mammals and other animals with noses. Thus I would have to punch an alligator in the nose if I ever had to fight one, though I doubted that the nose is the weak point of an alligator, as it must be for mammals. I also doubted that I would ever have to punch an alligator in the nose, or even have to fight an alligator in my lifetime. Waiting for a bear in order to punch it in the nose seemed futile and ludicrous, especially when I had no reason to believe that one might come. And it was unjust to the bear, so I tried to stop imagining a bear taking to its feet after I punched it in the nose.

The thought persisted, however, and I couldn't help but smile, picturing a scene in which a bear, extremely offended, continued to look back as it ran, unable to suppress its anger at me. Perhaps the bear, having been punched by a human, would only be able to swallow its anger after devouring wild strawberries, which always made the bear feel better, and of which the bear could never eat enough. I worried that eating wild strawberries might not be enough. I had heard somewhere that bears, being the gourmets that they are, love to eat sardines, wine, and honey. I hoped that the bear, its pride hurt from having been punched in the nose, would get lucky and find honey, which was the perfect thing to calm the bear, and devour it to sate its anger, restore its pride, and forgive me, for I had had no intention of hurting its pride.

I had been led into the forest by a thought about rabbits, had moved on to various thoughts about bears, and then imagined punching a bear in the nose in the woods where a bear might actually appear, though the possibility of it actually happening was rather slim. As if that were not enough, my thoughts wandered off to an incident involving a bear that escaped from the zoo and ran for the mountains. People shot the large bear with a tranquilizer gun to capture it alive, but the bear didn't fall. The bear pulled the darts from its flesh and fled into the forest. The bear was found in the end, and was killed by a real bullet. The thought made me a little bit sad. Having thought of all this, I felt that it had been worthwhile to wait for the bear that was not showing any sign of coming. I felt as though I had actually confronted a bear that lived in the woods, though I might have been slightly unrighteous in my imagination. I no longer felt the need to face a real bear, so I stopped waiting. Meanwhile, a bird had landed on the branch and begun chirping loudly. It was the same kind as the birds that had been perched there earlier, but I wasn't sure whether it was one of the same birds. Still, the bird seemed to be urging me to keep waiting for a bear. I told the bird that I was no longer waiting, and urging me to wait was fruitless. But the bird continued chirping, like a deranged person repeating meaningless sounds. I thought that most of the sounds that birds and other animals make might actually have no meaning at all.

The sound of the chainsaw continued. Richard seemed to work well even without anyone watching him. I continued to stand still. I felt that I needed a reason to stand still like that, but I could find no reason. Almost always, I do or do not do things with no special reason, and I'm in a state of not knowing what to do or how, and such a state gives me a certain comfort. This time, however, I felt a little flummoxed. I pictured a scene in one of my novels wherein a character becomes flummoxed in the middle of a forest. I tried to get closer to the psychology of the character, who is in a similar situation as I was, but all I could feel was the confusion that the character feels. I couldn't remember clearly how the character overcomes feeling flummoxed. I seemed to remember that he ends up becoming even more flummoxed as his thoughts wander.

I felt myself overlapping with the fictional character, whom I'd created while living a rather unreal, fanciful life. I remained in that flummoxed state a little bit longer, and thought that I often put characters in flummoxed states in my novels. All of my fictional characters experience some kind of emotional problem, cannot have real relationships with other characters, and find themselves in a flummoxed state that they share with no one. They mirror my reality. In reality, I don't form real relationships with other people, but with animals such as birds and bears, bodies of water, and clouds. I form intimate or awkward relationships with them as necessary, but even those relationships form in my mind only temporarily. I felt as though I had reached a point where no relationship I formed posed any problem, therefore I was unable to write novels in which relationships pose problems and the characters are conflicted. I felt as though I had a disability that kept me from forming relationships that pose problems in real life, but I didn't think it could be helped.

Quietly watching the speechless forest, it occurred to me that the sensations I feel most keenly whenever I'm in a forest are ominousness and covertness. Forests often feel ominous to me. I couldn't pinpoint the nature of that sensation, but I thought that it was derived from what hid in the forest and never appeared, or the very forest that hid it. I saw a fallen tree that must have been dead for a long time, though it certainly did not look ominous. I tried to think of something much more ominous than death, but nothing seemed ominous at the time. So I started thinking about covertness. Forests seem to possess a certain covertness that causes unwary travelers to become assimilated, putting them under the illusion that they are becoming a part of the forest's covert operations. Covertness seems inherent between the speechless trees and their bark, between the sky and the grass partially visible between the trees, between the sounds of the birds and the insects, and in everything else the forest is hiding. I reaffirmed that ominousness and covertness are the sensations that I feel most keenly in a forest, but was unable to define them or identify the exact cause of those sensations. Therefore, I was sure to resume thinking about the cause of those sensations the next time I found myself in a forest. Anyhow, thanks perhaps to thinking about ominousness and covertness, I seemed to have more or less freed myself from feeling flummoxed.

I let my mind wander wildly for a moment, after which I gradually became free of all thought. I remained in a daze for a while, as is natural in such a state. No thought came to mind, as though all thoughts had been washed away, and there also seemed to be nothing for me to say. I was at a loss for words, which led me to think about how much I like being in such a state, and then I returned to having no thoughts. I remained that way for a while longer before an uncomfortable thought began creeping in. Everything I was experiencing felt rather contrived. Even in that moment, I knew that I would do whatever it took to turn the experience into text, which made me suspect that I was steering the experience to make it suitable for turning into text. In fact, I thought about what form the text would take were I to write about my experience of getting lost in my thoughts in a forest in Mendocino, where nothing actually happened, and then I drew a vague outline of the story.

Somewhere along the line, rather than experiencing a moment in its purity, I began to manipulate the moment, even my consciousness and emotions, conscious of how I must process the moment in order to put my experience down in writing. This seems a gross fault, and I feel hypocritical. What I'm doing seems like an obvious ploy, but it doesn't feel all bad. It feels rather comforting. I believe that my comfort is the result of being at the center of a contrived world. For a long time, I have lived a contrived life, and being contrived has become natural to me. I have lived a contrived life because nothing in life feels real to me, and therefore I haven't been able to take life seriously, and cannot concern myself with the facts of life, but only with my thoughts on those facts. This is one of the greatest challenges in my life.

I felt as though a perfectly contrived world was waiting for me beyond that forest. I imagined a world that could be reached only through the act of contriving—a vague, awkward, confusing, unnatural, dark, hopeless yet inescapable world that was becoming ever deeper. Contriving seems to be the only way to complete the life laid in front of me. In my contrived world, where the lines between meaningfulness and meaninglessness, existence and nonexistence, and chance and necessity are blurred, everything is out of context, and I have no attachment to anything that happens or doesn't happen. It is a fictional world of strange idleness. On second thought, a perfectly contrived world was probably not waiting for me beyond that forest, because I'd already been living in that world for a very long time.

When I returned and told Richard that I hadn't seen a small pond, he said that the pond could be dried up. He said that there was a bigger pond a little bit farther away and that it shouldn't be dry. He told me to go look for it if I had time. He added that I would certainly see frogs there. He laughed as if he was joking, which made me think that I would have to go really far and get lost in the forest for the pond to magically appear. There I would find frogs floating leisurely on the surface. Richard seemed to be teasing me. In a short time, our relationship had evolved to a stage where we could tease each other within limits. This made me feel that Richard and I had become a little bit close.

That afternoon, we packed a picnic with wine and went to a mesa in Mendocino. We took up a spot in a field atop a sea cliff. This was one of the most impressive places on the California coastline. Many kinds of weeds, shrubs, and colorful wildflowers were growing in the expansive, flat field. This region, too, is often covered with fog, but it was a clear day, and I could look far across the Pacific Ocean under the blue sky. The waves were breaking calmly below us, and the breeze felt wonderful. It was a perfect day in every way. After drinking some wine, Richard and his wife went for a stroll, and I lay down in the grass. I couldn't ask for anything more. A moment later, however, I felt strangely helpless and uncomfortable, faced with this impressive, sublime, seemingly perfect scene.

Five years earlier, when I had gone on a group tour of Yosemite (on a whim), my predominant emotions had been helplessness and discomfort. I'd been sour at everyone visiting Yosemite, who had exclaimed with excessive delight at the scenery, as well as at Yosemite, at which they had exclaimed with excessive delight, but that isn't why I'd felt helpless and uncomfortable.

Yosemite's magnificent scenery overwhelms viewers and leaves them speechless. Faced with scenery that makes one speechless, all that one can do is be acutely aware that no words are appropriate. The flawless scene with its perfect composition is like a perfect circle or sphere, leaving no room for the viewer's mind to intervene or process contrived thoughts. This is the reason I felt helpless and uncomfortable. In order for the mind to intervene or process contrived thoughts, a scene with seemingly perfect composition must show a certain weakness, allow for the intervention of thoughts, or be mixed with a foreign element, none of which happened in Yosemite. I felt completely separated from all of its scenery, as if by a glass wall that blocked all sound. I lacked the mechanism to process my emotional reaction to the magnificent scenery, which gives inspiration to some. Thus, to me, the silent scenery was very dull, awfully dull.

Looking at the scenery of Yosemite, which did not conjure any special feelings in me, which, in other words, conjured only feeling enough to make me acutely aware of my helplessness and discomfort and nothing else, I became acutely aware of its lack of appeal. I thought that my helplessness and discomfort might go away if I rolled a few pebbles down a slope, but I couldn't find an appropriate spot. I had no choice but to leave feeling helpless and uncomfortable. When I took a last glance as I left, the place seemed to be nothing more than an enormous valley.

I had liked the scenery on the way to Yosemite: expansive fields covered with yellow grass interspersed with low hills, which didn't overwhelm the viewer. I liked it even more on the return trip. Most of the people on the bus were sleeping, and the rest paid little attention to the fields. Looking out the window, I saw a horse standing on a low hill rising above a wide field. That horse overlapped with an image of a horse I had in my mind, reminding me of a scene in a short story written by the English poet Ted Hughes. The scene is of a black horse standing on top of a small hill in a field, with the sky in the background. The horse I saw was not as impressive as the one in Hughes's story, because it was not standing with the sky in the background. The setting of the story is a field, a hill, and a forest. The horse in the story is a strange one. One rainy day, the horse chases a man who's visiting the place for the first time in twelve years. The man hides from time to time as he runs from the horse. The horse keeps a distance, repeatedly disappearing and reappearing, watching and chasing the man. The man, running on muddy ground, throws a rock as big as a goose egg and hits the horse. The horse chasing the man in the story, whether harboring malice, playing a game, or plain mad, was another image of a horse that was ingrained in my mind. I recalled that image and compared it to the horse on the hill in California, but the two images did not quite match. The horse I was looking at was brown, and it was grazing quietly. The weather was clear, and the sun was about to set. The red glow of the sun cast softly on the golden field. The story with the horse was the only story by Ted Hughes that I had read with interest. A story about a man being chased by a strange horse is the kind of bizarre story that I like.

I formed yet another image of a horse when I was driving on a country road in Germany. Under the gloomy sky, on a hill in the middle of an expansive field dotted with blackish spruce trees, I saw a lone horse with a peculiar reddish brown coat, standing quietly in the rain. The horse stood motionless, as if it were the core element of the landscape, completing the landscape, creating a flawless work of art. Like an image in a black-and-white photograph, the horse stood unwaveringly in a light fog that was rising from the rain, with the gray sky in the background. Looking at the impressive scene, I had the impression that the horse was consciously directing that scene.

I parked my car, walked closer, and watched the horse for quite a long time. As though it were hypnotized, the horse stood motionless with its head lowered, paying no heed to the rain dripping from its mouth, stomach, and tail. I felt a chilling sensation in my chest. Not suddenly, but gradually, I felt as though I'd been hit in the center of my chest by a rock someone had thrown at me. I don't remember whether it was in winter or spring, whether it was hard winter rain or soft spring rain that was coming down. Rain is an important element of this scene, and whether it was winter rain or spring rain changes the mood completely. Let us say that it was winter, and winter rain was coming down, so that the image will remain more impressive. I waited for the chilling sensation to gradually pass. As I left, I made sure that the horse, which seemed to be completing the winter landscape, remained motionless forever in my mind, thus bringing a perfect image of the horse into my contrived world.

On that sea cliff in Mendocino, I hoped for something to

happen to intervene in my contrived thought. Nothing happened in the end. Something needed to happen, like a herd of wild horses appearing from out of nowhere and galloping across the field. I felt completely separated from the scene, and I had almost no emotion. I saw a few gannets flying around. Like pelicans, they had a difficult time taking off because of their oversized wings, which are advantageous for long distance flights, but get in the way when flying short distances. But they were not fit to enter my contrived world, so I did not concern myself with their flying around. Whether an object or a landscape, only when something moves through memories and imaginations, takes on an unexpected form, and appears and settles in a different dimension, am I able to assimilate it.

12. An Unrevealing Revelation

THAT NIGHT, I saw the lights on at the old hippie's house until late. I walked up the driveway to his door, from which I saw the silhouette of the man moving quietly about in his living room, projected onto the curtains like a character in a shadow play. I wondered what he did as he moved quietly about at that time of night. I imagined that the interior of the old hippie's house was similar to the exterior, covered with weeds. He was strolling through the weeds inside his house, having no reason to go outside late at night to stroll through the weeds. I pictured the interior of his house, thick with ivy climbing the interior walls to cover the ceiling, entering the open closets, and climbing the dusty mirror on the wall. Strolling through the weeds inside his house, perhaps the old hippie, with a beard as untamed as the weeds, stopped when he passed the mirror, saw the blurry reflection of himself, greeted it as if meeting an acquaintance, and told stories that are told only by those who have lived in solitude for a long time and are understood by no others. It would be a long time before he resumed his stroll. Richard had reported that he could understand little of the man's endless stories.

I wondered what the old hippie ate. I suspected that he was a vegetarian and ate the weeds growing inside and around his house. There were weeds everywhere, so he probably had no worries about food. Perhaps he grazed on the weeds like a cow and spent sixteen hours a day chewing his cud. I was sure that his lights were on until late in the night because he had to stay up and chew his cud. I theorized that cows can move their mouths mechanically and chew their cud for sixteen hours a day because, luckily, they enter a sort of trance. Even for a cow, having to spend so many sober hours chewing their cud must be unbearable. Were it not for their ability to fall into a trance, chewing their cud might drive all the cows in the world to madness.

Though he yarned endlessly when he met people, I imagined

that the old hippie was mostly active at night and spent most
of his time alone, grazing on weeds and chewing his cud in a
trance, coming back to himself from time to time to entertain
bizarre thoughts and talk to himself. Red being his favorite color,
I imagined the hippie in his red underwear, spitting out words
that gave off a red sensation.

That night, the frogs offered me no help falling asleep, because
I could hear no croaking at all, as if all of the frogs had moved
away. I reasoned that the old hippie had invited the frogs to his
house that night, and the frogs, making an exception to their
principle of not accepting invitations from humans, had accepted
the invitation from the hippie, whose lifestyle resembled their
own. I imagined that they were all sitting in the hippie's living
room, playing a game that could be enjoyed by both humans and
frogs. I thought of what games they might play. For starters, they
could play a role-reversal game, though I was not sure what kind
of game it would be. Nevertheless, I imagined arrogant-looking
frogs sitting upright with their front legs propped on their waists,
and the hippie prostrating obsequiously. I didn't know what they
would do in those poses, so I figured they must be engaging in
activities only they knew about.

The lights suddenly went out at the old hippie's house. I
imagined that the frogs had decided not to return to their homes
and were sleeping next to the hippie, exhausted after partying
with the hippie until late. I could picture both the frogs and the
hippie sprawled out like slobs, snoring loudly. Some of them
could be dreaming about soldiers who had been abandoned after
a battle in a forest and did not possess weapons. I thought that
after dreaming that plotless, illogical dream, they might remember that the soldiers, who were named Richard, were wearing
camouflage reminiscent of frogs, and that they were marching
through the forest, playing cymbals and brass instruments now
and then like a military band.

The hippie and the frogs must have been out for the count.
I went back outside and smoked a cigarette in the bright, serene
moonlight. I wandered in the woods for a while before turning
back. I used to live in a house next to a hill in Seoul, and I often

wandered in the forest in the middle of the night. It is known that a notorious serial killer buried his victims on that hill. Even on dark, moonless nights, I strolled along the trail. It might seem impossible to walk in the woods without moonlight, but I could easily find my way because the earth gave off a faint glow, as if sunlight that had seeped into the earth during the day was slowly being released. I was not at all afraid of wandering in the woods where homicide victims had been buried, but there were moments when I feared myself and felt like a madman, and I was afraid of what I might do.

Under the desolate moonlight, I felt as though I could quite naturally behave very strangely. This feeling was not entirely responsible, but that night in the forest, under the moon, I collected very fragrant purple flowers with very long stems as if I were harvesting lavender, and I became convinced that I'd definitely gone mad. I brought the cut flowers into my room, put them in a vase, and placed it under a bedside table. I turned off the light, lay in the bright moonlight coming in through the window, and watched the flowers in a daze. It felt like a great night for strange ideas. I didn't want to make any effort to come up with strange ideas, so I waited for one to come to me, because I felt that I could only accept strange ideas that came to me. But no strange ideas came to me, so I kept staring at the flowers as if asking for help. Flowers are usually for looking at, but I wanted more, and felt the flowers with my fingers with the greatest care, as though searching for other uses. I felt as though I had never in my life paid so much attention to the velvety texture of flowers. I liked the coolness of the petals, which reminded me of a corpse's skin. A moment later, as if the flowers had helped me conceive an idea, it struck me, with no basis at all, that burning the flowers and rubbing the ashes on my forehead or eating them would help me fall asleep. I imagined, baselessly, that if I were to burn the flowers, the ghosts of some beings other than the flowers would appear in the guise of ghosts of flowers and take me to a place where ghosts of flowers and other beings that died in Mendocino forests congregated. I had a hunch that the ghosts of Mendocino forests had a playful side to them, and that we would be able to spend the night together doing something strange yet pleasurable. However, all of this was nonsense. I thought about the abundance of ideas with little or no basis that come to me without my trying to come up with them, and about how I cannot believe my own thoughts and words or take them seriously. In the end, I fell asleep thinking that I had not come up with more baseless ideas than usual. I awoke in the morning after an extremely vivid and strange dream about getting my fortune told by a fortune-teller.

The fortune-teller was a dwarf. She was as tall as a ten-year-old. She was wearing traditional Korean garb, with a snow-white jacket and bright red skirt. The two of us sat on the floor of a rather humble room, which was so narrow that we could not stretch our legs out comfortably. One of her feet kept on hitting my knee. A plastic bag full of foil-wrapped Hershey's Kisses was placed between us. She told me her name and described herself as a renowned fortune-teller, but I'd never heard of her. As if she needed them to become possessed by a spirit, she unwrapped and ate one Hershey's Kiss after another. She didn't offer me any. By the way she was behaving, she seemed to be telling me that I shouldn't eat them, or that it would be better to stay away from them. She seemed determined to eat them by herself and not give me any. I thought, *I see how it is. Have your fill.* I observed her mouth as pieces of chocolate entered continuously and thought that it was a little bit small for a whole Hershey's Kiss. She was cramming the chocolate into her mouth.

After being completely absorbed in eating chocolate for a long time, the fortune-teller lifted her head and scanned my face. She laughed amusedly, and told me that I was fated to die before my time due to my erratic temperament. When I told her that I already knew that, she didn't lash out, but she did make a face of disapproval. She had a very difficult time guessing my occupation. Seeing my long hair, she first asked me if I was an artist and I told her I was not. She then asked me if I was an actor and I told her I was not. She then asked me if I was a musician and I told her I was not. She then asked me if I was a sailor and I told her I was not. She then got red in the face and asked me

if I was a plasterer and I told her I was not. She then asked me
if I was a beggar and I told her I was not. She then asked me if I
was an ex-convict. I hesitated for a moment, then told her I was
not. Furious that she could not guess what I did for a living, her
face turned as red as the inside of a well-ripened watermelon.
She finally had to ask me what in the world I did for a living. I
could have lied, but I told her that I wrote novels. She slapped
her tiny lap, and as if by some kind of reflex, kicked me hard
in the knee. Suddenly speaking in the voice of a little girl, she
said that the reason she hadn't known that I wrote novels was
that I was a has-been. She then urged me to write *wuxia* fiction,
claiming that writing *wuxia* fiction would finally fix my fortune.

Her reasoning was that I had been a warrior in China's
Warring States Period, and had saved the life of a woman in a
high position. Although in this life I wouldn't be able to meet
the woman whose life I had saved in my past life, I would be
able to in the next life if I was lucky. This story seemed too obvious to me, a hackneyed story that fortune-tellers tell. I was not
convinced at all, but I nodded, and she kicked my knee again,
lightly, and shouted, "Straw!" I had no idea at first what she was
trying to say, but I took her word literally, and understood that
I should live as though floating down a river clutching at straws.
Seeming to think that I was following her, she once again kicked
me hard in the knee. Startled, I shouted involuntarily. My voice
had turned into that of a young boy, which sounded weird even
to my ears. I thought that she was a peculiar fortune-teller to
kick people as she told their fortunes.

When the fortune-teller talked, I could see her teeth, black
with chocolate, between her lips. They were black and ominous,
and I felt as though some negative force was pinning me down.
She told me that I had to keep a distance from other people and
write *wuxia* fiction. She then advised me to start considering
myself to be a donkey in heat, and I interpreted this to mean
that I should live in a mental state of utter chaos. She told me
to make a daily visit to some water's edge, and I interpreted this
to mean that I should engage in something until it becomes too
much. (This is not an exact transcript of our conversation. We

had a nonsensical conversation that can be replaced by what is written above. What is written above can be replaced by any other nonsensical conversation.) Continuing to speak nonsense to each other was not helping us gain a better understanding of each other. Nonetheless, I seemed to be gaining a better understanding of my own riddling thoughts.

As our nonsense continued, her eyes glazed over, and she looked sleepy. Her bleary eyes reminded me of a lizard's, and I felt as though I was talking with a lizard. My legs had gone to sleep, so I stretched my legs and placed them on top of hers, and she didn't mind. I felt that I had understood almost everything she'd said, and I told her that I would start living off the wall. She told me to stop being idiotic. She yawned and told me that it was time for her nap, and that chocolate, a lot of chocolate, makes her sleepy. She lay back where she was sitting. Her head and feet touched the walls at either end of the tiny room. Lying on the floor, she stared up at me with wide eyes. I asked idly what she had done for a living before she became a fortune-teller. She stared at me as if she didn't understand me. The reason became clear a moment later when she began snoring. Even as she slept, her eyes stayed open. Her eyes looked like those of an animal recalling its dark past.

I looked at the pictures and figurines that she kept in a shrine in her room. All of the various gods were depicted with glaring eyes. But the gods' attention seemed immersed elsewhere, and they didn't seem to be possessing the fortune-teller's body. If anything, my body was itching slightly as if some of the gods had entered my body and were tickling my body from the inside. In that state, feeling slightly itchy, I felt that I was supposed to become perversely stubborn and hit rock bottom. The fortune-teller had eaten all of the chocolate and left the foil wrappers in the plastic bag between us. I thought that the wrappers were the shells of our conversation, so I put one in my pocket and left the fortune-teller's house. Walking along the street in the middle of the broiling summer day, I played with the foil wrapper in my pocket, which seemed to help me understand the fortune-teller's words. I guessed that she was telling me to never escape chaos.

It was as if I'd come to Mendocino and received some divine revelation about my future, but I had already known that future for a long time—I was meant to never escape chaos.

13. Drowned Bodies

THE APARTMENT COMPLEX I stayed in was a square with a swimming pool in the center. The pool was not large, but it was landscaped with trees, and it provided a place for people to sunbathe on nice days. Swimming is one of the few sports I've ever been any good at. I even swam across the North Han River and back in my twenties. I often wonder what possessed me to make the arduous swim across that fairly wide river. At one point, in the middle of the river, I was helpless against the current and thought that I was going to drown. I felt as though I could understand the mind of a drowning person. After that near-death experience of crossing the river, I had to swim back across in a state of exhaustion, approaching nearer to death, because I was nowhere near a bridge. Thus I brought two near-death experiences upon myself in one day, although I didn't feel as though I was born again twice in that day. That event stands alongside the most ludicrous things I've ever done. I was with my then-girlfriend at the time. I cannot remember what happened between us that prompted me to swim across the river, or what she said about my swimming across and back, but I remember, or I can say I remember, waving several times to my girlfriend, who was sitting on the river bank, and her waving back. I must have struggled extra hard to wave to her, as I was already struggling to swim. As she waved to me, she might have thought that she could not date a man who behaves so recklessly. We broke up shortly after.

I seldom used the pool because the water was very cold. The pool was usually empty on weekdays, and I sat in a poolside lounge chair, reading or fantasizing about doing such things as swimming in a lake in my pajamas at night with the moon reflecting on the still surface of the water. I thought about various interesting facts, for example, that the *Epic of Manas*, a traditional epic poem of Kyrgyzstan, takes six months to memorize in its entirety; that soap is an ingredient of napalm bombs; that the English exploited the Burmese people during the colonial period as they began to build ships with Burmese mahogany, and the Burmese people suffered greatly because of mahogany; that there is a story set in the Bermuda Strait in Shakespeare's *The Tempest* (I had recently learned that fact watching television, but I'd been drunk, so it is possible that I had been channel surfing and had seen a show on Shakespeare on one channel, and another show on the Bermuda Strait on a different channel, and the details had become mixed up in my memory—I thought that I might or might not read *The Tempest* in order to check my facts); that marijuana strains are almost as numerous as cat breeds and include Shiva Shanti, Hindu Kush, Afghani #1, Ed Rosenthal Super Bud, Shiva Shanti II, Sensi Skunk, Skunk #1, Super Skunk, Shiva Skunk, Skunk Kush, Marley's Collie, Early Skunk, Ruderalis Skunk, and Early Girl, to name a few. I wondered why so many marijuana strains have the word *skunk* in their names.

Most of the time, however, I spent my time doing nothing. The poolside was a great place to do nothing, like a bed or a park. Sometimes I brainstormed ideas for pieces such as this one. I thought about how I marveled at my ability to finish a novel before I knew it, despite seemingly spending most of my days doing nothing. It sort of amazed me that despite being tired and exhausted, I continued to write stories that offered no help when I was tired and exhausted. Thinking that I wrote prolifically despite having nothing at all to say, and that I was writing another long-winded novel, I felt like a hopeless windbag.

One day, as I observed leaves floating on the water and clouds reflected in the water's surface, my thoughts naturally progressed to drowned bodies. Drowned bodies give me an especially peculiar feeling that I don't get from other dead bodies and that is difficult to describe. I have seen a drowned body from afar, being fished out of a river into a boat and carried away, and another one up close. One summer morning, I was at a popular beach in Korea. The sun was coming up and not many people were at the beach. I saw something rise to the surface near the water's edge, and a moment later it became clear that it was a drowned body.

People crowded around, and someone dragged the dead body onto the beach. The body was swollen as if it had been dead for days. An ambulance arrived momentarily and carted the corpse away to the hospital. I remember that I was with a woman at the time, but not what brought us there at that hour, or what we did that day. I cannot remember whether we talked about the drowned body that we'd seen or about other dead bodies, but I am certain that thoughts about the drowned body remained in our consciousness all throughout the day.

In addition to drowned human bodies, I have seen the drowned bodies of pigs, cows, and dogs, and those of frogs, snakes, and ants. Besides the drowned bodies that I have actually seen, there are countless other drowned bodies that I believe I have seen. I've seen them at various sites, such as rivers, lakes, ponds, and puddles. Among the drowned bodies that I believe I have seen are those of leaves, clouds in muddy water, rainbow-colored fish, shoes, clothes, mannequins, lotus-shaped lanterns, bookcases, and the pages of a book. There are drowned bodies that are brown, blue, foolish, pretty, flirtatious, playful, extraordinary, seemingly staunch, and spiteful. Everything floating or drifting in water looks to me like a drowned body. I like seeing or imagining drowned bodies. Some days I while away my time in the company of drowned bodies, thinking about nothing but drowned bodies.

What I like most about drowned bodies is that they are very quiet. There is no such thing as a drowned body that is loud. I think that a loud drowned body could be interesting, but not likable. Drowned bodies are most beautiful when they drift down calm rivers on moonlit nights. I find watching drowned bodies on such nights very pleasing, because they appear to be indulging in the joy of wandering while engrossed in thought. Among the drowned bodies that I've gleefully floated down calm rivers under the moon is the drowned body of a piece of paper with my writing on it. I have never seen the drowned body of a hippo or a rhinoceros, probably because I'm meant to see them if I ever go to Africa.

One hot afternoon, I was swimming in the pool. I stopped,

and leaned back in the water. Floating like a drowned body, I thought again about drowned bodies. They did not disappoint me, but reaffirmed the pleasure of thinking about drowned bodies. I imagined several more drowned bodies, including those of magic mushrooms and psychedelic mushroom clouds. As I thought about drowned bodies, I scooped out several drowned bodies from the water, and then sank things to make them drown again. I felt as though thoughts were floating in my head like drowned bodies, and I imagined that those thoughts were the drowned bodies of thoughts.

That night, after whiling away my time thinking about drowned bodies, I dreamt about spending the night with the drowned body of none other than Ophelia, the best-known drowned body of all time, the supreme drowned body. She emerged from the water. Water dripped from her body. Her body was dissolving gradually into water. On her face she wore a faint smile that I thought could belong only to a person who has drowned. At the end of the night, her form had completely disappeared. There seemed no better company to spend the night with than the drowned body of Ophelia. I thought that one day I might write a strange story about the drowned body of Ophelia.

14. Wasting of Time

I WAS DRINKING coffee one morning, skimming through the Marina Times, when an article caught my eye. To summarize, the article announced the refurbishing of the pet cemetery in the national cemetery in Presidio, a former military base located in northwest San Francisco, in celebration of American Memorial Day. Established in the early 1950s, the Presidio Pet Cemetery is the final resting place for animal friends of soldiers who were stationed in Presidio, including dogs, cats, birds, rabbits, hamsters, rats, mice, snakes, lizards, and fish. According to the article, the headstones in the cemetery bear inscriptions such as "A companion to the U.S. Army, to which he gave all his life," and a poem dedicated to Samantha, "a true military cat" who followed her master in the armed forces from Florida to Michigan, Germany, St. Louis, and finally California, where she died. According to an administrator, the cemetery may have been started with the burial of German Shepherd Dogs that guarded the missile sites on the property, though the exact beginnings are unknown. The cemetery was officially closed to new interments in 1963 and had fallen into disrepair by the 1970s. The article reported that the graveyard was located close to the remaining stables, but there was no evidence of any horses buried within the grounds.

I hoped to visit the cemetery, which wasn't far from my apartment, but I never ended up going, because I kept putting it off, thinking I could go there any time. On the other hand, I frequented the bunkers at a former military base close to the Golden Gate Bridge, not far from the pet cemetery. The bunkers, seldom visited by San Francisco tourists, were constructed in anticipation of the Pacific War, but were never used in actual warfare. The flat concrete structures with inclined roofs provided a peaceful space, a perfect place to lie back and watch the clouds or the Pacific Ocean. Lying there, I watched winged insects and thought about the unlaunched missiles, Samantha the cat who roamed the world, the Chinese men who died constructing the Golden Gate Bridge, the people who threw themselves from the Golden Gate Bridge, and other deceased people.

Reading the article on the pet cemetery didn't give me any motivation that I did not have before, but I tried to motivate myself a little. Knowing that staying home alone would depress me to no end, I went to the library to look at a photograph I had seen on a previous visit. I took out a thick collection of photographs by Helmut Newton and opened it to a photograph of Salvador Dalí. In the photograph, Dalí is lying in bed, wearing a comical mustache and a feminine-looking silk gown. Seemingly suffering from a severe illness, he is connected to a breathing tube. Over the gown, he is wearing a sash across his chest, with a badge that looks like one awarded by a king. Perhaps it is the Grand Cross of the Order of Isabella the Catholic, awarded to him by the Spanish dictator Franco, which Dalí spoke of proudly. Dalí looks brazen in every regard, as he does in the photograph taken after he nearly suffocated while delivering a lecture with diving equipment on his head at an art exhibition. I felt uplifted and invigorated after seeing the picture of Dalí. I was convinced that Dalí, who had lived all his life mischievously, was engrossed in mischievous thoughts in his last moments. In the collection was also a portrait of the film director Fassbinder. Until I saw the picture, I had assumed that he had a look that exuded frailty. But Fassbinder in the picture, drinking beer at a pub, looks like a country bumpkin who has just come in from milking a goat on the Mongolian steppe. I was not especially fond of his movies, but I liked that photograph. I flipped through other photographs in the collection. They were mostly nudes.

Leaving the library, I headed toward the Castro District. When I got off the tram, I saw an old, gay, nudist couple walking toward me stark naked. Nudists roaming the streets are not a common sight, even in San Francisco. One has to be lucky to see one (although some people might think it unlucky and creepy), so I considered myself lucky when I actually saw one. On a different street in San Francisco, I had recently seen more than forty nudists cycling by, being greeted with cheers from a crowd. About a month earlier, I had seen as many naked nudists as I liked at the San Francisco pride festival, a festival attended by many straight people as well as sexual minorities. The nudists, comprised mostly of old gay men, strode down the street naked, and posed lavishly in front of excited young women, as if to state that there was no reason to refrain from exposing their naked bodies. Although the pretext of the festival is celebrating sexual minorities, the real purpose seems to be throwing a rowdy party. It seemed to me the epitome of a dull festival. Regretfully, I didn't see any hot, young nudist men or women.

Having looked at many nude figures in the collection of Newton's photographs, the gay nudist couple didn't seem so out of the ordinary. Spectators glanced discreetly at the nudists' penises, and I kept spotting their discreet glances. Their discretion was natural, since staring at someone's penis would be faux pas on the street or anywhere else. I, too, glanced discreetly at the nudists' penises, but I couldn't get a clear view because they were bobbing too much from the motion of walking. Though smaller and more ambiguous than their penises, their balls were more noticeable, perhaps because they were bobbing more than their penises.

The nudists' penises triggered the peculiar feeling I get from penises and, further, they filled my mind with trifling thoughts. I thought about reflecting on my repeatedly becoming preoccupied with trifling thoughts, but I changed my mind and continued with my thoughts. The penis sometimes looks like a little imp, a hideous monster, or a wily beast, but never like an intelligent animal. Bizarre, freakish, and aberrant in some ways, the penis is unique among the organs of the human body in that it can change its shape by its own will or by the command of its master. It occurred to me that there has been no serious literary consideration of the penis, despite its having played a crucial role in the continued existence of the human race. It is probably unfair to the penis that it is treated like an unmentionable creature, and must be hidden away in a dark place most of the time, revealing its true self to the public in explicit pornography at best. Once again, I thought that there is nothing in the world that compares to the human penis, and that the only things that trigger as unique an emotion as human penises are the penises of other animals. Praying mantises trigger a peculiar feeling in me, but it doesn't compare to the feeling triggered by penises. I thought playfully that one might consider it obvious that the penis has the upper hand over the praying mantis in triggering peculiar feelings. However, drowned corpses, for which I have a special place in my heart, trigger as peculiar a feeling as penises. The contest between the two seems close.

In truth, neither drowned bodies, nor penises, nor praying mantises give me a remarkably peculiar feeling. Each of them arouses in me a particular reaction some of the time, but other times they arouse no reaction at all. They are merely things that I can talk about as if they trigger peculiar feelings in me. I could say the same for absolutely anything. Moving away from penises, I playfully thought about going through the streets naked, exposing my skinny body to make people frown, but I quickly gave up the idea, surmising that no one would frown. One thing that differentiates San Francisco from other cities, and might be considered one of San Francisco's strengths, is that residents and tourists alike are unaffected by nudists. In any case, it pleased me to think that if I wanted to, I could go around the streets naked any time in that city. The thought made me feel that San Francisco is a decent city. I am not a nudist, but if I had to have a position on nudists, it would be that all humans are born naked, and therefore should be allowed to walk around buck naked whenever and wherever they want.

There was a place that I hadn't yet visited because I had nothing but time, which made me procrastinate endlessly. I decided to go there that afternoon. I rode through downtown and the Mission District, which is like a humble Mexican city. I imagined that I had crossed the border for a moment, because I heard more Spanish than English being spoken and most of the passengers getting on and off the bus were Hispanic. Riding a little farther and up a hill, I arrived at Bernal Heights. While Castro is home to a gay community, Bernal Heights is home to a lesbian community. In the past, many lesbians lived in the Castro District, but for some reason, lesbians do not get along with gay men. They seem to have a tendency to believe that not getting along is for the best. I wondered if they think that living apart is a way to keep their relationship from growing sourer than it already is. It's possible to glean that they do not get along by the fact that they don't frequent the same restaurants and bars, perhaps because neither party enjoys when the other seems to be imitating them. I conjectured that lesbians might think that gay men are overly feminine, and gay men might think that lesbians are overly masculine, or that they might see each other as lacking finesse, and therefore find each other difficult.

The main stretch of Cortland Avenue in Bernal Heights, which stretches for four blocks or so, is lined with small shops. The atmosphere is very relaxed, arcanely feminine, and curiously, it feels like an ideal place for lesbians. Perhaps, lesbians, who do not like to face gay men on a daily basis, went on a search for an ideal place to live, and came to nest in Bernal Heights. I don't know whether they nested there for this reason, but without knowing anything about feng shui, I felt strong *yin* energy there, although that might have been the result of the lesbians having moved there.

Cortland Avenue is situated between two hills, one with a small park called Holly Park, and the other with only grass. I went to Holly Park. Below I could see houses painted in various colors, which gave me the impression of a small Mexican village. It was very quiet, and the shadows cast by the mid-afternoon sun were heavy and dark. A few people strolled by, but in the bright sunlight, the shadows seemed to have a bigger presence than the people. They seemed more alive. Lying in the grass, thinking that it was the hour that shadows become more alive than people, I closed my eyes and felt my shadow leave my body and flit about. When I felt that I had given my shadow enough time to flit about, I opened my eyes.

For a long time, I lay motionless and obsessively watched the drifting clouds. I thought about the way I spent my days, doing things only to kill time, which I had in overabundance, and the obsessiveness that required. The previous evening, I had boiled two ears of corn on the cob and spent quite a long time prying off and eating one kernel at a time. As I ate one ear of corn, I examined the other. I counted eighteen vertical rows, each with approximately forty kernels, amounting to around seven hundred and twenty kernels per ear of corn. I went on to examine the four ears of corn that I hadn't boiled, which had between fifteen and eighteen rows, with between thirty-five and forty-two kernels in each row. After finishing the first ear of corn, I began eating the other, one kernel at a time. Halfway through the second ear, my behavior suddenly seemed excessive and I quit. I felt that I was being perversely obsessive, and I became tired of being obsessive. I considered how I did or thought about things to the point that I became fed up, and I thought that my life would ultimately boil down to how I waste the remainder of my time. Counting kernels of corn didn't seem to me a good way of passing the time. It actually seemed to be slowing time, but it was the sort of thing I had to do to pass the time when time was not moving fast enough.

Later, at a souvenir shop on Cortland Avenue, I bought a carved wooden lizard. I hung it on the wall above my headboard, with its head pointing toward the ceiling. I was awakened in the middle of the night by something moving above my head. I saw that the lizard had moved down the wall and was sitting right above my head, with its head pointing toward the floor. I thought, *At that speed, it will disappear between the bed and the wall by morning.* "You can hang on to the ceiling if you like. Do whatever you want," I muttered to the lizard dreamily. Then I fell back asleep. That night, I dreamt about writing on a huge, strange computer. The keys on the keyboard were those of a piano. Attached to the computer was a typewriter lever and what looked like piano pedals. Every time I pressed a key to type, it made a noise. The sounds and the keys didn't match, and the keys kept entering wrong letters, so I was unable to write a proper sentence. As a result, strange words and sentences were created, none of which I could understand. When I woke up the next morning, I found the lizard on the floor next to the bed, and I left it there. For a while, I lay in bed and thought about the

wooden lizard on the floor. I thought that I might have bought
it because of the lizard-like eyes of the fortune-teller in the dream
I'd had in Mendocino. I thought about the unreal nature of the
world I was living in, the chaos from which I would never escape.

After contemplating how to waste another morning, I went
to Golden Gate Park. In addition to the many hobos who flock
to the park, there are many young vagrants hanging out in packs
like wild boar. Being the vagrants that they are, they sometimes
harass passersby. After being harassed by them several times, I
learned that the best way to deal with them is to ignore them.
This time, too, I ignored them as I passed. I was reminded of a
sign I had seen on a mountain trail in Seoul where wild boar had
been sighted. The sign warned that people who encounter wild
boar should neither show any aggressive behavior toward the
wild boar, such as throwing rocks, nor show signs of weakness
or submission, such as turning their backs. I had been perplexed
as to what else I could do in that situation. I'd thought about
staring straight into the eyes of a boar, but feared that it might
seriously offend the boar. But after being flustered by such a sudden encounter, it would be useless for me to drastically change
my facial expression to look bashful, or to gaze at the boar with
a mellow and calm expression.

Ultimately, what happens when one faces a wild boar on
a mountain probably depends on how the boar feels at that
moment. Depending on the boar's mood, the person might be
let off the hook without any trouble, or something might happen that both the person and the boar will remember shame-
fully for a long time. I wished that there was a sign in Golden
Gate Park that was similar to the one instructing visitors how to
behave when confronted by a wild boar on the mountain, but
that instead unambiguously delineated what to do when passing
by young vagrants. Perhaps the sign could instruct people to pay
no heed to the vagrants' jeers and carry on looking straight ahead
into the distance. The thought made me see the young vagrants
of Golden Gate Park as wild boars.

I entered the park and proceeded to Stow Lake, which is one
of my favorite places in San Francisco. The lake's water looks

as though someone has stirred in green paint, presumably due to algae. I imagined that the water had magical properties, and sipping it would turn me into some weird, mysterious-looking aquatic organism. The first time I went there, I'd been drawn inexplicably to the green water. I thought that I might have entered a phase of being especially drawn to the color green. Then I wondered if my buying green socks had been a result of seeing the green water of Stow Lake. Sitting by the lake, I thought about people who created unique gardens, such as James van Sweden, Ganna Walska, and Roberto Burle Marx. I thought about designing my own strange garden. I thought that I might like to be a landscape architect if I were born again, but I didn't want to be born again for any reason.

After a little while, I walked over to a place with a wide lawn, where I saw a homeless man taking a sweet nap in the grass, under a small, child-sized blanket. His two feet sticking out from under the blanket made me smile. The blanket was so small that his feet would have stuck out no matter what. As if he were a child, he was using a pillow that was also child-sized. On his blanket was a printed illustration of a flock of geese flying in formation. He was talking in his sleep, his hands shaking above the blanket, as if in his dream he was flying through the sky, clinging to the neck of a goose, demanding that the geese take him higher. When I passed by him, I was hit by a rank smell. As I took in the odor, it occurred to me that among all of the home-less people, beggars, vagrants, and hobos, who never, seldom, or only occasionally wash themselves, there must be some who, like dogs, choose their partners by body odor. The homeless man must have been sleeping in his underwear, because laid next to him were his clothes and tattered shoes. I thought that when he took off his shoes and fell asleep, cicada larvae or other bugs that like to burrow might crawl into his shoes to rest.

I watched the homeless man for a time and mused, all the while wondering why on earth I was thinking what I was think-ing, that even though it appears that becoming a bum requires no effort, and some people become bums as a result of doing nothing, becoming a bum is not easy for everyone, and almost no one becomes a bum after working to realize his lifelong dream of being a bum—I must assume, however, that those bums exist, for it takes all kinds, and among them, there are likely those who didn't like to do anything from a young age and became bums after deciding that there is no occupation better than being a bum for doing nothing. In fact, most bums become bums despite their effort not to become bums, so the process of becoming a total bum cannot be easy, and going through that process could be considered effort, rather arduous effort at that. In other words, most bums become bums after devoting considerable effort to it. I thought about how much I like to advance half-baked theories, and decided to delight for a moment in the fact that I had advanced a theory on the process of becoming a bum. Then, I delighted in it.

I left the homeless man, who appeared to be the happiest person in the world, at least in his sleep, and walked a little farther and found a place on the lawn to lie down. Feeling the sunbeams beating down on my forehead pleasantly, I thought that certain pleasant sensations are transmitted through the forehead. It felt as though the pleasant feeling was being transmitted from my forehead, down my spine, out my buttocks and into the ground. In a moment, it seemed to actually be slowly draining into the ground in that way. Lying still, I began to think about moles. In addition to vagrants and homeless people, there are many kinds of animals living in the park. Among them are moles, which could be considered the principal residents of the park. All over the park, there were many holes dug by moles, which looked like tiny craters. I never saw a mole in the park, however, and it seemed that moles come out only at night, when few people are around and birds of prey sit quietly on branches, holding their breath, waiting to spot a mole. Nevertheless, I could see that there are quite a lot of moles there. Somewhere else in the world there might be a park with more moles, but I could not imagine a park with more moles than Golden Gate Park, which made the park seem to belong to the moles.

Lying in the park and thinking about the moles in the tunnels below, I became curious about the fate of the moles of San

Francisco when the city was devastated by the earthquake of 1906. I was certain that no record of the San Francisco earthquake mentions the harm suffered by moles. I suspected that some moles were buried alive in crumbling tunnels. I wondered if mole tunnels are designed to withstand earthquakes. Peerless burrowers and born civil engineers, the moles might have quickly restored crumbled tunnels, demonstrating their characteristic solidarity in times of crisis. Perhaps the surviving moles buried the victims of the disaster and held respectable funerals for them. Or they might have been wise enough to predict the earthquake and evacuate. I thought that moles must have worries, as people do, and wondered what the biggest worry might be for a mole. I thought some more about moles, and thought that it was generally pleasing to think about animals that burrow, such as moles and rabbits. But the excitement of thinking about moles faded. I became fed up with my habit of useless and absurd contemplation of the most trivial things, and the uncontrollable stream of thoughts that constantly plague my mind. I became upset, as if I'd had an argument with someone. I got up and headed home, feeling as though I'd just come out of an intense quarrel with countless inconspicuous moles.

I saw a raccoon on the street near my apartment. I had never seen a stray cat in San Francisco, but I'd seen several raccoons. I walked right past the raccoon, paying it little attention. A few days prior, I had seen another raccoon in the area. I had watched it with great interest as it stopped at the crosswalk, watched the signal turn green, crossed the street, and continued down the sidewalk toward the beach. The raccoon had shown solemn determination in the way it crossed the street and walked toward the ocean. Despite their cute appearance, raccoons have the reputation of being ferocious. I had wanted to ask the raccoon why it was so serious, and why it was headed for the beach, but I'd been afraid to get in its way. Not knowing how to salute a raccoon, I had raised my hand and waved good-bye. It was near sundown, and the raccoon seemed to be on its way to the beach to see the sunset. On that day, everything, including the raccoon and the moles, seemed to have nothing to do with me. Some days, my heart becomes suddenly lukewarm, making it difficult to even think about sharing the moment with anyone.

It was hot and sunny the following afternoon. Lying in my bed, I heard a piano. I'd heard it several times before. The sound seemed to be coming from next door or upstairs. The pianist played a tune that I was familiar with, but I could not remember the composer. Then the pianist played a modern yet lyrical, impressionist-sounding piece by a composer I could not guess. The composition had characteristics similar to Debussy. It could have been the pianist's own composition. I couldn't tell whether the pianist was a man or a woman by the performance alone, but I leaned toward it being a woman, so I imagined her long, pale fingers crisscrossing the keys nimbly like butterflies. The first piece was over ten minutes long, and the second piece went on for nearly twenty minutes. She slipped in several places and repeated the measures, but I did not mind at all.

Listening to the piano, I let the notes take over my body and I sank into the music. At least I felt that I did. For some time, I hadn't been moved by music, so I had distanced myself from music. This music was suddenly resonating with me so closely that it was difficult to believe that I'd been able to distance myself from music. There was a time when I listened to music as if music alone could give me solace, but I never found anything close to solace. I find most music to be unbearably boring, and I can only tolerate certain modern compositions that make me feel quite uncomfortable. Regardless of my intentions, every time I am exposed to music that does not soothe my heart, I feel physical pain. I don't know what it is exactly, but there is something oppressive about music, like everything else in the world.

I felt very relaxed. I could hear seagulls between the notes. Outside, I could see cypress trees under the intense sun, the tip of the Golden Gate Bridge between the trees, and the weathercock on the roof of the auburn brick building across the street, the conical tower of which reminded me of a medieval European monastery. Everything seemed so far away, and I felt a languid sorrow coming over me. The expressive melody seemed to be awakening a sorrow that I had ignored for a long time. But that sorrow felt thin, like a gauzy mist, so I tried to push it away. I was gazing at a piece of decorative fabric with a picture of a house on a prairie from a European country scene. It was hung on the white wall of my room, which otherwise reminded me of a hospital room. Watching the fabric sway gently in the breeze that was coming in through the window, the languid, thin sorrow became vivid and heavy, and I suddenly realized that once I sank into that sorrow, it would not be easy to get out.

Some forms of sadness seem to require impossibly fine perception and sensitivity to experience the emotion, while other emotions, joy and depression, for example, do not seem to require the same level of perceptiveness and sensitivity. If I lack perceptiveness and sensitivity in experiencing those forms of sadness, the emotion often feels sour, and as soon as I realize this, the emotion requires great concentration. This is how I was feeling at that moment. But I had a difficult time concentrating, and I couldn't muster enough perceptiveness or sensitivity. I felt as though I could own that sadness wholly through an accurate analogy, and I came up with the expression *calcic sadness*, but this didn't seem entirely appropriate. It seemed that I was not going to be able to own that emotion, because once again I could not find a suitable analogy. More importantly, despite being aware that one should feel sadness for what it is, I tried to feel it through some thought process, which likely altered the emotion severely. In the meantime, the sadness seemed to have transformed from an uncharged emotion to an insignificant emotion, and then finally to a trivial emotion. From some point in my life, my thoughts have always intervened and ruined emotions in this way, which seems like an emotional disability.

Lying in bed, I felt as though the sorrow that I was determined to feel was laid by my side, looking as ugly as a badly crumpled piece of paper, or the slough of a snake. So I left the apartment and walked along the coast. I saw a South Korean container ship passing by San Francisco Bay. The ship was close and enormous. For a while, I walked side by side with the ship as if I were walking with a person. Walking with an enormous ship gave me quite a different feeling from walking with a person. Actually, I felt that I was walking with an enormous person, a giant perhaps. The ship was moving slowly, but a little bit faster than walking speed, and it soon got ahead of me. I thought that I would be able to move side by side with the ship if only I ran. I did not run, so little by little I fell behind, and little by little the ship and I became farther and farther apart.

The receding freighter from South Korea reminded me of everything about Korea that I was fed up with. This put my pent-up anger on the verge of boiling. In order to get through some insufferable days, I have to boil up some pent-up anger and swallow it quietly. On certain days, my anger boils several times, and it happens regardless of the time of day. Personally, evening is my favorite time to watch my anger boil—anger settles well within me in the evening. On that evening, too, I hoped to watch my anger boil, preferably with a view of the ocean. Evening was still hours away, however, so I thought that I would put off my anger boiling for a while. But before I could put it off and wait, terrible, not-so-quiet, pent-up anger began to boil in me. There was no need to try to feel an indescribable emotion, because the anger that arose in me seemed to be composed of indescribable emotions. This anger was not easy to swallow quietly, sitting alone. It was the kind of anger that needs to be released or relieved, but this was also difficult. In the end, I was forced to swallow it quietly. I tried to visualize the size and shape of the anger I was feeling, as if this would help me swallow it. I could not determine the approximate size of my anger, but the shape I recognized as something akin to a distorted rhombus. Once I reshaped my anger into something akin to a distorted rhombus, I thought that its shape was actually closer to a circle sector.

Feeling my anger and thinking about the things about Korea that I was fed up with, I fell into a bitter mood and my heart became heavy. I am often surprised by how uncommonly rare it is that I find anything interesting in Korea, aside from the work of a very few authors. But there is nothing surprising about this. Uninteresting people do not do interesting things. There is something like a social climate that dictates that one should not do interesting things. The number of people who are willing to engage in interesting activities is extremely small and wanting. Most everything in that country is driven by nothing better than common sense, and rarely does anything transcend common sense. However, few people recognize this to be a problem. If anything is changing in that country, it's that many things are getting worse. The already bad situation is only going to get worse. I think that there is an evil in all that is commonsensical and conventional, because it makes life not only trite, but shallow. Devolution into shallowness is perhaps the worst kind of devolution.

The anger that boiled in me in the afternoon did not subside even after nightfall. (A properly pent-up anger should not subside easily, and I could, therefore, call my emotion properly pent-up.) I thought about trying to feel grief on the side, but this was too daunting, so I focused on my anger. In the end, I drank myself to sleep, and dreamt that I was in a meeting with strangers in a room in a building right next to a canal, sitting in a chair with a back that was almost as tall as the ceiling. Outside, a very large cargo ship was cruising slowly through the fog, which reminded me of a large ship passing through a canal in a film directed by Michelangelo Antonioni. The inside of the room was also thick with fog. Like distant mountain peaks poking through the fog, faces were occasionally revealed and covered again. Sound echoed as though bouncing off a distant mountain. Words were spoken, but it was impossible to tell who was speaking to whom. Some of these words penetrated the fog and reached the ears of another, but these words lost something inherent to words, becoming non-words. I woke up and thought about the countless dreams I had dreamt, but I was incapable of finding any revelation or meaning in them. I like dreaming meaningless, incoherent dreams, because I consider such dreams a reflection of my meaningless, incoherent life.

The next morning, I lay around in bed after waking up. My body smelled strangely of metal. I suspected jaundice. I have a habit of suspecting jaundice whenever I feel something wrong with my body. I went in the bathroom to take a look at myself, but my face didn't appear sallow. To my disappointment, I did not seem to have jaundice. Nevertheless, my saliva tasted like rust, and my stomach felt as though it was full of sand. I thought of a few diseases and conditions that could be self-diagnosed from my symptoms, but I couldn't figure out my condition. My neck felt stiff and strange. Looking closely, I saw that a large, dark red boil had broken out ostentatiously below my chin. Looking more closely, it looked like a flower bud on a tree that was about to bloom, and I thought that the boil might bloom like a flower if I was lucky. I was unsure whether the tender protrusion was a cyst or a boil, but based on the fact that it had erupted overnight, I leaned toward it being a boil. I thought that a cyst would take more time to form, slowly and with difficulty.

It was red and swollen all around the boil, changing the topography of the entire neck area. I thought that the boil might be the fruit of the previous night's anger. The moment I discovered it, the boil began to throb. *What a lousy and useless boil*, I thought. It didn't seem to have broken out without a reason, however, because no boil would or could break out without a reason. From the point of view of the body, there must be no such a thing as a boil that breaks out without a reason. Because of the sheer size and the serious shape of it, I was hesitant to squeeze and pop it, or to leave it alone. I decided to monitor its progress for the time being. I tend to harbor a lot of unhealthy thoughts, and I think that certain abnormalities are caused by my useless or lousy thoughts. I felt the boil again, like a physician examining a patient's body, and I became certain that it was caused by my useless or lousy, absurd and preposterous ideas. I thought that the boil wasn't so unsightly that I could not look at it. Had the boil broken out on my forehead, I would have imagined that I was about to grow horns. For a moment, I contemplated the phrase *to grow horns* and its other meaning in Korean: to show anger.

Raising the blinds, I was delighted to see that the air was heavy with fog. San Francisco is known as the fog city, but I'd never seen such thick fog there. It was colossal, and moving very slowly. I brewed and drank some coffee. Possessed by a thought,

I began to perform every action in slow motion, like a person with seriously poor motor skills. The slow-moving fog might have had something to do with this, but it was mostly because the boil below my chin was throbbing. I spent an interminably long time taking a sip of coffee and swallowing it. I lit a cigarette and smoked it very slowly, thinking about how I was going to waste another day. The thought was enough to put me at a loss. Every day was far too long, and passing each day was like crossing an open sea. I greeted each day feeling dread, hopelessness, and misery, and every day I felt as though I was meeting my end.

15. My Thoughts on Vengeance

THAT AFTERNOON, I went to Haight-Ashbury. Having a boil under my chin, refraining from going out seemed the right thing to do as a human being, but I didn't think that staying home was going to make it disappear. In fact, I felt as though my anger would grow if I stayed home, and the boil would consequently increase in size. A part of me wanted to see how much the boil would grow, but it didn't feel right to hope for the boil to grow just to see it. I bought a pair of red checkered pants at a clothing store. I have opinions about all kinds of things, some strong and others not so strong. I have never liked checkered patterns, and I believe that checkered shirts in particular should be avoided, but I thought the checkered pants would go well with my theatrical jacket. I went out into the street in my new pants. I felt like a clown whose circus troupe had just been disbanded and who had to find a new way of living. I trudged along the street, imitating a clown who had worked for the circus all his life and didn't know which road to take next, let alone how he should live. This made me feel like a clown who had been a clown all his life and could never be anything else, who no longer performed in front of people, but occasionally played the clown when left alone, and smiled a clown's smile.

Here and there on the streets of the district that was once home to hippies were groups of youngsters who looked like the descendants of hippies. They seemed determined to lead lives that were as idle as possible. They looked as though they were in a conversation about how to lead an idle life. Leading an idle life can be as challenging as or more challenging than leading an active life, and their worries could therefore be substantial.

I saw a beggar slouched against a building. This triggered a thought, which set off another train of trifling thoughts. The City of San Francisco was provoking controversy by trying to adopt an anti-loitering law. The bill was mainly supported by store owners who were displeased by beggars and vagrants sitting or lying in front of their stores and obstructing business. People who were for protecting the socially disadvantaged opposed the bill. I was against the bill, but the issue was not a simple one. One could raise many tricky questions regarding the bill. For example, if lying down was not permitted, but sitting down was, would one be required to keep his buttocks off the ground? To what extent would "sitting" be permitted? Would they permit hunkering down with the buttocks off the ground but not sitting sloppily? Is slouching against a building considered sitting or lying down? If lying down was permitted conditionally, how would the City impose a time limit? Would they permit lying down momentarily, but prohibit falling asleep? If lying down was permitted, what position would be appropriate? Would propping one's head up with an arm and lying sideways be permissible? How about lying on one's back or on one's stomach?

There are perhaps many more details, beyond those mentioned above, that must be considered when introducing an anti-loitering law. In the end, a city might deem sitting or lying down in a position that might upset most good citizens to be illegal, but this would likely provoke a quarrel among interested parties. If the regulation is ambiguous, people might find loopholes and assume ambiguous positions that appear to be sitting down or lying down, depending on how one looks at it, but that are, technically, neither sitting down nor lying down. I felt slightly troubled by my train of thoughts, which had little to do with me, so I tried to clear my mind.

I walked without thinking for a long time, and ended up near Alta Plaza Park. I walked by the Victorian houses, which I had seen before. In an alleyway next to a house painted entirely in black—the roof tiles, shingles, and all—which I thought rather groundlessly might be seen in Scandinavia or in a Russian village west of the Ural Mountains, I found an abandoned green loveseat. It was slightly worn, but I thought it would be a nice addition to my apartment. My apartment had come with a red loveseat that I didn't care for. I made up my mind to put the green loveseat in the place of the red loveseat, move the red

loveseat into the corner and never sit on it again, and to shame it
every time I looked at it. Contemplating how I would move the
green loveseat, I walked aimlessly toward the main road. When
I looked back, I saw a girl sitting on the loveseat.

I walked back to the loveseat and told the girl that I was
planning to take it away, but she insisted that she had found
it first, which made it hers. It was no use telling her that I had
found it first. The girl might have been seven. She was blond
and very pretty. The dense freckles on her cheeks added to her
charm. There was nothing common about her dress to clash with
her pretty face. Her blouse, skirt, and shoes were all very pretty.
Nevertheless, she had quite a personality, stubborn and brazen.
Regretfully, we ended up squabbling a little over the abandoned
loveseat. She became angry, but I couldn't understand her or
what made her angry. I thought to myself, *What an obnoxious
girl you are!*

I could tell that the girl was feeling flummoxed as she was
losing her temper, which I considered natural. In most cases, a
person loses his temper because he is angry, but in some situations a person loses his temper because he does not know what to
do with himself. In those moments, loss of temper reveals a flummoxed state. I held back from showing the girl how ferocious I
can be. Squabbling made me feel like some twisted child. Being
the twisted child that she was, the girl did not seem to have any
desire to right herself. I thought that appearing too serious in
front of a girl with quite a personality but with an innocent face
would not be right, so I tried my best to appear only a little bit
serious, and I felt ludicrous.

The girl's face was so pretty that it seemed to glow. Her
attractive blue eyes sucked me in, and I felt myself crumbling
under her charm. I believe that I must become weak-kneed in
the presence of a pretty or beautiful thing, whether it's a flower,
an object, a bird, or a human, and it has become a habit that
I become hopelessly weak, or act so, in front of a pretty thing.
At those times, I cannot steel my heart enough to keep myself
from becoming weak-kneed. If she'd been my age, I might have
fallen head over heels in love with her, letting her run wild and

tolerating her obnoxious personality. She was looking straight up into my eyes. Her blue eyes seemed to be commanding me to yield to her, or rather to give up. I thought that if I ended up yielding to her or giving up, it would be because of her magnetic blue eyes. She was cute despite being angry. I thought that she looked like an angry, fierce little mermaid.

I couldn't tell by her puerile face whether she was being serious or teasing me. Perhaps she'd seen my clownish checkered pants and decided to tease me. She certainly didn't appear to be from a poor enough family that her parents would have told her to keep an eye out for a nice-looking piece of furniture. I couldn't figure out why she was obsessing over the loveseat. Maybe something about the green color of the loveseat drew her in. I held myself back from acting menacing or tough. *Peculiar things happen in old age*, I thought. But this seemed false. First of all, the experience was not particularly peculiar, and I was not that old. It is a habit of mine to attribute peculiar things to old age. I think, *I had better live a long life, if only to have peculiar experiences.* But I am sure that no matter how long I live, life will never become more peculiar, because no experience is that peculiar.

None of my thoughts seemed useful in that situation, and I had to give up in the end. I didn't give up easily, however. I acted somewhat petty, thinking that the situation called for acting that way, and acknowledging how petty I can be if I allow myself. First, I told myself that I could take the abandoned loveseat or leave it. Thinking so was unsatisfactory, so I steered myself toward thinking that I could hardly say that I would prefer to have it. Still, I was not satisfied. Assuaging myself as much as possible, I convinced myself that I would rather not have the loveseat. Moreover, it was a matter of time before someone, possibly the girl's parent, was going to come and press me, a stranger, about squabbling with a little girl. The odds were certainly against me in that case. I didn't wish to fight with a seven-year-old girl over an old, abandoned loveseat. I never like to fight with anyone over anything. What ultimately led me to give up the loveseat was the sudden thought that the girl looked like a cute rare fox, and that fighting with a fox is ridiculous. It also helped that I couldn't see myself fighting with anyone while wearing clownish checkered pants and flaunting a boil under my chin, which had grown larger in the meantime. With that appearance, I didn't seem to stand a chance against anyone, let alone this blond girl, who was cute like a fox. In the end, I was going to have to admit defeat. I felt as though the little girl was staring at my boil, reading my thoughts. I thought that my boil was made uneasy by her piercing stare and was about to pop open. With a boil like that, I decided that I could not keep a straight face, let alone fight a little girl. I admitted my defeat. From some point in time, I have lost all fights, no matter who the opponent has been. Actually, I choose the losing side willingly, so I'm unable to beat anyone.

"Have a good life with your loveseat!" I said to the girl on the loveseat, but she didn't seem to understand me. Walking away, I wished divine retribution on her, but I had to admit that divine retribution was excessive. At any rate, I maintained that she deserved some kind of punishment, albeit nothing as extreme as divine retribution. When I looked back, the girl's long blond hair stood out more than anything else. I decided to avenge myself one day on another blond person. My reasoning was that although vengeance is one's response to harm inflicted on him by another person, getting perfectly even with that person is difficult. It seemed to me that people commonly settle for a strange redirection of vengeance, wherein one responds to harm inflicted on him by another by inflicting the same or a greater or lesser degree of harm on a third party, rather than getting vengeance on the person who caused him harm in the first place. Quite possibly, the girl was punishing me to avenge a hurtful event that involved someone else. Oddly enough, that was not the first time I contemplated revenge on a blond person.

Five years prior, I'd been living in Iowa City, participating in an international writing workshop at the University of Iowa. On Halloween, I met a graduate student from New Zealand, a blond woman dressed as a witch. I developed a crush on her, and when my plan to take her away from her boyfriend fell through, I contemplated revenge.

The woman looked like the girl I was squabbling with over

the loveseat, only twenty years older. She started dating a guy around her age, whom I thought she outclassed. Their relationship appeared to heat up quickly. Although I did not attempt to break them up, I wished wholeheartedly that they would break up. I was unsure whether she knew how I felt about her, because I behaved rather ambivalently toward her. She was probably quite confused about whether I had feelings for her. In truth, I only thought about acting ambivalently toward her, and hid my true feelings away completely. Later, when we met every three days for a joint project, I felt as though I was deceiving her in a way. I felt almost cunning to have hidden away my feelings so completely. Naturally, she could have no notable reaction to me. In the end, I was hurt by her noninterest despite having shown her nothing. I contemplated revenge on the blond woman, but I've done nothing to this day. I don't think that I will ever actually take revenge on the woman, because the kind of vengeance I enjoy and believe myself to be capable of is acted upon not in reality, but in my thoughts.

It dawned on me that vengeance is an extraordinary example of man's thought and behavior. Vengeance, directed by a resolve to seek justice through retaliation, seems to be a complicated and sensitive issue, concerning damage and compensation, hurt and reprisal, and the extreme dignity and vulgarity that are revealed in the process of revenge. Vengeance requires both great passion and equanimity, but maintaining one's cool in an impassioned state is tricky. It tickled me to think about how people resolve to seek vengeance, then deprive themselves of sleep, starve themselves, forget to wash, and vehemently curse others in their minds. I felt that sitting down was necessary to think about vengeance properly. I went to a cafe, ordered a cup of coffee and a sandwich, and settled at a table outside to continue thinking.

In a novel titled *Vaseline Buddha*, I advanced a theory on vengeance that is slightly off the wall in my opinion, but so far no one has expressed agreement or refuted it. The theory is about the kea, a species of parrot found in the high country of New Zealand, and sheep. The kea is known for its vicious attacks on sheep. It lands on the back of a grazing sheep and sinks its beak and claws into the sheep's body to rip out and devour its kidneys, leaving the sheep to die a slow, miserable death. Sheep seek revenge on man, who has slaughtered sheep for ages, by burping quietly and gravely, releasing methane into the air. The kea takes revenge on the sheep that moved in with the immigrants and invaded its territory. The sheep take revenge on man, and man, in turn, takes revenge on everything for no good reason. There is something missing from this theory. The following might supplement this theory: humans are the only animal that can seek revenge on other species without having been harmed by them. Humans have a special capacity for revenge. They preemptively seek vengeance even on aliens, which may or may not exist, albeit in their imaginations. Perhaps this trait is what separates humans from other animals.

My sandwich came, and I saw that the contents were swimming in mayonnaise. I had been careless and forgotten to ask about mayonnaise when I ordered. I more than dislike the taste of mayonnaise. I have developed a rather particular animosity toward mayonnaise, an emotion that I cultivate attentively. Every time I find mayonnaise in food, I try to find fault with it. I look for ways to degrade mayonnaise further, comparing it to such things as the mucus of a sea lion that has caught a terrible flu, or inadequately fermented camel milk. Consequently, I cannot bring myself to put mayonnaise in my mouth. I believe that if I ever get over my aversion to mayonnaise, I will be a different person.

Laboring to scrape off the white, sticky, greasy, rich and stinky mayonnaise, I realized that mayonnaise reminds me of a freckled blond girl named Mayo, specifically her nose, red from the cold. I concocted a new plan to seek revenge on mayonnaise as I began eating my sandwich. Seeking revenge on mayonnaise didn't seem so simple. I saw no way to take revenge on all the foul, rich, stinking mayonnaise in the world. It seemed that I had no choice but to seek revenge on something else and pretend that I was getting revenge on mayonnaise. Nevertheless, I continued to think about seeking revenge on mayonnaise, and revenge in general. It dawned on me that there was one form of vengeance that I'd been acting on incessantly: revenge on fiction. I had been seeking revenge on fiction by writing fiction.

By writing fiction, I seemed to be taking revenge on fiction as well as something other than fiction, though I couldn't quite put a finger on what. There was nothing I could do about the lingering mayonnaise taste in the sandwich. I tried to neutralize the taste by spreading mustard generously, but I could still taste the mayonnaise faintly. Fixating on the taste of the mayonnaise in the sandwich, it occurred to me that I was writing fiction to seek revenge on nothingness, meaninglessness, and the baselessness of existence. I had been doing this for a long time, but I hadn't thought about it in that way or put it in those terms. The phrase *revenge on nothingness, meaninglessness, and the baselessness of existence* did not sound bad, so I chewed on taking gruesome revenge on those things. I don't like anything to be too gruesome, however, so I toned it down to a lukewarm vengeance. But lukewarm vengeance seemed inadequate for those things, so I switched back to gruesome vengeance. I finished my sandwich, thinking that dreaming of getting revenge on mayonnaise and blond women was futile and that the only revenge I could get was on fiction, nothingness, meaninglessness, and the baselessness of existence, chewing on gruesome revenge, telling myself that in order to get that revenge, I had no choice but to live an ever weirder life with ever weirder ideas.

I left the cafe as though I had come to a conclusion. I was walking down the street when something fell on my head. I wiped it with my finger and found that it was bird shit. I could not believe it, and I thought briefly about what an unbelievable bird shit it was. But the bird that had shat on my head was flying away as if to prove that it was not a lie. The bird perched on a tree branch nearby, and crowed as if announcing itself as the culprit. I felt as though someone was already seeking revenge on me, as I renewed my determination to seek revenge on nothingness, meaninglessness, and the baselessness of existence. With that incident, I felt as though my theory on a strange redirection of vengeance had been proven. A bird did not actually shit on my head, but I imagined it to support my theory on vengeance.

16. Wild Hawaiian Rooster

I NEVER HAD any intention of going to Hawaii. After the author in residence program at UC Berkeley, I was given the opportunity to go on a trip, and theoretically I could have gone anywhere I wished. I thought long and hard about where on the entire continent I might travel, from Alaska to Punta Arenas on the southern tip of South America, but nothing piqued my interest. I did, ever so briefly, entertain the thought of going to Costa Rica to hear the peculiar cry of a certain parrot in a tropical jungle. That thought could have been triggered by having once dreamt about searching all over the Costa Rican jungle for a particular orchid and hearing parrots letting out cries that sounded like those of monkeys. It could just as well have been triggered by having met a parrot with vividly colored plumes that appeared to hail from Costa Rica, sitting on a bench with its owner in a small park on Haight Street.

I stroked the parrot's head with the permission of its owner, but it did not talk to me in response. Thinking that stroking its head hadn't sufficed, I stroked its neck lovingly, but the parrot still did not talk. *This parrot doesn't know how to talk. Does it have an unmentionable reason for not talking? Is it retarded?* The parrot did not suddenly speak in an indecipherable language as though it had read my mind. The parrot's owner, who was perhaps of German Jewish descent, told me that the bird's name was Kaspar, and that it knew a few words in German, English, and Hebrew. I even touched its beak with my fingertips, but the parrot still did not talk, or even cry. There was still some time until sunset. I felt as if the sun had to go down in order for the bird to say something. The parrot looked a little bit frightened even though no one was trying to scare it. I wondered if it always looked so frightened. For some reason, it cocked its head mechanically from left to right from time to time, and then suddenly stopped to stare blankly at the huge standing statue in the park. The statue didn't blend well with the rest of the park. Like so many statues in the world, it made one wonder why such a thing was there. It was an iron statue of a very large woman with long hair. The statue probably didn't know herself how she'd ended up there, but she seemed to be standing there as if it were her fate, accepting her fate. There were so many unknowable things about the statue, and about the parrot. No matter how much the parrot's owner urged the bird to talk, it didn't say a word. It seemed to have shut its mouth tight, unwilling to talk to me for some reason. I was disappointed, but the parrot's owner seemed even more disappointed, because his bird, which could speak three languages, would not talk. It felt as though dusk would never come as long as the bird said nothing. I wished for the parrot to forget everything else if need be, and to say something in Hebrew. It did not. I began to think that the bird would not say anything even after the sun set and night fell. I imagined that right at midnight, it might say *Guten Tag!* I did not think that the bird had any concept of time.

A few days later, I went back to the park. I was disappointed not to see the parrot again, though the bird was not my reason for going there. I felt as though my disappointment would be dispelled if I went to a Costa Rican rainforest and heard the peculiar call of a certain parrot. I thought that if I ever went to Costa Rica, I might go to a hair salon and dye my hair to look like a Costa Rican parrot that boasts exotic, colorful plumes. I thought that the sight of my hair might puzzle an exotic Costa Rican parrot. But traipsing through a Costa Rican jungle teeming with insects seemed like too much work just to puzzle a parrot, so I gave up the idea of traveling there.

Hawaii was the last place that I considered as a travel destination. My decision to go to Hawaii might have been influenced by a story, either written or told by Brautigan, which I had read somewhere. It was about the author's experience in Hawaii. Brautigan visited the island for some business (I think it was a lecture), and after finishing all of his responsibilities, he found himself with no more obligations or desires on that

terribly boring island. He suddenly felt an urge to find a live
chicken and get his photograph taken with the chicken in his
arms. After much hassle, he actually found a chicken, and actually got his photograph taken with the chicken in his arms.
After that, he was able to leave Hawaii, feeling that he had done
all he'd come to do. By his actions, perhaps he'd taken revenge
on Hawaii, which was a terribly boring place to him. I do not
remember whether he specified if it was a rooster or a hen, but
I have a hunch that it was a hen. It is only a hunch, and I could
be wrong since it is only a hunch. This is a rather unfounded
speculation, based on my impression that Brautigan was quite
fond of women. This impression is also rather unfounded. It is
based on the fact that he used photographs of himself taken with
women he had been with on the covers of several of his books.
If I am remembering correctly, Brautigan committed suicide
shortly after returning from Hawaii, unable to overcome his
alcoholism, which was brought on by depression.

Before leaving for Hawaii, I reread *The Hawkline Monster:
A Gothic Western* by Richard Brautigan. Hawaii appears at the
beginning of this strange story, which is about killing a monster
that lives in the ice caves below Miss Hawkline's house. Hawaii
is mentioned only briefly, in a scene where two hit men from
San Francisco find themselves unable to finish their job when
they see their target teaching his child to ride a horse in a field
planted with pineapples, and decide to leave eerie Hawaii. Here,
Brautigan reveals his scorn for Hawaii. This story, while not
being a very complete work of literature, demonstrates that a
story can be good if it is sufficiently strange, regardless of its com-
pleteness. On the cover of the book, which includes two other
stories, is a photograph of Brautigan leaning on a mailbox that
is standing among tall grasses, presumably in front of a country
house. He looks like an ugly Persian cat with a fierce expression
of irritation. His arm is resting atop the mailbox and the fingers
of his hand are curled up almost unnaturally, like the claws of
a cat about to pounce on a mouse. Scowling, Brautigan looks
foul, but in a kind of cute way. He might have been consciously
trying to mimic a Persian cat.

I cannot say that I went to Hawaii because of the story about Brautigan getting his photograph taken with a chicken in Hawaii, or because of the strange story he wrote with a small part set in Hawaii, but I might not have gone to Hawaii had I not read those stories. Perhaps my decision to go to Hawaii was influenced by my going to a historic hotel in downtown San Francisco for an appointment, while still undecided about my travel destination, and hearing that both former U.S. President Warren Harding and the last king of Hawaii died sudden deaths at the hotel. The hotel had been restored after it burned down on April 18, 1906, in a fire caused by the Great Earthquake. Enrico Caruso, who was staying at the hotel during the earthquake, swore that he would never return to the city. I do not know whether he kept his word.

Drinking coffee at the hotel, I thought about the last king of Hawaii, who had died there. I felt a sudden desire to go to Hawaii, and I made up my mind. Vaguely hoping to see a statue of the last king of Hawaii, I chose Oahu over the Big Island and Maui. Wanting to see a statue of the last king of Hawaii felt like a somewhat selfish motive for going to Hawaii, but I decided that that degree of selfishness was harmless, and would be easy to satisfy. In fact, there is nothing selfish about intending to see a statue of the last king of Hawaii in Hawaii, but I felt like I had to at least have a selfish motive for going to Hawaii, and that my motive was reason enough to go to Hawaii.

As I expected, Hawaii was a typical vacation spot, and a very boring place. The unique boredom that I felt in Hawaii was so deep that I could almost sink into it. I went to Hawaii even though I was not unaware that a person who enjoys Brautigan's chicken story would not find Hawaii to be fun. It was painfully clear to me how bored Brautigan must have been there. Hawaii is a sad tropical island that embodies the tragedy of this era, with conventional things ultimately winning out over unconventional things.

From the day I arrived, I regretted going to Hawaii. In my week's stay in Hawaii, the only thing I did with any purpose was visiting almost every hat shop downtown and trying on hats. I tried on more than one hundred hats, but I did not buy any, because I could not find one that would suit a Javanese monkey who became the first monkey to ever reach the North Pole and became deranged. The hat I was looking for had to look nice on my head as well as on a hat rack—nice enough to keep it hung all the time. But all of the hats I tried on made me look uncomfortable, zany, and pedestrian. I wanted a hat that made me look zany yet comfortable. I didn't mind looking somewhat pedestrian. I thought that while many hats in the world can make a person look pedestrian, they are pedestrian-looking things to begin with. I had failed to find the hat to match my theatrical jacket in San Francisco, and I failed again in Hawaii. Still, I felt as though I met all the hats I was to meet in my lifetime, and this gave me some sense of fulfillment. Moving from one hat shop to the next, I got a good tour of downtown Honolulu, but nothing caught my interest.

I was indifferent to everything. I felt no difference at all between doing and not doing. I felt that everything I did, I could just as well not do. I have always thought that when there is no difference between doing and not doing, not doing is certainly the better choice. I felt as though my existence in this all-too-dim world was all-too-thin. I felt I had no presence. I wanted to do nothing. I was devoted to doing nothing. No, I didn't want to devote myself to anything. My every volition felt cruel and harsh, and cruelty and harshness seemed to be the very nature of volition.

At a loss as to what to do about anything, I spent most of my time in my hotel room on Waikiki Beach in a delirious state from lack of sleep. For long stretches, I stared out the window, emotionlessly, coldly, or heartlessly, at the towering wall of mountains that had been formed by volcanic eruptions long ago. I thought that what I truly wanted was to stay right where I was and do nothing. I thought about the name *Honolulu* and how it sounds like a word that describes the narcotic root of a certain tropical tree. I got drunk and thought about how the word *alcoholism*, which refers to a chronic disorder marked by excessive drinking, could be interpreted, when translated into Korean, to mean a distinctive sort of doctrine or principle. Recalling the countless nights I had spent drinking, alcoholism seemed to be a doctrine that prescribes acting purposelessly. I sensed my thoughts, which felt like the product of the organs other than my brain, slipping through my fingers as I stared at my hands.

I also thought about the parrot in the Costa Rican jungle that I had lost the chance to see because I'd come to Hawaii, but I didn't regret having missed it, because I recalled a story about another parrot, which was a member of a Columbian mafia organization. It was trained to stand guard and signal other members to run when the police approached. I do not know what became of that bird. Perhaps it was arrested and lived a life of confinement. Or it might have reinvented itself as a beloved pawn of the police, living a somewhat checkered life for a parrot. Had I gone to the Costa Rican jungle instead of Hawaii, I might have written a story about a parrot that I saw there, but I did not regret having missed the chance to write that story.

I recalled several events that I wanted to forget about. Those were events I'd wanted to forget forever but forever lingered and came back to me. They were nothing significant, and not forgetting them did not really bother me. I recalled feeling bad one night in Seoul, when I ignored an acquaintance of mine who was inebriated and staggering down the street. Plastered, he was barely keeping his balance and narrowly managing not to fall down. His narrowly managing not to fall seemed like some kind of a trick. I remembered watching him stagger away, thinking that when people reach a certain level of drunkenness, they start walking in a zigzag, which seemed like some profound and mysterious truth. One year prior, when I had seen him last, he'd been barely alive, having just had a cancerous organ removed as a result of extended, excessive drinking. Usually, when I see a person who is almost certainly dying, I feel as though I am going to die sooner than that person. When I see a person dying, I feel as though I am dying. And when I see a dying person, I do not feel apart from that person. But at that time, he felt like a total stranger. I recalled that he had been illogical and ineloquent when sober, but illogical yet eloquent when drunk. He seemed to be doing fine despite having lost an organ. He seemed to be trying to prove that he was doing fine despite having lost an organ. I saw him narrowly managing not to fall, but I did not walk over to help. Instead, I kept repeating a spell in my head: *Fall over. Fall over.* This had troubled me for years, but recalling the memory this time, it did not trouble me much.

I also thought of a time when I saw a person I knew well from Korea dining with a group at a restaurant in a European city and I walked away without acknowledging him. Had I walked into the restaurant, we would have likely greeted each other and chatted happily, but I didn't feel like greeting him and chatting happily. Somehow, recalling this incident did not trouble me at all. I felt the same when I remembered having been troubled after the two summer months that I stayed in Iowa City three years prior, when I was so bored that I desperately hoped for a tornado, which actually came and caused damage the day after I left the city. The more I thought about things that troubled me, the less they troubled me. Nothing troubled me in the end, and the fact that nothing troubled me did not trouble me either.

Three days before leaving Hawaii, I went on a sightseeing tour of Oahu, even though I was not really in the mood, because I felt that I was doing Hawaii wrong by doing so little in Hawaii. The group of about forty American tourists, mostly from Texas and Alabama, was very loud on the bus, and I immediately regretted having opted for a group tour. The crafty-looking Hawaiian guide and driver was overly into his job, and for the nearly eight hours of the tour, he talked constantly without breaking for even a minute, except during lunch time. He treated the group like children, and this seemed to make everyone like him. He made lewd jokes in the presence of children, and this made the adults excited like children. It also made the children excited like children. I felt alone and alienated.

I sat next to a man that one might call a redneck. He was in his fifties, and had a short, thick neck. He and I did not exchange a word. With the concentration of a person reading an abstruse philosophy book, the man was absorbed in a sports magazine, on the cover of which was a photograph of a glamorous woman in a swimsuit, dripping water as she walked out of the ocean. He closed his eyes quietly as if thinking about a half-nude woman, then he began to snore. He might have been dreaming about the half-nude woman. I felt like twisting the man's nose, but I refrained, thinking that I might get myself in trouble. I was afraid that I would end up with a nosebleed or a broken nose. The snoring man had a rather healthy-looking complexion, almost to the point of looking too healthy. I thought that looking too healthy makes one look strangely unsightly. I was the only grumpy one in the group. I saw a valley that looked like dinosaurs might live there, where a well-known movie featuring dinosaurs was actually filmed, but I felt no inspiration at all. The valley also looked grumpy. If dinosaurs lived there, they, too, would probably have been grumpy.

Later we went to a fairly high, elevated observation platform in a thick forest. The view from the top was not bad, but I still felt little inspiration. I realized again how unmoved I can be when viewing impressive scenery. Instead, my energy was being drained by too many excited people with their mouths agape with awe, all preoccupied with capturing their joy in photographs. Watching the awestruck people unable to close their mouths, I wondered why mouths must open when people are in awe, which seemed like a riddle that I couldn't figure out. It seemed strange that mouths open so easily when people are awestruck or surprised, and that they don't close easily, but I could understand why people react by covering their mouths with their hands. A mouth that does not close easily must be covered by something, be it a hand or anything else. I was puzzled, too, by the gestures that people make when feeling awkward or embarrassed. I wondered how it came to be that they scratch their faces or heads, for example. Thinking this, I tried scratching my head, but I still felt puzzled.

I stepped into the forest where it wasn't so crowded, and I saw a wild rooster. It was hard to believe, and it gave me the greatest pleasure. The rooster was perched on a branch right near me, scanning its surroundings, cocking its head left and right in a motion characteristic of birds. Three or four other tourists were watching the rooster with amazement. I was not sure whether it was fully mature, but it was small for a mature rooster. Perhaps roosters in the wild don't grow as large as those raised on farms. The rooster was not afraid of people. Rather, it looked at us somewhat condescendingly. It looked especially condescending because it was in a high place. I wasn't at all put off. The rooster's seemingly condescending attitude was very impressive. It looked as though it was boasting its sovereign power over the land it inhabited.

The rooster did not crow. Instead, it made a noise that sounded like a person clearing his throat, as though displeased by the people who were not paying enough respect to the king of the land. When the people failed to pay due respect, and instead pointed and laughed at it, the rooster gave up putting on airs and began flying from branch to branch, as if trying to prove that it was a bird. Looking at the rooster, which seemed a little too flippant for a king, I thought, *Enough of that. Now let's hear you crow.* Whenever I see a bird, I want to hear its cry. But the rooster would not crow.

It seemed unlikely that the rooster lived alone in that dense forest. I suspected that there were other chickens around, but they did not show themselves. Perhaps the hens were angry at the rooster for losing its dignity as a chicken and preferring to mingle with people over them, and the other roosters were scheming to dislodge that rooster, with whom they were thoroughly displeased. Alternately, the rooster might have left the forest it hailed from and moved to the one it was living in, seeking some sort of political asylum after a dispute among the roosters. Looking at the rooster while thinking that it could be in political exile did not make the rooster look any different, nor did it make the rooster appear critical of a regime. Nevertheless, that chicken in the dense, primeval forest evoked a unique feeling in me.

In fact, chickens in general evoke a unique feeling in me. This can possibly be traced back to my childhood memory of learning about hypnosis and making concentrated efforts to hypnotize chickens in my front yard. The thought of putting a living thing in a hypnotic trance fascinated me. I would approach a chicken that was sitting relatively still and concentrate hard on hypnotizing it, looking directly into its eyes, swinging something tied to a string, or repeating certain syllables. Each time, I felt as though I was the one being hypnotized, not the chicken. A few of the chickens fell asleep, but I was unsure whether they fell asleep because of the hypnosis or because they were sleepy. One time, I fell asleep trying to hypnotize a chicken, and I was woken up by a rooster's crow. In my childhood, I always liked to watch chickens as if possessed, because chickens were a good thing to watch as if possessed.

Watching the rooster, I recalled the time in my youth when I spent a lot of time sitting on tree branches like a chicken on a roost. I tried to recall what I had thought about at that time, with little success. The rooster flew away and disappeared into the trees. I was disappointed that the rooster had disappeared so soon. I thought about chickens for a moment to ease my disappointment. I thought of the classic English-language riddle *Why did the chicken cross the road?* There is not one but countless possible answers to this question, which is not different from the question *Why did Bodhi Dharma go east?* The subject of the question doesn't have to be a chicken. It can be replaced by anything with legs that can cross a road, such as a raccoon, a frog, a camel, or a dinosaur, or anything with no legs that cannot cross a road. The question can be changed to *Where did the chicken come from?* or *Where did the chicken go after crossing the road?* To the question *Why didn't the duck cross the road?* one might answer, "Because it was not a chicken." For the question *Why did the chicken cross the road?* which is like a Zen riddle, people have made up various answers. The following answers have been given from the perspective of historical figures:

Buddha: If you ask this question, you deny your own chicken nature.
Ernest Hemingway: To die. In the rain.
Charles Darwin: It was the next logical step after coming down from the trees.

Zeno of Elea: To prove it could never reach the other side.
William Wordsworth: To wander lonely as a cloud.

Asking *Why did I come to Hawaii?* was not different from asking
Why did the chicken cross the road? and the number of possible
answers could be none or countless. I thought that Brautigan
might have thought of the chicken from the riddle *Why did the
chicken cross the road?* when he thought to get his photograph
taken with a chicken. I felt as though I had done everything
I needed to do in Hawaii by sighting a wild rooster that flew
from branch to branch in the Hawaiian forest. I took three photographs in Hawaii, all of which were of the rooster. One is of
the rooster perched on a tree branch, the second is of its profile,
and the third is of it flying from one branch to another. I got
them printed when I returned from Hawaii. These photographs
seemed to be the only evidence of my trip to Hawaii.

On the way back to Honolulu, I saw a girl of about seven
years old playing on a slide in the front yard of a farmhouse next
to a two-lane road. The bus stopped at the perfect time for me
to watch the girl for a moment. A large, black dog was standing next to the girl, watching her play. The two of them took
a quick glance at our bus, then immediately returned to what
they were doing. The girl was barefoot and had disheveled hair.
The girl played on her slide, and the dog watched her. The two
of them probably did the same thing every day at that hour.
The scene had a feeling of loneliness, and the lyrical quality
of a softly colored painting. Behind them was a shabby house
that presumably belonged to a poor family. Behind the house
and beyond the mountains, the setting sun was dyeing the sky
beautiful colors. Perhaps the girl will later recall playing on her
slide when she felt lonely in her childhood, which was poor and
lonely, and think about the beloved dog that accompanied her
and the setting sun dyeing the sky beautiful colors. This memory
will perhaps become part of her lyrical landscape. I was not the
only one watching that scene. A white cat was watching the girl
and the dog from under a nearby tree, and a bird was watching
everything from the branch of different tree. Strangely, I felt as
though I was going to recall that scene over and over again like

a troubling thought. Strangely, that scene felt like a faded photograph that I'd never seen, even though it had been in my photo album for a long time.

Two days before leaving Hawaii, I went around Honolulu on a trolley bus. At one point, the bus driver pointed at a black statue in front of a royal palace and said that it was of the first king of Hawaii. Seeing a statue of Hawaii's last king had not been my reason for going to Hawaii, and I had forgotten completely about having thought that I might see one. The statue I saw was not of the king that died in the historic hotel in San Francisco, but it occurred to me that the two kings could have been related by blood. From a distance, the king's complexion was dark, and he was wearing a golden outfit. One of his hands was empty and raised up to the sky, and the other was holding what appeared to be a spear. I later learned that the first king of Hawaii had a nickname that is translated as *hard-shelled crab*, but I don't know why he came to be called that. In the end, I did not see a statue of the last king of Hawaii, but this didn't bother me at all.

That night, I was eating at a restaurant, and a blond girl sitting with her family at the table next to me caught my eye. Seeing her put me in a strangely good mood. She looked like a lion cub, though I could not put my finger on what made her look that way. Maybe it was her frizzy, curly hair that reminded me of the fur of a lion cub, or the shape of her nose. She made me feel that I was eating in a restaurant with a lion cub. Looking at her, I felt my need for revenge on blondes disappear. I mean, this is a strange way to put it, but I felt the vengeance that I thought I no longer harbored leaving me.

I spent the next afternoon at the beach. I recalled a story about Brautigan that I had heard from an old poet I'd met five years prior in the United States. The poet, who had been personally acquainted with Brautigan, only said of Brautigan that he'd been a peculiar man. It seemed to me that the poet had not forgiven Brautigan for doing something that was hard to forgive, and had never seen Brautigan again. He seemed to still be harboring a negative impression of Brautigan, and was reluctant to talk more about him. In expressing this, he reiterated that Brautigan had been a peculiar man. He appeared to be biting back his desire to slander Brautigan.

I imagined the conversation that I might have with Brautigan if I met his ghost in Hawaii, which to me felt like Brautigan's island. Our conversation would be focused mainly on chickens. Trout fishing and noodling in America would likely come up. We would probably talk about the last king of Hawaii and the fog in San Francisco. Perhaps Brautigan would tell me about the time he shot himself with a large firearm, the kind one would expect a large man like Brautigan to use. We could talk about the triviality of everything in life, which is simultaneously a philosophical issue, like ennui and death, and an aesthetic issue, like kitsch and ugliness. On the other hand, we could mainly talk about clouds, or ignore everything else and talk only about clouds. As we talk, the conversation itself and the act of conversing might seem trivial, so we might stop talking, and as if it is the natural order of things, we might keep our mouths shut, and like two men sulking after a fight, glare at the waves that are rushing in and out with no purpose whatsoever.

That evening, I was looking at the volcanic mountains out the window when a sudden thought led me to take the toilet paper out of the bathroom and place it on my bed. I sat in a chair and looked fixedly at it. Of all things, I probably chose the roll of toilet paper because I wanted to face the thing that evoked the least feeling in me in all of Hawaii. Like many objects, the roll of toilet paper appeared to have reached Nirvana, having no consciousness or senses. It had no substance, and evoked no feeling in me at all. A roll of toilet paper is certainly not something to look fixedly at, nor a great thing to look fixedly at, nor a great thing to contemplate while looking fixedly at—it is certainly not as exciting to look fixedly at as a comet that approaches the earth every few decades or a volcanic eruption that occurs every few centuries. At any rate, a roll of toilet paper is a great thing to look fixedly at while thinking that it is not a great thing to look fixedly at.

Obviously, there is nothing dramatic about a roll of toilet

paper, and it has no element of the horror that is found in dramatic things. So I couldn't consider it a horrifying roll of toilet paper, and this pleased me. Looking fixedly at the roll of toilet paper made me feel as though looking fixedly at toilet paper was the true purpose of my coming to Hawaii. When I look fixedly at an object for a long time, the object sometimes loses its concreteness and becomes abstract. I felt as though this phenomenon of reversal was about to occur. The phenomenon never occurred, and I was unable to look at the roll of toilet paper as an abstract entity in the form of toilet paper. Looking fixedly at the roll of toilet paper led me to think about Gödel's Incompleteness Theorem, which demonstrates that there are mathematical propositions that cannot be proven despite their being true, and about the relief this theorem provides. I continued to stare fixedly at the roll of toilet paper, and felt as though I was sinking comfortably into some predicament. I didn't think that it would be so comfortable when I sank completely into it. Still, I let myself go, hoping to sink into some uncomfortable predicament, but I was unable to sink completely. Spending time with the roll of toilet paper, I felt like a monkey playing with a coconut in the Arctic.

Thinking negative thoughts about Hawaii, fighting in my head with other tourists on the bus, seeing a wild Hawaiian rooster, and entertaining pointless thoughts had been the extent of my activities in Hawaii, but I felt as though I had done everything I needed to do there. Then something completely unexpected happened on my last night. I was drinking in my hotel room, delighted that I was going to leave boring Hawaii the next day, when I felt an excruciating pain in the left side of my chest, and my heart beat irregularly before stalling like the engine of a car. It was the first heart attack of my life. I felt as though my heart was splitting in half. I believe that my heart was stopped for scores of seconds, and began to beat again after I pounded on my chest with my fists several times. The sensation I had when my heart stopped was quite peculiar, and I have not found an appropriate analogy for that sensation to this date. The heart attack came to me not in the way that I had imagined, but it was similar. The state of having a stopped heart was not serene like death. It was excruciating. The pain lasted for a long time. When it finally receded, I was slightly tickled that my fist-sized heart began to beat again only after I had beaten on it with my fists several times. Other than that, I was rather calm about my first heart attack. I knew that I would never forget the fact that Hawaii is the place where I experienced my first heart attack. No one can easily forget the place of his first heart attack. From then on, when I thought about Hawaii, I would recall the wild rooster and my heart attack.

That night, I took several sleeping pills before finally falling asleep late at night. I had a strange dream. I went to a Native American village, where real American Indians lived. There were no dead American Indians on the highway. The Indians were performing some ritual around a bonfire under the full moon. I was handed a drink that was red like chicken blood. I drank from the cup, and immediately felt discombobulated, but I was not so discombobulated as to hallucinate. I thought, *How nice it would be if I could hallucinate*, but no matter how much I tried, I could not hallucinate, so I thought, *I feel fine as is*. I felt as though I was roving across a vast and blurry landscape between sopor and hallucination. The place looked like the snowy tundra, but with a warm climate. As if they understood my needs, the American Indians told me to wait, lit one end of a chicken bone, and handed it to me. I took a drag off it, which gave me a magnificent, dizzying hallucination. Blue smoke rose from the chicken bone pipe. It was very trippy, and discombobulating.

A moment later, the dream scene changed completely, and turned into what is perhaps one of the saddest dreams of my life. It was a dream about my own death. I regard it as something akin to a near-death experience. My soul seemed to be leaving my body and rising into the sky, and the next moment I was in the sky. I felt that I was somewhere in outer space, as if I were in Stanley Kubrick's *2001: A Space Odyssey*. (I actually thought this in my dream.) In that place, where gravity had no effect at all, my body drifted very slowly toward some point, as if being sucked in. Actually, it seemed that my body no longer existed, and only my senses and consciousness remained. In the distance, I saw an enormous hole, which I presumed to be a black hole, rotating slowly. I half expected to hear the soundtrack from *2001: A Space Odyssey*, but there was only absolute silence. Strangely, I felt as though I would be sucked into the hole that looked like a black hole if I let go of my string of consciousness, and that would end everything. I felt greatly tempted to be sucked into the hole, while at the same time I resisted and strained not to be tempted. Meanwhile, I continued drifting toward the black hole at a painfully slow pace. When I awoke from the dream, which felt tediously long but was actually not very long, I was overcome with sadness for a moment. Then I became devoid of all feelings, as though my mind had met its death.

Upon my return from Hawaii, I thought that perhaps I had had a vague notion that I would write this story, and that writing this story was ultimately the reason I had gone to Hawaii. Rereading what I had written about Hawaii reminded me of how bored I'd been the whole time while writing it, and of how being bored had allowed me to write such a story. Boredom is perhaps what allowed me to write this novel, of which this story is a part. This entire novel, which I wrote as if it were about my idea of fun, is a lengthy expression of my indescribable, intense boredom.

17. Drifting Clouds

THE DAY BEFORE I left San Francisco, I revisited Golden Gate Park, which is one of the many parks in San Francisco where I had spent much of my time. I spent the afternoon lying on a low, grassy hill, under the blue sky, surrounded by woods. There were people strolling, sunbathing, and reading. There were women hula-hooping and men throwing a Frisbee. Here and there on the lawn were dogs chasing after tennis balls thrown by their masters. American dogs really like to play catch.

I recalled a time when I had returned home to Seoul after several months traveling abroad. Something unexpected was waiting for me: cockroaches. The roaches wandered around the apartment in a leisurely manner, as if they had taken over the empty apartment in my absence. They welcomed me gladly, and I gladly did away with a few of them. Having lived by themselves in an empty apartment for so long, the roaches did not seem to know how to behave in front of a human. I was clueless as to how to teach them to behave in a way they might understand. Despite having no reason to be desperate, I looked at them with desperation, and tried in vain to think of a desperate measure for dealing with them.

An idea struck me, and as a last resort, I put on Beethoven's "Moonlight Sonata" for the roaches and watched them roam the apartment floor. Together we appreciated the lyrical piece of music. The roaches seemed to be enjoying the music, and roamed more actively. They even appeared to be dancing to the music. I was about to faint from exhaustion after my long flight, but the cockroaches were brimming with energy. They scurried around the apartment indifferently as if to mock me. I could barely lift a finger. The apartment seemed to belong to them, and I was so freaked out that I ended up sleeping at a nearby motel that night and returning home the next day.

It was August. I spent the day lying on my bed, under a

mosquito net, waiting for the mosquitos to appear. Strangely, there were no mosquitos. August is the time of the year that mosquitos pester people, but none came as I waited. It was a strange day, lying on my bed inside the mosquito net, waiting for mosquitos that wouldn't come. However, the mosquitos appeared the next morning, when I had stopped waiting for them. Throughout August, I killed a great many mosquitos, thinking that I was spending my August killing mosquitos.

It wasn't only cockroaches and mosquitoes that tortured me. Cicadas chirped incessantly in the trees outside my window. Listening to the sound of the cicadas, which I felt was gouging my brain, I became vividly aware that I was in Korea. I was unsure, however, whether the sound of the cicadas or my having returned to Korea tormented me more. I lay on the bed, trying to figure out the answer. The little energy I had left was drained by the sound of the cicadas. I cursed the cicadas calmly, and tried in the same spirit to curse that strange country to which I'd returned, but this I was unable to do very well, because I had become completely dispirited and disheartened by the vigorous chirping of the cicadas. I felt a surge of anger, followed by a rush of despondency. These two emotions took turns overwhelming me. After perceiving my anger sufficiently, I felt despondent, and after feeling sufficiently despondent, I felt ready to move on to a different emotion. Not knowing what to feel next, I felt another surge of anger and repeated the cycle.

I expected that when I again returned to Seoul in August, I would, as always, struggle desperately with inconsequential things, like cockroaches, mosquitoes, and cicadas. I would return to my life in Korea, where I'm one of the people with the most bizarre ideas. I was lying in a park where everything was peaceful, but morbid ideas kept popping into my head. The peaceful park was not a good place to think morbidly, so it was difficult to think that way, but I persisted in thinking morbidly, propelling those ideas forward. The grass had grown too tall and lanky under the trees near me, and it gave me a strange sense of foreboding. The foreboding that I sensed in the grass seemed to actually be coming from within me. The foreboding seemed to be indicating that I would continue obstinately to write this kind of insubstantial story, or possibly that I would never write anything again. No, it was actually indicating that I was like a ghost, living a life with virtually no expectation, hope, or solace, a life from which even laughter had nearly vanished. I would not live obstinately, but I would continue living a life that was itself obstinate, or possibly, I wouldn't be able to continue living that way, and I was already aware of it.

I looked at the grass intently, and I imagined that everything was changing before my eyes. As if I had closed my eyes for a while and the wrong season had come, everything turned strange. Everything wilted, and soon all the wilted things disappeared—the dogs that were running across the green grass, the green balls the dogs were chasing, the hula-hoopers, and the Frisbee throwers all disappeared, and a strange season of nothing but bleak hills came. All of these things in my imagination formed a realistic image of my inner landscape. Everything might have frozen in that state were it not for a dog that barked and ran past me, chasing a ball that had been thrown in the air.

Normally, I would have watched the dog as my thoughts meandered endlessly, marveling at how much the dogs in the park liked to play fetch, conjecturing that a dog that doesn't like to fetch balls must be considered abnormal by other dogs, and imagining that a dog that has led a happy life might visualize itself jumping for a green ball as it closes its eyes for good. But I was no longer thinking about the dog or the ball it was chasing. I was no longer thinking about anything. I watched the drifting clouds blankly and didn't even think that there is nothing better than clouds to watch blankly. I was free of all thoughts, the thought of which makes me shudder.

(In this last chapter, I had intended to write only about clouds, but somehow I ended up going off on a tangent. But this chapter, and this entire novel, is actually about clouds, because it is a cloud-chasing story about chasing clouds. I might title this novel *Drifting Clouds*, because drifting clouds, in my opinion, are the thing in the natural world that best demonstrates that there's no point to anything, and because this novel, which is no more than a confused play on thoughts and words, has no point at all, like drifting clouds.)

JUNG YOUNG MOON is a novelist, short story writer, translator, playwright, and teacher. He was born in Hamyang, South Korea, in 1965 and graduated from Seoul National University with a degree in psychology. He made his literary debut in 1996 with his novel *A Man Who Barely Exists*. He has also translated more than forty English-language books into Korean.

MAH EUNJI and JEFFREY KARVONEN are the recipients of two Literature Translation Institute of Korea Translation Grants and a Daesan Cultural Foundation Grant for Translation of a Korean Literary Work.

MICHAL AJVAZ, *The Golden Age.*
The Other City.

PIERRE ALBERT-BIROT, *Grabinoulor.*

YUZ ALESHKOVSKY, *Kangaroo.*

FELIPE ALFAU, *Chromos.*
Locos.

ANTÓNIO LOBO ANTUNES, *Knowledge of Hell.*
The Splendor of Portugal.

ALAIN ARIAS-MISSON, *Theatre of Incest.*

GABRIELA AVIGUR-ROTEM, *Heatwave and Crazy Birds.*

DJUNA BARNES, *Ladies Almanack.*
Ryder.

DONALD BARTHELME, *The King.*
Paradise.

SVETISLAV BASARA, *Chinese Letter.*

MIQUEL BAUÇÀ, *The Siege in the Room.*

RENÉ BELLETTO, *Dying.*

MAREK BIENCZYK, *Transparency.*

ANDREI BITOV, *Pushkin House.*

ANDREJ BLATNIK, *You Do Understand.*
Law of Desire.

IGNÁCIO DE LOYOLA BRANDÃO,
Anonymous Celebrity.
Zero.

BONNIE BREMSER, *Troia: Mexican Memoirs.*

CHRISTINE BROOKE-ROSE,
Amalgamemnon.

MICHEL BUTOR, *Degrees.*
Mobile.

G. CABRERA INFANTE, *Infante's Inferno.*
Three Trapped Tigers.

JULIETA CAMPOS, *The Fear of Losing Eurydice.*

ANNE CARSON, *Eros the Bittersweet.*

ORLY CASTEL-BLOOM, *Dolly City.*

LOUIS-FERDINAND CÉLINE, *North.*
Conversations with Professor Y.
London Bridge.

MARIE CHAIX, *The Laurels of Lake Constance.*

HUGO CHARTERIS, *The Tide Is Right.*

ERIC CHEVILLARD, *Demolishing Nisard.*
The Author and Me.

MARC CHOLODENKO, *Mordechai Schamz.*

JOSHUA COHEN, *Witz.*

EMILY HOLMES COLEMAN, *The Shutter of Snow.*

ERIC CHEVILLARD, *The Author and Me.*

ROBERT COOVER, *A Night at the Movies.*

STANLEY CRAWFORD, *Log of the S.S. The Mrs Unguentine.*
Some Instructions to My Wife.

RENÉ CREVEL, *Putting My Foot in It.*

RALPH CUSACK, *Cadenza.*

NICHOLAS DELBANCO, *Sherbrookes.*
The Count of Concord.

NIGEL DENNIS, *Cards of Identity.*

PETER DIMOCK, *A Short Rhetoric for Leaving the Family.*

ARIEL DORFMAN, *Konfidenz.*

COLEMAN DOWELL, *Island People.*
Too Much Flesh and Jabez.

ARKADII DRAGOMOSHCHENKO,
Dust.

RIKKI DUCORNET, *Phosphor in Dreamland.*
The Complete Butcher's Tales.
The Fountains of Neptune.

JEAN ECHENOZ, *Chopin's Move.*

FRANÇOIS EMMANUEL, *Invitation to a Voyage.*

PAUL EMOND, *The Dance of a Sham.*

SALVADOR ESPRIU, *Ariadne in the Grotesque Labyrinth.*

JUAN FILLOY, *Op Oloop.*

ANDY FITCH, *Pop Poetics.*

GUSTAVE FLAUBERT, *Bouvard and Pécuchet.*

KASS FLEISHER, *Talking out of School.*

JON FOSSE, *Aliss at the Fire.*
Melancholy.

FORD MADOX FORD, *The March of Literature.*

MAX FRISCH, *I'm Not Stiller.*

FOR A FULL LIST OF PUBLICATIONS, VISIT: www.dalkeyarchive.com

Man in the Holocene.

CARLOS FUENTES, *Christopher Unborn.*
Distant Relations.
Terra Nostra.
Where the Air Is Clear.

TAKEHIKO FUKUNAGA, *Flowers of Grass.*

WILLIAM GADDIS, JR., *The Recognitions.*

JANICE GALLOWAY, *Foreign Parts.*
The Trick Is to Keep Breathing.

WILLIAM H. GASS, *Life Sentences.*
The Tunnel.
The World Within the Word.
Willie Masters' Lonesome Wife.

GÉRARD GAVARRY, *Hoppla! 1 2 3..*

C. S. GISCOMBE, *Giscome Road.*
Here.

WITOLD GOMBROWICZ, *A Kind of Testament.*

PAULO EMÍLIO SALES GOMES, *P's Three Women.*

GEORGI GOSPODINOV, *Natural Novel.*

JUAN GOYTISOLO, *Count Julian.*
Juan the Landless.
Makbara.
Marks of Identity.

JACK GREEN, *Fire the Bastards!*

JIŘÍ GRUŠA, *The Questionnaire.*

MELA HARTWIG, *Am I a Redundant Human Being?*

JOHN HAWKES, *The Passion Artist.*
Whistlejacket.

KEIZO HINO, *Isle of Dreams.*

KAZUSHI HOSAKA, *Plainsong.*

NAOYUKI II, *The Shadow of a Blue Cat.*

DRAGO JANČAR, *The Tree with No Name.*

MIKHEIL JAVAKHISHVILI, *Kvachi.*

GERT JONKE, *The Distant Sound.*
Homage to Czerny.
The System of Vienna.

JACQUES JOUET, *Mountain R.*
Savage.
Upstaged.

MIEKO KANAI, *The Word Book.*

YORAM KANIUK, *Life on Sandpaper.*

ZURAB KARUMIDZE, *Dagny.*

JOHN KELLY, *From Out of the City.*

HUGH KENNER, *Flaubert, Joyce and Beckett: The Stoic Comedians.*
Joyce's Voices.

DANILO KIŠ, *The Attic.*
The Lute and the Scars.
Psalm 44.
A Tomb for Boris Davidovich.

ANITA KONKKA, *A Fool's Paradise.*

GEORGE KONRÁD, *The City Builder.*

TADEUSZ KONWICKI, *A Minor Apocalypse.*
The Polish Complex.

ANNA KORDZAIA-SAMADASHVILI, *Me, Margarita.*

MENIS KOUMANDAREAS, *Koula.*

ELAINE KRAF, *The Princess of 72nd Street.*

JIM KRUSOE, *Iceland.*

AYSE KULIN, *Farewell: A Mansion in Occupied Istanbul.*

EMILIO LASCANO TEGUI, *On Elegance While Sleeping.*

ERIC LAURRENT, *Do Not Touch.*

VIOLETTE LEDUC, *La Bâtarde.*

EDOUARD LEVÉ, *Autoportrait.*
Newspaper.
Suicide.
Works.

MARIO LEVI, *Istanbul Was a Fairy Tale.*

DEBORAH LEVY, *Billy and Girl.*

JOSÉ LEZAMA LIMA, *Paradiso.*

ROSA LIKSOM, *Dark Paradise.*

OSMAN LINS, *Avalovara.*
The Queen of the Prisons of Greece.

FLORIAN LIPUŠ, *The Errors of Young Tjaž.*

GORDON LISH, *Peru.*

ALF MACLOCHLAINN, *Out of Focus.*
Past Habitual.
The Corpus in the Library.

RON LOEWINSOHN, *Magnetic Field(s).*

YURI LOTMAN, *Non-Memoirs.*

FOR A FULL LIST OF PUBLICATIONS, VISIT: www.dalkeyarchive.com

MINA LOY, *Stories and Essays of Mina Loy.*

MICHELINE AHARONIAN MARCOM,
A Brief History of Yes.
The Mirror in the Well.

BEN MARCUS, *The Age of Wire and String.*

DAVID MARKSON, *Reader's Block.*
Wittgenstein's Mistress.

CAROLE MASO, *AVA.*

HARRY MATHEWS, *Cigarettes.*
The Conversions.
The Journalist.
My Life in CIA.
Singular Pleasures.
Tlooth.

HISAKI MATSUURA, *Triangle.*

ABDELWAHAB MEDDEB, *Talismano.*

GERHARD MEIER, *Isle of the Dead.*

HERMAN MELVILLE, *The Confidence-Man.*

AMANDA MICHALOPOULOU, *I'd Like.*

CHRISTINE MONTALBETTI, *The Origin of Man.*
Western.

WARREN MOTTE, *Fables of the Novel: French Fiction since 1990.*
Fiction Now: The French Novel in the 21st Century.
Mirror Gazing.
Oulipo: A Primer of Potential Literature.

GERALD MURNANE, *Barley Patch.*
Inland.

YVES NAVARRE, *Our Share of Time.*
Sweet Tooth.

DOROTHY NELSON, *In Night's City.*
Tar and Feathers.

WILFRIDO D. NOLLEDO, *But for the Lovers.*

FLANN O'BRIEN, *At Swim-Two-Birds.*
The Best of Myles.
The Dalkey Archive.
The Hard Life.
The Poor Mouth.
The Third Policeman.

CLAUDE OLLIER, *The Mise-en-Scène.*
Wert and the Life Without End.

PATRIK OUŘEDNÍK, *Europeana.*

The Opportune Moment, 1855.

BORIS PAHOR, *Necropolis.*

FERNANDO DEL PASO, *News from the Empire.*
Palinuro of Mexico.

ROBERT PINGET, *The Inquisitory.*
Mahu or The Material.
Trio.

MANUEL PUIG, *Betrayed by Rita Hayworth.*
The Buenos Aires Affair.
Heartbreak Tango.

RAYMOND QUENEAU, *The Last Days.*
Odile.
Pierrot Mon Ami.
Saint Glinglin.

ANN QUIN, *Berg.*
Passages.
Three.
Tripticks.

ISHMAEL REED, *The Free-Lance Pallbearers.*
The Last Days of Louisiana Red.
Ishmael Reed: The Plays.
Juice!
The Terrible Threes.
The Terrible Twos.
Yellow Back Radio Broke-Down.

JASIA REICHARDT, *15 Journeys Warsaw to London.*

JOÃO UBALDO RIBEIRO, *House of the Fortunate Buddhas.*

RAINER MARIA RILKE,
The Notebooks of Malte Laurids Brigge.

JULIÁN RÍOS, *The House of Ulysses.*
Larva: A Midsummer Night's Babel.
Poundemonium.

ALAIN ROBBE-GRILLET, *Project for a Revolution in New York.*
A Sentimental Novel.

AUGUSTO ROA BASTOS, *I the Supreme.*

DANIËL ROBBERECHTS, *Arriving in Avignon.*

JEAN ROLIN, *The Explosion of the Radiator Hose.*

OLIVIER ROLIN, *Hotel Crystal.*

ALIX CLEO ROUBAUD, *Alix's Journal.*
RAYMOND ROUSSEL, *Impressions of Africa.*
VEDRANA RUDAN, *Night.*
PABLO M. RUIZ, *Four Cold Chapters on the Possibility of Literature.*
GERMAN SADULAEV, *The Maya Pill.*
LUIS RAFAEL SÁNCHEZ, *Macho Camacho's Beat.*
SEVERO SARDUY, *Cobra & Maitreya.*
NATHALIE SARRAUTE, *Do You Hear Them?*
Martereau.
The Planetarium.
STIG SÆTERBAKKEN, *Siamese.*
Self-Control.
Through the Night.
VIKTOR SHKLOVSKY, *Bowstring.*
Literature and Cinematography.
Theory of Prose.
Third Factory.
PIERRE SINIAC, *The Collaborators.*
KJERSTI A. SKOMSVOLD, *The Faster I Walk, the Smaller I Am.*
JOSEF ŠKVORECKÝ, *The Engineer of Human Souls.*
GILBERT SORRENTINO, *Aberration of Starlight.*
Blue Pastoral.
Steelwork.
Under the Shadow.
MARKO SOSIČ, *Ballerina, Ballerina.*
ANDRZEJ STASIUK, *Dukla.*
Fado.
GERTRUDE STEIN, *The Making of Americans.*
A Novel of Thank You.
LARS SVENDSEN, *A Philosophy of Evil.*
PIOTR SZEWC, *Annihilation.*
GONÇALO M. TAVARES, *A Man: Klaus Klump.*
Jerusalem.
Learning to Pray in the Age of Technique.
LUCIAN DAN TEODOROVICI, *Our Circus Presents . . .*
NIKANOR TERATOLOGEN, *Assisted Living.*
DUMITRU TSEPENEAG, *Hotel Europa.*
The Necessary Marriage.
Pigeon Post.
Vain Art of the Fugue.
ESTHER TUSQUETS, *Stranded.*
DUBRAVKA UGRESIC, *Lend Me Your Character.*
Thank You for Not Reading.
TOR ULVEN, *Replacement.*
MATI UNT, *Brecht at Night.*
Diary of a Blood Donor.
Things in the Night.
ÁLVARO URIBE & OLIVIA SEARS, EDS., *Best of Contemporary Mexican Fiction.*
ELOY URROZ, *Friction.*
The Obstacles.
LUISA VALENZUELA, *Dark Desires and the Others.*
He Who Searches.
BORIS VIAN, *Heartsnatcher.*
LLORENÇ VILLALONGA, *The Dolls' Room.*
TOOMAS VINT, *An Unending Landscape.*
AUSTRYN WAINHOUSE, *Hedyphagetica.*
DIANE WILLIAMS, *Excitability: Selected Stories.*
Romancer Erector.
MARGUERITE YOUNG, *Angel in the Forest.*
Miss MacIntosh, My Darling.
REYOUNG, *Unbabbling.*
VLADO ŽABOT, *The Succubus.*
ZORAN ŽIVKOVIĆ , *Hidden Camera.*
LOUIS ZUKOFSKY, *Collected Fiction.*
VITOMIL ZUPAN, *Minuet for Guitar.*
SCOTT ZWIREN, *God Head.*

AND MORE . . .